PRAISE FOR
ALONG WOODED PATHS

A skillfully written blend of Amish and "Englisch" lives that will have you rooting for both sides. *Along Wooded Paths* draws the reader into Marianna's complex choices and swirling emotions, while exposing her deep-seated desire for a stronger faith. Tricia Goyer's beautifully woven tale captured me from beginning till end.

—Miralee Ferrell
author of *Love Finds You in Sundance*

Every once in awhile I read a book that draws me in as a reader and challenges me as a writer. *Along Wooded Paths* is such a book. The story is gripping, the characters so well drawn I hated to see this installment end, and the faith element challenged me to deepen my walk with God. *Along Wooded Paths* is a beautiful story that will compel you to consider what God really asks of us.

—Cara Putman
author of *Stars in the Night* and *Ohio Brides*

A sweet, tender story about God's gentle workings in the hearts of His own. Tricia Goyer has a true talent for creating believable characters readers can identify with and empathize with. Anyone who enjoys Amish fiction will appreciate this moving tale.

—Sally L̶ nd coauthor of House trilogy

If you read only one Amish book this year, make sure it's Tricia Goyer's *Along Wooded Paths*. With her elegant prose and deep insights into the human heart, Goyer has crafted a poignant story of a young Amish woman forced to choose between the love of two very different men. My heart ached at the realization that one man would have his heart broken, and yet when I reached the end, I breathed a sigh of satisfaction that Marianna had chosen the right one. This beautiful story of love and faith should come with a warning label, though, for one Goyer book is not enough. Fortunately, the first of the series, *Beside Still Waters*, is still available, and *Beyond Hopes Valley* is coming. I've made space for them all on my keeper shelf.

—Amanda Cabot, author of *Tomorrow's Garden*

Set amid the majestic Montana countryside, Tricia Goyer's gentle tale of love, loyalty, and longing will keep your heart guessing until the last page.

—Cathy Elliott, author of *Medals in the Attic:
An Annie's Attic Mystery*

I was pulled into Tricia Goyer's *Along Wooded Paths* from the first page! A devastating past, a heart-breaking choice, this story has it all. Endearing, lovely in every way. If you love heartwarming Amish fiction you can't go wrong here. I can't wait to read the next book in the series!

—Traci DePree, author of the Lake Emily series
and *Into the Wilderness*

Tricia Goyer

Along
Wooded
Paths

TRICIA GOYER

ALONG WOODED PATHS

B&H
PUBLISHING GROUP
NASHVILLE, TENNESSEE

ISBN: 978-1-4336-6869-2

Published by B&H Publishing Group
Nashville, Tennessee

Dewey Decimal Classification: F
Subject Heading: AMISH—FICTION \ FAMILY LIFE—
FICTION \ SPIRITUAL LIFE—FICTION

Published in association with the Books & Such Literary
Agency, Janet Kobobel Grant, 52 Mission Circle, Suite 122,
PMB 170, Santa Rosa, CA 95409-5370, www.booksandsuch.biz.

Scripture references marked NIV are taken from the
New International Version, copyright © 1973, 1978,
1984, 2011 by International Bible Society.
Scripture references marked KJV were taken from
the King James Version of the Bible.

Cover photo by Steve Gardner, PixelWorks

2 3 4 5 6 7 8 9 • 16 15 14 13 12 11

In their hearts humans plan their course, but the LORD establishes their steps. (Proverbs 16:9 NIV)

DEDICATION

Dedicated to my grandson Clayton William Goyer.
May you always seek Jesus with all your heart.

ACKNOWLEDGMENTS

Every good and perfect gift comes from above and the greatest gifts to me are the people God has brought into my life. This book would not be written without the love of my family: my husband John and my kids Cory, Leslie, Nathan, and Alyssa. Also, my wonderful daughter-in-law Katie and my first grandchild Clayton. Grandma Dolores is always wonderful about caring for me as I pour so much out, and for sending up prayers. I'm thankful for my church home of Mosaic Church and the new community God has planted me in, in Little Rock, Arkansas.

I'm always grateful for my stellar agent Janet Grant and my editor Karen Ball. Also, Julie Gwinn and the B&H team are amazing to work with! Thank you!

CHAPTER ONE

The hammer weighed heavy in his hand. Aaron Zook hit the nail again and again, securing the iron hat hook. Finally done, he placed the hammer on the windowsill and stepped back. His heart weighed heavy too. Bruised as if it received similar blows. Aaron removed his straw hat and placed it on the hook, then he turned and scanned the room. For months he'd poured himself into his work, planning for the day he'd complete the cabin, but it meant little now. The windows were bare, like large blank eyes staring into his soul, mocking his pain. He'd done his part, but it needed a woman's touch—white, plain curtains, a rag rug by the door, green plants by the window.

He'd set up a bed in the larger room, but he wouldn't sleep here. Not yet. Another blow struck his heart. He'd always imagined his first night with Marianna by his side, snuggled under the quilt she'd been working on. He swallowed hard and wiped his eyes, telling himself to push those thoughts from his mind.

Aaron cleared his throat and strode, steps determined, into the kitchen. His eyes scanned the simple cupboards and the table and two chairs he'd made. He took a deep breath and imagined the fragrance of homemade bread wafting from the wood-burning stove he'd picked up at a local auction. From there he moved through the living area to the simple bathroom, and then to the larger bedroom, making sure the last nail had been driven. All looked *gut.* The wooden floor was laid. The trim around the doors finished. Aaron refused to go in the smaller room—the one he'd made for a child. Their child. He crossed his arms over his chest, pulling them tight.

Marianna would love that room best, especially the view of the meadow. The window bench still needed cushions, as did the cradle.

His mother had declared the room "fancy," giving a toss of her head, but Aaron didn't care. Marianna deserved something special. As he'd worked on the window bench, he'd pictured her watching sparrows dance in the tree limbs, cradling his child in his arms, humming a lullaby.

Who was he kidding? He pictured her in every room. Even though she'd never stepped through the door, her presence haunted this place. If only she'd taken the time to come and see the home he'd built for her.

He approached the bare, queen-sized mattress and sat, placing his elbows on his knees and hiding his face in his hands. Anger coursed through him, followed by desperation.

Why had she turned back?

His mother had heard from Marianna's best friend Rebecca that she'd packed up her things and boarded the train to Indiana, but at the next station she got off and returned the way she'd come. Why? Did guilt chain her to that place—to her parents? Was it something else? Some*one* else? His stomach clenched and a soft moan escaped his lips.

He'd seen her urgency to live right. Determination to follow every rule often straightened her eyebrows and tightened her lips into a thin line. Didn't she realize all could see the pain she attempted to hide?

Losing her sisters impacted Marianna in ways he doubted she understood. It also made Aaron love her even more. It made him want to take her away from the haunted memories tucked away within her family home and cherish her as she deserved. To show that he loved her just for *her*. Making this cabin had been his first step, but it did little good if she never saw it.

I need her to return. She has to come back. She has to know . . .

He stood and paced from the bedroom window to the door and back again. If this place were to ever be filled with the life he'd planned on—the woman he'd dreamed of—he'd have to do something about it.

Aaron's heart seemed tangled in a thousand knots. He placed a hand to his chest and forced in a breath. He had to let her know he wasn't giving up.

His only chance was to go to her. Marianna had to know his heart.

As much as it scared him to leave, he had no choice.

Aaron looked at the borrowed suitcase. It was only half full. He'd put in a few changes of clothes and an extra hat. He'd borrowed a book on cattle from Mr. Stoll. Under it all he'd tucked his sketchbook.

Turning to his dresser, Aaron picked up the last two things. A stack of letters and a paper sack with a lunch Naomi had packed. Tears had filled her eyes as she'd handed it to him. She hadn't wished him a good trip. She hadn't begged him to stay. She'd come to him months ago in her desperation, hoping to find companionship. For a while he'd tried, for the same reason. But he knew better now. Lying was something he'd been raised to hate. And letting Naomi think he cared about her the way he cared for Marianna . . .

That was a lie.

That was why he was leaving. To find the truth.

He sighed as he set the lunch inside the suitcase. Many in his parents' generation married for a home and family. His own mother said it was foolish for him to travel so far for love. Marriage did not take love, she insisted.

His younger sister called up the stairs. "Your driver's here!"

"*Ja, ja*," Aaron yelled back.

He clenched the stack of letters, still unsure if he'd give them to Marianna. There were fifteen letters. Nearly one for every week she'd been gone. He'd shared so much on those pages—his dreams, his hopes. He'd left nothing hidden. Which was why he hadn't mailed them yet. He had to go to Montana. He had to look into Marianna's face, peer into her eyes—her soul. Only then would he know if he'd be willing to hand over his heart.

Lifting his suitcase, he took one last look around the room he'd slept in since a babe. Then, in determination, Aaron straightened his back, turned, and walked out the door.

CHAPTER TWO

The crisp air stung her nose, and Marianna pushed her gloved hands deeper into the pockets of her wool coat as she walked. Yesterday the sky had been cloudless and sunshine danced on the fall colors—especially the bright yellow of the larch needles—bathing the forest with patches of gold. Today gray clouds filled the sky. The hills behind her house rolled upward toward those clouds.

Beyond the hills, expansive mountains loomed. They rose into the gray mist, their tops unseen. She'd like to climb those mountains one day. To see beyond. When she lived in Indiana she'd spent her entire life within thirty square miles, but the more of God's creation she witnessed, the more she wanted to see.

Tall pines rose around her. She stepped over fallen logs as she walked toward the pond. There was no trail to guide her, but Marianna's heart knew the way.

Since returning on the train more than a month ago, she realized the more she sought God the more she longed for Him. Looking back now, she knew she made the right choice, yet what stood out to her most about that day wasn't her father's words as he sat by her on the train. Even now she could hardly remember what he'd said. What she remembered was her dog Trapper's excited bark as she stepped off the train. Even more . . .

The look on Ben's face as she approached.

Her heartbeat quickened even now. Though she'd tried to keep her distance—him being Englisch after all—she allowed a soft smile to tip her lips at the memory.

The yellowing grass and fallen leaves crunched under her feet. She didn't doubt snow would soon come. She'd heard the stories of winters in these parts. Snow piled up to doorposts. Her Uncle Ike had even bought sled runners to replace the wheels on his buggy. She didn't like the thought of trudging through the snow on the way to work. Even worse, she wouldn't be able to meet God at her special spot until spring.

She'd come to treasure the quiet moments when she sat on a fallen log overlooking the still pond. She'd often brought Dat's English Bible to read God's words. And as she sat amongst the trees, with bird song filling the air, it was as if God sat beside her, whispering words of hope and promise to her heart.

After reading, she often bowed her head in silent prayer. The traditional silent prayers of her childhood were different than how she prayed now. Then, she focused on the length of the pause and the slightest noises around her rather than on her praying. Now, she was immersed in her prayer. A few times, from her place on the log, she'd lifted her voice in song, letting her words drift through the tree branches swaying in the wind. The songs were those she'd learned growing up in church, but the words seemed deeper now, richer, as they slipped from her lips to God's ear.

A squirrel chattered from a nearby tree. Trapper pranced by her side, perking his ears to the sound, but he refused to be distracted. The small dog strode ahead as if he were the leader.

TRICIA GOYER

With his eyes fixed on the hill leading to their destination, his feet barely touched the muddy ground, like a show pony on parade. His gray fur looked dingy again. Maybe she could bribe David or Charlie to bathe him. It amazed her what she could get her young brothers to do for a few extra cookies.

They crested the hill and the wind picked up, stinging her cheeks. Marianna blew out a surprised breath. The moisture of her breath danced on the air as a fine mist before her. Trapper flapped one ear and then shook his head as if trying to toss off the wind.

"We won't stay long. I jest want once more chance before—" Marianna's words caught in her throat as she noticed a figure sitting on her log. She knew that blue jacket. Her eyes moved to the dark hair and the man's profile. *Ben.*

All thoughts of bringing her prayers before God got pushed to the side as she eyed him. Her heartbeat quickened again and heat rushed to her cheeks. Even her fingers and toes warmed.

Her footsteps slowed and she considered turning back. From Ben's lowered head and still posture, she guessed he'd come here for the same reason—to be with God, to pray.

Instead of returning the way she'd come, something propelled her forward. It was as if Ben had tied a string to her heart and reeled her in.

Trapper paused, noticing Ben for the first time, and then with a bark the small dog shot toward him.

"Trapper, no!" She called too late. Trapper's tail wagged and he leapt over a small dry bush in a single bound. Two more long jumps and he was at Ben's feet, dancing and spinning.

Ben's head jerked up and his laughter split the air. He said something to Trapper, and the dog stilled. Ben patted Trapper's head. When the dog sat at Ben's feet, Ben turned to her. His eyes locked with hers and a smile filled his face. His lips moved, and she almost thought he whispered her name.

Marianna pulled her gloved hands from her pockets and crossed her arms in front of her, as if that one motion could protect her heart.

"I'm so sorry. I didn't mean to interrupt."

Ben waved a hand in the air. "I'd never consider you an interruption, Mari. You ought to know that. Anyone else, yes, but . . ." He ran a hand through his hair. "Well, you can surprise me any day you'd like."

She nodded and focused on his eyes. There was truth to his words. He wanted her near him, she could see it in his gaze.

Marianna turned her attention to the pond. In the summer it had appeared bright blue, but fall had darkened it to a bluish-green. The beaver lodge seemed a few feet higher than she remembered and she pictured the furry family snuggled inside, resting from all their hard work.

A sigh escaped her lips and she turned back to him. "I came down to just sit and enjoy the place one more time—"

"Before the snow hit?" He chuckled. "I was doing the same. Even though I know I can meet with God sitting in my warm cabin, it's just not the same."

"*Ja.*" Marianna touched her kapp. It still seemed strange to be talking so openly about God. The Amish protected their privacy. She'd lived her whole life amongst a community that loved God, but to them that love was a private matter. Even her parents kept their faith to themselves. In fact, if her father hadn't left the English Bible sitting out—and if she hadn't caught him reading it a time or two—she would have never known about his search for truth.

"You can join me if you'd like." Ben scooted over on the log, moving closer to the gnarled roots. "I warmed it for you."

She shook her head. "Uh, no thanks." She curled her toes in her boots. "Don't want to stay out too long. Jest . . ." She tried to think of an excuse, but none seemed to work. She couldn't confess that the pounding of her heartbeat would increase the nearer she got to him. "I just better head back."

Ben nodded and stood, nearing her. An ache filled her chest as she imagined taking up his offer and sitting next to him. It ached even more to see him striding toward her. She'd pushed him away time and time again, but he'd never lost that small smile that played on his lips—or the intense care in his gaze—whenever he saw her.

"Let me walk you back, then." He swooped his arm wide, as if directing her to lead the way. Even though she gave no evidence of her returned affection, though it was obvious they couldn't be anything more than friends, Ben made it clear he'd take what he could get.

"Have you settled back in?"

She knew he referred to the return trip to Indiana—the one she'd abandoned. "Oh, yes, weeks ago."

"And do you still think coming back here was the right choice?"

His questions were so direct. She cleared her throat. "I believe so. Dat says he couldn't imagine what the house would be like without me."

"So are you going back in the spring?"

She paused, and Trapper stopped at her side. Marianna placed a hand on her hip. "Are you trying to get rid of me?"

Ben chuckled. "Just the opposite, Marianna. I just wanted to know how long the sun would be hanging around. My days always seem brighter with you in it. Even on cloudy days like today."

She nodded but didn't respond. She continued her pace, slower than normal. She should be spending as little time with him as possible, but something inside urged her to linger.

As they walked, the only sounds were the dry brush scraping against their clothes and the crunching of frozen grass. When the roof of her house came into view, Marianna paused.

"I like to hear you say things like that, Ben, but I tell myself I shouldn't. Amish folks don't talk in such a manner. We focus on humility."

"I'm sorry. I didn't mean—"

She lifted a hand, halting his words. "Do not worry. You jest don't know these things. Unless you were one of us, you couldn't know."

Ben nodded and fixed his eyes forward. If she wasn't mistaken, his shoulders slumped.

Marianna's heart ached as if she'd slapped him in the face. She could see the sting of rejection in his gaze, but what else could she do? She couldn't allow him to continue such nonsense. Marianna trudged on. They emerged from the woods behind her parents' house. From the corner of her eye she saw movement from the back cabin window, but when she looked again, there was only a slight fluttering of the curtain.

She considered inviting Ben in. If he were any other neighbor—Amish or Englisch—she would have. People were like that around here, friendly, sociable. But Marianna cared for Ben in a different way than she cared for others in the community. Deep, romantic notions refused to be locked away. If she invited Ben inside, Mem no doubt would see through her act of "just being neighborly." It would bring up too many questions. And concerns.

So she glanced down the road as if looking for a way out from this conversation.

"Have you seen my uncle? I've heard he's preparing his buggy for winter. I imagine—"

"I saw him yesterday, Mari." Ben's voice quieted. He studied her face and she could tell he understood. They must say good-bye. His lips turned down, and he brushed something off his pants leg—though nothing was there.

"Speaking of your Uncle Ike, I need to drop by his place. He wanted to talk to me about some deliveries I need to make tomorrow."

"That's fine. Trapper will make sure I get *all the way* home. Surely we won't get lost." She forced a small laugh but it sounded as dull as the chilled world around her.

"See you later, then?" He picked up the pace and veered the direction of the road. She continued toward their log house. Her lip trembled as she watched him go, then she lifted her chin and told herself to stay strong.

"It's how things have to work, Trapper." She spoke to the dog trotting by her side, but her eyes were still fixed on Ben's departing form. "I suppose someday we'll both be comfortable just being friends."

Marianna entered the house. David and Josiah were at school. Charlie—his leg still bandaged from being burned in an accident over a month ago—read a book on the couch. Both Ellie and Joy napped. She could hear her father's heavy footsteps upstairs as he worked on one project or another. He finished up a building project at Kootenai Log Homes yesterday and would start another tomorrow. Today was his day to take care of things around their house, and Marianna had to admit she enjoyed seeing his smile and hearing him whistle as he worked.

Life here was so different from life in Indiana.

She glanced to her mother in the kitchen as she took off her coat. Mem was busy washing dishes and didn't look Marianna's way. Something about Mem's slouched posture and lowered head made the hairs on the back of Marianna's neck stand on end.

Nearing, she noticed silent tears streaming down Mem's face. Her mother pulled a hand out of the dishwater, wiping them away and leaving small, bubbly suds on her cheek.

Marianna placed a hand on her shoulder. "Mem, what is it?"

"Maybe you were right, Mari. Maybe we shouldn't have come here. Who knows, you could be planning a wedding by now." She spoke in a low whisper. "You were so determined when we left, and Aaron had worked so hard on the cabin . . ."

Marianna rinsed off the last of the dishes in the basin of water, then placed them in the dish strainer. Her chest felt heavy, as if each of Mem's words was a brick, piling on top of it. Her mother no doubt had seen her and Ben walking outside. She'd also probably noticed Marianna had written less frequently to Aaron. How could she tell her mother things had changed? That *she* had changed. It took all her energy to keep her feelings for Ben at bay. She didn't have the emotional strength to communicate with Aaron or consider what possibility there was for a relationship with him.

Marianna looked to Mem again. Her face had grown pale. With frantic motions, Mem scrubbed a pan that already looked clean. There had to be something more. Something else bothering her.

Marianna took her time drying the dishes, waiting.

"I got a letter from an old school friend." Mem said it as if trying to make Marianna believe she was switching topics, but the look in Mem's eye told Marianna different.

"Really? Good news?"

"*Ja, ja*, yet another grandchild. It makes eight. Eight grandchildren. And to think we went to school together, are the same age."

Marianna picked up the dishtowel. Had her sisters lived, they would have made their mother a grandmother many times over by now. Had her older brother Levi joined the church and married Naomi, then they could've had a baby by this time too.

A few rays of sunlight filtered through the kitchen window, but the gray clouds made it impossible for any warmth to break through. Her heart ached for Mem's losses—unfulfilled dreams— but a new emotion stirred too. Anger. Why did this pressure have to fall on her? She had enough to worry about. Now she had to carry Mem's burden too?

God, it doesn't seem fair. Couldn't You have made it easier? Help me here. She waited for His peace to come, but instead the glass pane of the window radiated more cold.

"I . . . I didn't say I would never consider marrying Aaron. It's jest I'd like some time to think some more. Maybe whenever I do go back, I can see him and we can talk about things."

Was it just her imagination or did Mem's shoulders straighten a bit?

"Yes, *gut*, but don't wait too long. There are other young women . . ." Mem let her voice trail off. "There are rumors."

"Rumors?"

"That Aaron was in a relationship. Or at least it appeared as such."

Mem didn't mention Naomi's name. Marianna wouldn't either, but they both knew. She thought back to the letters from her friends talking about how close Aaron and Naomi seemed to be at Clara's wedding.

"I've heard the same, but you know rumors."

"Don't break his heart, Mari." Mem's whispers sounded like a low hiss. "He has yet another woman who'd give her heart to him. And where would that leave you? Don't walk away from your dream and live with regrets for the rest of your life. Don't let your heart get caught up in what it ought not."

"Mem, you don't understand—"

Mem turned to her. "Really? Do you honestly believe that? Do you not think I was young once?"

"Of course, I know you were—"

Mem raised her hand. "Don't believe yer the only one whose eyes have turned to a handsome Englischman, Marianna Sommer. There was a time I—"

Dat's steps sounded, and Marianna turned toward his approach.

"Ruth." Dat walked into the kitchen. "Do you have any more clean rags? I'd like to change the dressing on Charlie's wounds."

Mem brushed a strand of hair back from her face and patted her kapp. Then she forced a smile. "*Ja*, of course. I washed some and have them hung to dry upstairs. I'll fetch them."

"I can do it—"

"Nah." Mem raised a hand. "I should check on Joy. She hasn't eaten in a while."

Mem rushed from the room. Dat seemed oblivious to the pain on her face, but Marianna hadn't missed her mother's furrowed brow, red cheeks. Anger and something else . . . shame?

Who was this Englischman Mem spoke of?

CHAPTER THREE

W hitefish, Montana, next stop!"

The conductor's voice echoed through the car as he strode by. Aaron straightened in his seat and looked out at the town coming into view, at the mountains stretching into the sky. He'd never seen such mountains! They were beautiful, but their sharp peaks and jagged cliffs reminded him he was far from home. Give him a field and a dozen cattle any day. Give him lumber and some nails. Those he could control. Here?

Nothing seemed in control.

Maybe he should have let Mrs. Sommer tell Marianna he was on his way. For the first hundred miles on the train he pictured Marianna's smile as she saw him. But the closer he got, the more he questioned if that would be the case. Had the distance ruined any chance of the love he'd once counted on?

First he felt a shudder, then the grinding of wheels locking up. Finally a loud clanging sounded as the train slowed to a stop. Aaron adjusted his straw hat and grabbed his suitcase, eager to leave behind the movement of the train that caused his stomach to rumble as if it were filled with a hundred bees.

Descending the train steps, he scanned the old-fashioned platform. The crisp, cold Montana air hit him and his stomach ached. People moved about, unloading and loading, all of them Englisch. He'd been the only Amishman on the train, and it looked like he was the only one here, too. If it hadn't been for Mrs. Sommer's letter, talking about the small Amish community in West Kootenai, he would have thought he was getting off at the wrong stop.

A steady snow fell. Large white flakes landed on the wet ground with a plop.

Aaron carried his small suitcase onto the platform and scanned the faces. Was one of these folks his driver? A few people gazed at him, but none approached. *Maybe he's inside.* His chest felt hollow. He'd never felt so alone.

Aaron entered the station and looked at the rows of wooden benches and the ticket desk. Everything within him told him to go back. To get on that train and head home—back to everything he knew.

But his longing for home paled in comparison to his longing for Marianna. He had to know if she still loved him.

The air was warm in the station. People filled the space. A television mounted overhead gave a weather report—more snow coming. Most people sat with computers on their laps and music devices attached to their ears. A girl sitting tugged her mother's arm and pointed at him. Others eyed him, their curiosity evident in their widened eyes. One teen took a photograph.

His chest tightened, and he found it hard to breathe. All confidence in who he was and what he stood for had been left behind on the train platform in Indiana. He was nothing here—worse than nothing. A spectacle.

"Hey there." A voice sounded behind him, and Aaron turned to see an older man staring at him with a gapped-tooth smile. "Are you the Amish guy who needs a ride up to Rexford?"

"Sir, it's West Kootenai, but yes, I do need a ride."

"Rexford, West Kootenai—it's close enough. Do you need help with your things?"

Aaron glanced down at his one suitcase. "I think I got it."

The man wore a thick fleece jacket and an even thicker beard. He seemed tired, jittery. He rubbed his eyes. "Yes, well, I suppose you do. We best get hurrying now. I need to make it up the hill afore supper. There ain't nothing worth missing supper for." He strode off with quick steps. Aaron had no choice but to follow. Just outside the train station the man climbed into a white van parked in a no-parking zone. The filthy, dented van had seen better years.

Aaron climbed in. The snow fell faster now and a layer of slush covered the road. As soon as Aaron's door slammed shut, the man started up the van and gunned it. The van moaned and slid onto the road, the vehicle's back end wiggling like the tail of a fish.

Go back! his mind shouted to him again. He fumbled for the seatbelt and snapped it in place. He looked around them. They were the only ones on the road. If Aaron needed help, he'd only have the man driving this van to turn to.

Go back!

He pushed the voice away. He had to do this. Had to see her. But what if he'd come all this way and Marianna didn't want him there?

What if he'd come this far for nothing?

The snow and fog filling the Montana sky outside the van window made Aaron feel like he was in a dream. Or maybe a nightmare. His hand gripped the handle of the passenger side door.

How long had they been on the road? It seemed like forever, though they'd left town only thirty minutes before. And the man's driving was only getting worse. Why hadn't Aaron told the driver to stop when he still had the chance? He couldn't tell him to pull over now. Fields and forests stretched out on either side of the road, and beyond unfamiliar mountains mocked him, reminding Aaron he didn't belong.

When he decided to leave Indiana, the only thing on his mind was Marianna. He'd thought of her every day as he built a home for her. He'd thought about her when she was gone. Even those days he'd spent with Naomi, Marianna had never been far from his thoughts. He tried to come up with the perfect thing to say when he saw Marianna again, but he'd yet to come up with anything good.

Go back.

He removed his hand from the door handle and crossed his arms over his chest. The heater groaned on high, but it did little good.

His eyes darted to the majestic mountain ranges, but he barely saw them. Instead he looked to his rimmed hat resting on his knee. He ran his hand down his face. The smoothness of the skin on his cheek mocked him. Fear caused his heart to thud in his chest. Fear that he'd come all this way and not see the love in her eyes he desired. For many years he believed in her love just as he believed the sun would rise the next day. But now?

The driver fiddled with the radio dial, then turned to Aaron. "You talk English?"

Aaron's head darted up.

"*Ja.* I mean, yes, uh, sir."

"That's funny. I was wondering. You haven't said more than two words since you loaded up."

Aaron shrugged. "Got a lot on my mind."

"Ever been to the West Kootenai before?"

"No, sir."

"What's yer reason for coming?" The man took a sip from a thermos of coffee.

"Mrs. Sommer didna tell you?" Aaron eyed the man. His jeans looked like they hadn't been washed in a week. A large mustache covered his lip and wiggled like a trapped animal when he talked.

"Na. She just sent a mess—"

For a moment it seemed the van floated off the pavement. Aaron's stomach lifted, like it did when he pumped his legs on the old tire swing back home. His eyes darted to the driver, and the man's eyes grew wide. The driver's hands were fixed on the steering wheel, unmoving, but it was as if an outside force had caught hold of the vehicle. The man's mouth opened in a silent scream. The road, black, shiny and glazed with snow, continued straight, but the van spun toward the opposite lane, heading straight for an oncoming car.

No! Aaron leaned hard against the passenger side door as if his weight alone could push the van back into its lane.

Then, as if hit in the side by a large hammer, the van jolted and spun the other direction, gliding toward a cluster of tall trees.

"Hold on!"

Aaron's vision sharpened as he focused on the large row of pines on the shoulder of the road. As if in slow motion, the van slid toward trees. Aaron braced his hands on the dashboard, his nails digging in. The tree trunks neared, and then—

The front corner of the van hit, causing a deafening crunch. Then, still in motion, the van spun and turned. Aaron's door hit first and the sound of bending metal and shattering glass filled his ears. The crushed metal opened, like some monster widening its jaws, and closed around his leg. His breath caught as the tree before him quivered and then snapped, falling, falling. Aaron heard a terrified scream. Only when he felt tears wetting his face did he realize . . .

. . . it was his own voice.

CHAPTER FOUR

*B*en crested the hill, newly fallen snow crunching under the tires of his old truck. The tools he'd loaded up in the back for Marianna's dad, Abe, and her Uncle Ike did a good job weighing down the back. He was taking the tools up to the old Meberg place. Folks had moved into the area a few years ago and started an ambitious building project during that summer. Then winter hit and the snow piled high. They'd abandoned the house half-finished then headed back to a milder climate. Abe and Ike were part of the crew now finishing the job.

Ben was glad. It bugged him to see that house sitting half-done all those years. It seemed only right the brothers would finish what was started. Half-realized dreams did no one any good.

Seeing that electric lights had already been set up inside, Ben smiled. Sure, the Amish in the area keep plain homes, but when it came to work, most of them used the modern tools their bosses provided. They never seemed conflicted by that, and he never brought it up.

He parked in front of the house and jumped out. He was just about to open the tailgate when he noticed Abe striding toward him. Marianna's father usually wore a wide smile, but not today. Ben ran a hand through his hair. What could be wrong? He hoped nothing was wrong with Marianna.

"Ben." Abe approached, pausing near the rear of the truck. "It's good of you to bring our supplies up. Our buggies would have had a hard time getting those things this way."

Ben opened the tailgate. "No problem. Glad I can help." He reached for a wooden sawhorse, but Abe's hand stopped him.

"Hold up. Can we talk a few minutes first?"

"Do you need help with something else? Another load?" Even as Ben asked he could tell from the older man's face this conversation had nothing to do with work.

"No. I'd like to talk to you about my daughter. Do you mind taking a short walk?"

"I don't mind. I believe from the top of the hill behind the house there's a great view of Lake Koocanusa."

Abe nodded and headed that direction.

Sucking in a deep breath, and willing his pounding heart to calm, Ben stepped into pace next to the older man.

They walked toward the top of the hill, and Abe cleared his throat. He glanced over at Ben and let out a low sigh. "What I'm gonna say should have been said months ago. I've seen the signs, but Ruth finally convinced me that I should say something to you."

Ben pressed his lips into a straight line. "Signs?"

"The care you and my Marianna have for each other. It's plain to see for anyone looking."

Ben nodded. His guess was that Ruth—Mrs. Sommer—had been watching when he and Marianna had emerged from the woods yesterday and that had been the last straw. He could try to explain—tell Mr. Sommer they'd met by accident, which was the truth—but it didn't really matter.

Abe was right, and Ben knew it.

"As much as I like you, Ben, our Amish community has its own ways. To be baptized into the church you're not just dedicating yourself to God, but your people. Relationships with outsiders are not to be. Fer as long as Marianna has been old enough to consider staying Amish, she's made it clear she would. It's all she's wanted. To live by our ways, to marry, and to raise children to do the same."

It's all she's wanted. Those words played through Ben's mind. Was that what this was about? Abe was worried that if their affection continued to grow Marianna might leave the Amish way of life? Ben clenched his fists by his side. Part of him understood their worries, their pain. This family had been through a lot. They'd lost two children to death and one to the world. No wonder they were being protective.

"I understand, sir, and I'd be lying if I were to say I didn't care for your daughter. I do. I care so much in fact that I want what's best for her. I mean if the Amish way of life is her choice—"

"It is."

Ben nodded and his footsteps slowed as they neared the top of the hill. The trees were sparse and the world seemed to open up before them. There was not only a clear view of the lake, but additional mountain ranges beyond that. Ben wished he could crest an emotional hill and get such a view of his own life. To see in every direction and know the right way to walk.

"I understand what you're saying, Abe." Ben crossed his arms over his chest, and he turned to him. "And I will honor your wishes. I won't push Marianna. I won't attempt to draw her away. I can promise you that. But I do have one question."

Abe stroked his beard as he met Ben's gaze.

"You've been reading God's Word for a while. Do you believe, sir, that one can be a follower of Christ without being Amish? That they have the same chance of getting into heaven?"

Abe's gaze narrowed. He opened his mouth and then closed it again.

Ben lifted a hand. "You don't have to answer me now. It's just something to think about. But know I will do my best to be Marianna's friend and look out for her best interest, just as I look after yours."

Abe nodded once, took a final scan of the valley, and then turned and headed back down the hill. Ben wasn't sure if he'd insulted the man. He hoped not.

Dear Lord, may You use my feeble words to do good, not harm.

Back at the truck they unloaded the tools and supplies together. They chatted about the project, about the snow, but Ben knew what weighed heaviest on both of their minds. When Ike came out to help, it was clear he sensed the awkwardness between them, but he didn't say anything. It was only after Ben closed the tailgate and drove away, heading out the way he came, that he released the heavy breath bottled up inside.

It's all she's wanted.

Those words haunted him as he drove back home. As he settled before the wood-burning stove in his small cabin and opened his Bible, Ben knew what he wanted. He wanted Marianna. But did he want her at the cost of all she knew, loved, longed for?

To share his love would be to draw her away. To bring her shame. To put a wall between her and her family and community.

Yet he also knew God's heart, and even though he cherished his relationship with his Amish friends, he couldn't help but question their commitment to tradition, to their old ways. While he appreciated their dedication to family, church, community, an uneasiness had settled deep in his gut. Something just didn't sit right with him.

Over the past three years Ben's relationship with God had grown. Following God by obeying outside rules—like rules of dress or whether or not to have electricity—was not necessary. And that's where he struggled. Marianna could love him *and* love God. Her salvation depended on her heart, not her kapp. Problem was, mentioning such things to her would take away any chance of friendship, let alone the hope for more. He might have already ruined everything by questioning her father.

Ben closed his eyes to pray, but no words came. He wanted to trust God, but defeat gripped his throat, refusing to release. Pursuing Marianna—as he wanted—would bring more harm than good.

It was a hard decision, not pursuing her romantically. He wanted to be with her. He wanted to see her, but he knew something else. When he looked into her eyes, Ben saw she cared. And to confess his love would lead to something he never desired.

How could he ask the woman he loved to choose between him and the only way of life she'd ever known?

CHAPTER FIVE

*M*uddy footprints from yesterday's slush lay buried under a layer of white snow that sparkled like the diamonds in Millie Arnold's wedding ring. Marianna held her gloved hand out. Glittery flakes sparkled on the black wool. Not that she'd ever have a wedding ring like Millie's. Well, unless she married an Englischman.

Not that she'd marry an Englischman.

She shook her glove, scattering the diamond snowflakes.

With wide swishes of her broom, Marianna swept snow from the front steps, but it fell faster than she could sweep. Millie Arnold had arrived not five minutes prior, settling into the table closest to the kitchen for warmth from the woodstove and conversation from the bakers. Now it wasn't clear where her footprints had been. White flakes had smoothed the landscape with a frosting of white.

Marianna blew out a frosty breath. The bone-chilling air, whipping through the tall pines, stung her cheeks. Finished with the steps, she turned and swung open the door to Kootenai Kraft and Grocery. She stepped into the embrace of the warmth and stomped her snow-caked boots on the front doorstep. Snow ringed the hem of her plain blue dress like lace—the only lace she'd ever wear—and she attempted to brush it away.

She moved to the dining room area to warm her hands by the fire, and discovered Millie'd moved from the kitchen area and now sat in the wooden booth next to Jebadiah Beiler. Millie's red lips made an *O* shape and wrinkles extended out from her mouth, splayed like cracks in weathered paint. Her eyebrows lowered in two straight lines and her concerned eyes were fixed on Jebadiah.

"The van must've been taking the corner too fast." She pointed to the copy of *The Daily Interlake*, the newspaper spread on the table before him. "Did ya read an Amish man was the passenger and he's up in the hospital in Kalispell?"

"*Ja*, I can't say I know of anyone missing." Jebadiah looked toward his bushy eyebrows as if doing a mental count. Leaning forward, arms on the table, he stroked his beard, which reached the second button on his simple blue shirt. "Maybe they're mistaken. Coulda been someone dressed plain."

"Or maybe someone coming for a visit." Millie's voice and mannerisms were fit for a chow line. A rancher's wife all her life, her face was as weathered as the leather saddlebag hanging on the dining room wall. But Marianna had discovered Millie's interior wasn't nearly as tough. Weeks ago the older woman had bought two sacks of groceries and loaded them in the back seat of Jenny Avery's compact car while the young mom shared a bowl of soup with her four-year-old daughter, Kenzie. Jenny had asked around, but no one spilled the beans. Millie even tucked a hundred-dollar bill into a box of Pop Tarts, Marianna later heard.

Marianna grabbed up the carafe of fresh coffee to top off her customers' mugs and to get a glimpse of the photo in the newspaper. Her heartbeat always quickened at any news of a vehicle accident, whether buggy or automobile. Her two sisters had died in such an accident on the very night she was born, when a semitruck hit their buggy. Even though she'd never met Marilyn and Joanna, the fast falling snow reminded her of their loss. No sooner had she swept off a layer of pain over heart, than another layer fell. What muddy footprints hid underneath the thin covering of protection she'd built around her soul?

All those years she spent always trying to be the perfect Amish girl to make up for her sisters' loss. . . . All that changed when her family moved to Montana. Here she discovered maybe God had a plan for *her* alone.

"Heard that passenger got his leg broke real bad." This from Howard Anderson, who sat across the dining room. "My wife Annabelle called down to check on him. It's a young man from Indiana come to Montana for a visit. Goes by the name of Aaron Zook."

"Aaron?" The whispered name escaped Marianna's lips. There could be another Aaron Zook, but she knew it wasn't. It was her Aaron—the man she'd always thought she'd marry.

"Whoa there!" Millie's voice split the air, and Marianna looked down. Hot coffee poured over the mug and onto the table.

"I'm so sorry." Marianna set the carafe on the table and grabbed up her apron, wiping the spill. "It didn't get on you, did it?"

"No, just soggied up my napkin." Millie chuckled. "I'm still a bit chilled from the elements, but I wasn't wanting to get warmed up that way."

"I'm so sorry." Marianna hurried to the kitchen for a soapy towel. Her hands trembled as she plunged them into the sink. The hot water stung, but she barely noticed as she rung the washcloth out. Her chest tightened, as if someone had poured concrete into her lungs. Months ago she hadn't wanted to leave Aaron, and now?

She felt trapped.

She hurried back and wiped up the table. Should she call home and ask her parents if they knew about Aaron being here? Would they answer the phone? Should she talk to Annie, who worked on the schedule in the back office, and ask for the day off? To trudge back home. To discover what Aaron's being here meant. Why he hadn't told her he was coming? He wouldn't just show up without an invitation. He would have written a letter . . .

Mem.

The heaviness on her chest increased. She pulled back her shoulders, sucking in a breath.

Ever since Marianna got off the train and returned to West Kootenai, Mem had acted strange. When Marianna entered the front door a month ago, she'd expected her mother to cry tears of joy. That wasn't the case.

Mem expressed concern when Marianna left a quilt for Ben. Then, when she'd walked back in the door with Ben at her side, one would have thought from Mem's reaction that Marianna stopped at a chapel on the way home and married the Englischman! It was later, in the month following, when Marianna had little contact with Ben, that Mem had seemed less worried. But only slightly.

Had Mem brought Aaron here for a surprise visit to ensure her heart didn't stray toward the Englischman?

Marianna swallowed hard and returned to the kitchen. She pulled the dishtowel off the bread dough. It had doubled in size. Just to make sure it was ready, she poked her index finger into the dough. Mem had showed her the trick. If the hole she made stayed in the dough without filling in, the dough was ready to punch down. But if the hole closed—even a little—the dough wasn't ready and needed more time to ferment. If the dough collapsed—which had happened to her more than once—it had risen too long and would not rise again.

This dough was perfect. Her fist punched it down, gently pushing her knuckles into the center of the dough. Then she pulled the edge of the dough toward the center, punching it down again. Satisfied, she turned it over, giving it time to rest.

Mem *had* been acting peculiar. She'd been talking a lot, asking Marianna about every aspect of her work. She'd commented how nice it would be for Marianna to have her own home and family some day and not have to brave the cold, watching her footing on winter's icy paths.

Mem had also cleaned the house from top to bottom.

How could she do it? How could Mem invite Aaron here without telling her?

The bell on the front door jingled. Marianna washed her hands and then hurried out to greet the customer. Edgar had called in sick, and it was the other Amish girl, Sarah's, day off. Annie, the owner, would come out to help if Marianna needed, but maybe being busy would keep her mind off the fact that Aaron Zook lay in a hospital bed just an hour's drive away by automobile.

An Amish man entered, his head lowered as he brushed snow from his hat. When he lifted his face, she recognized Dat, looking more tired, more stooped than she'd seen in a while.

Dat's eyes drifted toward her. His face molded into the same look she witnessed the night Levi left. Her father offered her a blank stare that gave evidence of rejection, disbelief.

Marianna dried her hands on her already damp apron and then stepped toward him, trying to control quivering hands. Keeping her breathing even.

"Is it true that Aaron's here? That he got in an accident and he's in the hospital?"

"Yes, and no." Dat's words were slow and heavy, like the large icicles hanging from the porch outside. "He did get in an accident, but he's not in the hospital." Dat removed his hat from his head, brushing it. He repeated the motion of a moment ago even though snow was no longer on the rim. "They released him this morning. He's back at our house."

"But what is he doing here? Why didn't you tell me he was coming?"

"I didn't know. It was Ruth." The way her father said her mother's name told Marianna the sting of betrayal pierced him too. "Mrs. Zook sent a letter to your mother. She returned one, sending an invitation for Aaron to come. Mem thought it would be a nice surprise for you since you didn't go back."

She could tell from his tone that there was more to it than Mem wanting to give her a "nice surprise." She lowered her voice and stepped toward him. "Mem had no right to do this. To assume—"

Dat placed a hand on Marianna's shoulder. This type of touch was rare, but it spoke volumes. *This is how things are,* the look in his eyes stated. *We'll not mention it again.*

Two years ago she would have let the matter drop. Even six months ago she would have done the same. But now? Marianna balled her fists at her side. She wouldn't be able to hold the words in if she tried. Maybe, as those back in Indiana believed, she'd already been corrupted by the Englisch ways.

Dat studied her, frustration reflecting in his gray eyes.

Her words poured out. "I can read it in your eyes, Dat." She tried to keep her tone respectful. A heavy weariness came upon her, surprising her. "But we both know that's not the truth. She didn't want him here for a surprise. She—she's worried about me. Worried I'm not going to carry through with my plans to marry Aaron." Marianna clenched her fists then slowly released them. Her mother did what any Amish mother who'd already lost three children would do. Marianna cleared her throat. "Like I've told you before, Ben's a good friend. Nothing more."

Even as he nodded, she could see her father didn't believe her. Dat rubbed the back of his hand against his forehead, as if wiping away a memory. Maybe the memory of her and Ben in this very room. He in his Englisch clothes, she in Amish dress. Her with his guitar in her hands, and him—with his arms around her. His cheek close. Her body resting against his. She guessed that's what Dat thought about.

Maybe because the memory always hung in front of her, like frozen breath on the air.

It was a memory she'd have to pluck from the surface of her heart and plunge deeper inside. She had Aaron to think of now. He needed her. And a good Amish girl never turned her back on a friend.

CHAPTER SIX

*D*at had only to explain the situation and Annie gave Marianna the day off. She and Dat walked home through the snow. The exertion of wading through the calf-high drifts kept her warm, but neither spoke. Disbelief sealed her lips, and Dat's far-off gaze held a hint of betrayal. His own wife had lied to him. Not by words, but by silence.

Arriving at home thirty minutes later, Marianna stepped through the front door. Her scraggly dog Trapper greeted her first, jumping against her leg. His tail wagged as quick as the beating of hummingbird wings. She patted his head, enough to satisfy him, and then her eyes fell on Aaron. He partly sat, partly lay on the sofa. Three pillows supported his leg, casted to mid-thigh.

Charlie sat on a cushion on the floor, his own leg bandaged. It had been nearly a month and a half since his accident, and the burn was healing. The doctor asked Mem to keep him home from school for at least another month. The other two boys were at school and the baby napped in her cradle near the woodstove. Ellie was nowhere to be seen, and Marianna assumed the young girl was upstairs. Charlie's eyes fixed on Aaron, a look of camaraderie between them.

Aaron wore no hat and the glow of the fireplace radiated off his blond hair, which looked silky smooth and fell across his forehead in straight bangs. Her heart did a double beat—something she hadn't expected.

His eyes fixed on her and his lips curled into a close-lipped smile. Then his lips parted. "Surprise, Marianna. Although this wasn't how I imagined things."

In an instant the angst over him being here vanished. It was Aaron. Even if she didn't have the same strong, romantic feelings she once had for him, he was her friend. They'd attended school together since the first year. He'd put frogs in her lunch pail. She'd tied his shoelaces together under the porch as he sat and chatted with friends. Even now a giggle threatened to bubble up as she remembered the look on his face when he stood only to tumble.

"Well, you always have been clumsy." She removed her gloves, unbuttoned her heavy wool coat and hung it, then placed a hand on her hip. Then, all joking aside, she moved toward him, her smile fading. "So what happened? I heard at the store it was some type of automobile accident."

"*Ja.* It happened so fast." He shook his head. "I bet when my letter finally reaches my mother she'll smile and nod."

"That you're hurt?"

"No. She just likes to point out how many more car accidents there are compared to buggy. She always complains when she needs to ride in an automobile to town. The buggy accidents just make the news more because folks get hurt worse—"

Aaron's eyes widened and he looked to Dat, as if realizing what he'd just said. But her father paid no attention. Instead, as he removed his hat and coat, Dat's eyes were fixed on his wife.

"'Tis a dangerous time of year to be traveling these roads." Dat hung up his coat, then sat on the chair next to Mem. His hand reached over and took hers. "If I woulda known Aaron was coming I would have picked a driver I trust. Ben Stone—he's a good driver. Would've got Aaron here in one piece."

Mem's upper lip flinched, but she said nothing.

Hearing Ben's name, heat rose to Marianna's cheeks. She hoped Aaron didn't notice.

"Of course, nothin' we can do about that now." Marianna sighed and then turned to Aaron. "What's done is done and we have to get you on the mend. How did it break? How long did that doctor say you must be in that cast?"

"My leg is broken right above the knee. They put in a plate and screws."

Marianna could tell his energy was fading fast.

Aaron forced a small chuckle. "I wonder what the bishop will think of all the technology in my leg." He sighed. "But that means I can't move around much. Not for six weeks soonest. Could be longer."

Six weeks? Marianna looked to Mem.

Mem's jaw tensed, and her lips moved as if chewing down words that rushed to break through. She glanced at Marianna, then averted her eyes as if realizing she'd dug a hole that swallowed them all. Marianna would have a chance to spend time with Aaron, all right. No going around that now.

Marianna scooted a kitchen chair closer to Aaron and sat. "I'm sorry to hear that. It's a long time to lay around, but we'll do our best to tend to you."

Aaron wet his lips and his eyes met hers. He blinked and she could tell he attempted to find words to turn their conversation to a more pleasant subject, but pain reflected in his eyes. His face reddened. Sweat beaded on his forehead. She reached for Aaron's hand and he wrapped his large hand around hers tight—as if holding it would provide the relief he needed.

Her throat tensed and tears pooled. How selfish she'd been to worry that Aaron's being here would be a bother to her. He was in pain. This was a serious injury. And it could have been worse.

I could have lost him. Could she imagine her life without Aaron?

Her thumb stroked the top of his hand—the most physical contact they'd ever had. Somehow it seemed natural, right. "Do you need anything? Did they provide you with medication for the pain?"

"*Ja, ja.* But it's not working as I'd like." Aaron squared his shoulders. "The ride up here . . . think I tensed up because of the snow on the road. Couldna rest. Could not get comfortable. And when we passed the spot where the accident happened . . ." He shook his head.

"How'd it happen?" Charlie piped up, for the first time being brave enough to join the adult conversation.

"Charlie, he don't need to be sharing." Marianna looked to her hands. The roads up to the West Kootenai were dangerous even during good weather. The highway ride wasn't bad, but then it turned onto a small, windy road. Then, once over the bridge, a wide, gravel path wound up the mountain with a steep cliff on one side, falling to the lake. Who would have guessed a whole community used that as their main thoroughfare. She disliked automobile travel on these roads as it was, although she agreed with her father. If she had to travel with anyone, it would be Ben who she'd trust.

She fixed her gaze on her brother. "I'm sure Aaron needs to rest. We don't need to bother him with that now."

"I don't mind. Just an icy road, that's all. Happened so fast. The van turning, sliding. My side hitting a tree. The tree falling." Aaron closed his eyes and swallowed hard.

The room fell silent. The tension in the air made the heat from the woodstove feel heavy, dense. Though no one said it, all thoughts were on her parents' buggy accident so long ago. Charlie shifted on his cushion as if waiting for Aaron to give more details. Aaron lowered his head instead. Charlie glanced around. Something was wrong but he wasn't sure what. Unlike Marianna, to the young boy the accident long ago was only a story. All he knew was his family now—his one older sister. He hadn't grown up with the pain of the loss of two others. Marianna and her parents had hid their pain well.

The dog's yawn broke the silence, and Marianna glanced over to see Trapper open his eyes and stretch. Then Trapper rose and trotted to her from in front of the woodstove where he'd been napping. He wagged his tail, as if forgetting he'd already greeted Marianna not ten minutes ago. He sniffed Aaron, then sat next to the sofa near where his hand rested. Aaron patted the dog, much to Trapper's approval.

They sat there in silence. Finally Marianna took a deep breath. "At least yer on the mend, cared for by friends."

Aaron's eyes darted to hers. He studied her face as if searching for the meaning behind that word friends. She wished she could explain—ease his fears whatever they were. But this wasn't the time. Her parents and brothers still sat, listening. She could tell from Mem and Dat's faces they, too, wondered how things would turn out with Aaron around.

"Yes, it is nice to be with folks I know. And now that I'll be around fer a while I wonder if you could introduce me to some of your other friends."

"Oh, yes—we have a nice Amish community." She touched her kapp for emphasis.

"Those friends and others. I'd like to meet them." Aaron released her hand and leaned back, allowing his head to sink deeper into the pillow. "I hear that Englischer driver your dat mentioned has become a close friend."

Ben? How much did Aaron know about Ben? What had he heard?

No doubt he'd heard rumors circulating around the community. Rebecca had written just last week about all the ideas spreading on why Marianna had purchased a ticket, boarded a train, then before she got far returned home with an Englischman driving her back. How they learned even that much Marianna didn't know. She'd written to Aaron, Rebecca, and Aunt Ida, explaining that her family still needed her. Hadn't they believed her?

Obviously not. Aaron was here, wasn't he?

Aaron shifted as if he sat on nails, not a soft cushioned couch, then he touched Marianna's arm. "At least I have no worry of yer family tossing me out in the cold. To the barn maybe . . ." He forced a pained laugh and Marianna joined him.

She rose, placing a balled fist on her hip. "You don't know that yet." Then she lifted her finger and wagged it. "I grew up with you, remember? I know the type of pranks you like to play, Aaron Zook." She cocked her head, lifted an eyebrow, and eyed him. "Least I can keep you in my sights with your leg all plastered up like that. If anything we'll get to talk about all the things neither of us got around to writing about."

Aaron nodded. "It's true. There is so much—" He glanced around, as if remembering her parents were still in the room. "I'd like that, Marianna." Aaron scratched his leg just above his cast. "Really I would."

Dear Journal,

There are things that surprise me, but mostly it's my emotions that can't be hidden under a kapp or plain dress. Can truth be seen in my eyes? Sometimes I worry. The fact is I remember the feeling of Ben's arms wrapped around me and his breath on my cheek most. Why can't I sweep the memories away?

I'm surprised by what I forgot, too, like how much I care for Aaron. I forgot how handsome he was. I forgot how much he cares. He built a house with me in mind. That's all I could think about tonight. When my family sat in the dining room, eating Mem's hamburger potato dish, I sat in the living room, in the flickering evening light, next to Aaron with a plate on my lap. For a moment in time the voices in the kitchen faded and it was just the two of us. I wondered about the house he built that I never yet saw. I wish I could see it. Maybe some day I'll ask him to draw me a sketch. Or maybe I won't. Will it be hard to stay when I know what's waiting in Indiana?

Why did I stay?

When I looked into Aaron's eyes I realized I hold part of his heart. Like the flowers that had been waiting in my bedroom when I arrived in Montana, Aaron's heart was pressed and kept—not between the pages of a book but deep inside me.

Tonight Aaron's sleeping on the sofa. Tomorrow he's moving into my room, then he won't have to go upstairs and it's close to the indoor bathroom. Tomorrow I'll be sharing quarters with Ellie and Joy, but maybe I can find a place to tuck this book. There are things I couldn't write to a friend or talk about out loud, but that doesn't mean they're not whipping through my mind all day like the icy wind outside the window. Putting them here helps.

Maybe God can help me settle my mind, just like He settled my heart this summer. Even though it's still fall, the cold comes quick in these parts. With the snow here now, I doubt I'll get back to my pond till spring. Yet it warms me to think of the still waters and to remember they're there, even when I can't see them. And that God's with me, even when I canna see Him.

CHAPTER SEVEN

*A*aron's leg throbbed, the pain unrelenting. Heat traveled up his body, down to his toes. His arms trembled and even lifting a glass of water to his lips seemed like too much work.

Waking up in the hospital, he'd almost talked himself into just finding a way back to Indiana. He hadn't wanted to see Marianna—not like this. He'd come to win her over, and now? He couldn't even cross the room to the toilet without help.

Yet, when she'd walked through that door, the pain had subsided for a moment, and he remembered again why he'd put so much work into the house. Why he'd come.

For a few months he'd tried to convince himself Mari wasn't the one he needed by his side. Naomi had become a dear companion during the days after Marianna had left. She was thoughtful and kind. She made him smile. He'd even allowed himself to be swept away in her kisses. Yet being here—seeing Marianna, reminded him of all he loved about her. Her beauty. Her kindness. Her care for others. There was something else too. The nippy air outside had made her cheeks pink and full. Her eyes sparkled.

The sadness he remembered in her gaze had faded to a shadow. Aaron liked the way she looked now.

For as long as he could remember, he'd wanted to marry Marianna Sommer, and she made it clear he held her interest too. When he and the other boys had played baseball at recess, he'd always looked to the sidelines to find her eyes on him. She'd been the one to kindly comment on his drawings, and then there were little things she shared. Growing up it had been a cookie, a jar of jam, a small basket of strawberries.

Aaron attempted to turn and stretch, tucking the pillow under his cheek. Pain shot up his leg, turning his stomach. He covered his mouth in his hand, willing himself not to be sick.

He'd been feeling ill all day. The tension from the ride. The pain. He'd eaten dinner because all eyes were on him, but now he wished he'd hadn't. His body seemed to protest digesting the food when it worked so hard just to deal with the pain.

Would Marianna come if he called out to her? He guessed she would.

She was just on the other side of that wall, in her room. He looked to the living room window and the bright moon outside. Did she lie there, awake, looking at the same moon and thinking of him?

He'd been worried, he had to admit, when the train from Montana had arrived and she hadn't been on it. He'd understood more the next day when her letter showed up in his mailbox. She'd planned on returning, but her family needed her. She said things had changed, that she changed, and that God still had a plan for her in Montana.

What Aaron had read between the lines—what his heart had

feared—was that her feelings for him had changed. Surely if she loved him as much as he loved her, she would have come.

Now, seeing her again, took away some of those worries. Her smile had brightened when she'd glanced at him, and a special spark lit her eyes—despite his mind being fuzzy with pain medication, he'd seen that.

Even with the pain of his leg it was worth comin'. He'd be here—close to her. He had nowhere to go, neither did she. A soft smile curled his lips as he imagined telling the story in years to come about how their love grew after a broken leg brought him into their family's home for a spell. Would their children have gray eyes like hers? He hoped so. To him Marianna was the prettiest girl he'd ever seen, and he couldn't wait to make her his—for good.

Outside the sound of the trees rustled, and in the distance Aaron thought he heard a wolf howling to the moon. On the other side of the bedroom door Trapper growled. Aaron perked his ear and listened. The dog's footsteps clicked on the floor, then the creak of the door. More footsteps followed as Trapper trotted into the room.

"Hey there." Aaron rubbed his eyes then stretched out a hand to the dog. Trapper sniffed the air and eyed Aaron.

"You comin' to check on me, boy?"

"Trapper." Marianna's voice called from the door in no more than a whisper. "C'mon, you're gonna wake him."

Aaron smiled. Should he tell her pain kept him awake? Maybe she'd have sympathy. Maybe she'd come and talk to him for a while.

No. He settled his head into the pillow once again. He didn't want her to think him too weak. Besides, she had a job to go to tomorrow. As much as he did not like that she worked with the Englisch, he understood. Her parents needed her help for a time. That's what he told himself anyway. She'd work until she returned to Indiana. After that she'd have to do it no longer.

That had been his plan all along—for her work to be in their home. Most Amish wives didn't work outside in stores and such, but they often sewed or baked for others. He didn't want that for Marianna. He wanted to prepare enough ahead of time to give her a comfortable life. His herd had been a part of that. His job on the Stoll farm too. And the cabin, most of all. Sometimes he wondered what would have happened if he'd worked faster—stayed up later at night to get the job done. If he'd finished just three months prior, they'd be heavy into courting before her family decided to move.

Nah. He shook his head, ignoring how his neck, too, still ached from the accident. As his dat always said, a task takes as long as it takes. No use rushing around—not like the Englisch did. Hard work got everything done. He'd given it his best. He had to trust that now.

Trapper approached and placed his paws on the sofa, nuzzling Aaron's cheek with his wet nose.

"Yer not minding yer master. Or rather mistress," Aaron whispered. "I'm all right. I'm a crippled one—the kind the wolves like—but they're not coming in."

The sound of footsteps interrupted his words. Not the clomping of shoes, but the softness of bare feet. He glanced up and saw them first—Marianna's bare feet on the hardwood floor, her toes curled up. Just a few inches of her nightdress could be seen under the hem of her robe. He glanced up to see Marianna pulling the collar of the robe tight to her neck. On her head she wore a white sleeping kerchief. Her eyes were round, wide, innocent. Aaron's heart pounded to see her dressed so—so intimately—but he tried not to let it show.

He pulled his hand off Trapper's ear and pointed to Marianna. "See, you're in trouble now."

"Sorry he woke you, Aaron."

The way she whispered his name was a mix between a question and a statement, as if she still didn't believe he was really here.

"It's all right. I wasna sleeping yet."

"Is it the pain in your leg?" She took a tentative step forward, stretching her hand toward Trapper, then paused.

"Some of it." Aaron didn't know how to tell her the pain in his leg mattered little in comparison to the questions of his heart.

Marianna, do ya still love me? Did you ever? He swallowed hard looking to her hair, braided and hanging over her shoulder. He hadn't seen it down like that in years—eight at least—but it was different than her childhood braids. What it would be like to untie it, to run his fingers through it? Did it feel as soft and silky as it looked?

"I don't know why he's not coming to me." She hunkered down and stretched out her hand to Trapper.

Why didn't Marianna come closer to get the dog? Did she feel the charged air in the room as he did? It reminded him of the time he'd first been digging the foundation for his house and a lightning bolt had struck a tree not too far away. The hairs on his neck had stood on end as they did now. Aaron tried to sit up but pain shot through his leg. The deep ache had been there all along but had been forgotten as soon as she walked into the room.

"He's never done this before." She patted her legs, and still Trapper sat there, close to Aaron.

Aaron smiled. "I guess that's a good sign. Maybe he likes me."

"*Ja.*" Marianna stood and cocked her head. She placed a hand on her hip. "Maybe he wants to stay with you tonight. If you don't mind." She sounded disappointed.

"I don't mind. But will you be okay?"

She sighed. "I think I will." Her eyes stayed on him and he saw something there. Care. Appreciation. Love? He wasn't quite sure, but he hoped.

"Yes, Aaron. I'll be *gut.*" She moved toward her room, her nightdress swishing against her bare calves. And for some reason Aaron had a feeling she wasn't talking about the dog any more.

CHAPTER EIGHT

*B*en Stone straightened the quilt on his bed. What had he done to deserve such a gift? He'd made his bed everyday since Marianna gave the quilt to him, running his fingers over her careful stitching, sending up a prayer or two. First time in his life bed making had become a habit. First time he'd prayed so intensely for a beautiful woman.

Sometimes he wanted to pinch himself that Marianna had stayed. Other times he kicked himself for not telling her more when she got off that train. In his dreams he ran toward her, sweeping her up in is arms, burying his face in her neck, and breathing in the scent of her. Every time he awoke, a powerful sense of loss assaulted him. She was here, but he could not hold her. He couldn't see her . . . well, at least not often. Even though Mr. Sommer had made that fact clear, Ben had known it already. He understood all Marianna risked to return his affection.

Some days he couldn't help it. He'd visit the store despite his stocked pantry. A few times he'd chatted to her about nonsense things. Other times he'd entered quietly, so she wouldn't notice. He watched her working in the kitchen, her hands busy with bread or pies. Her eyes looking out the window, lost in thought.

The scent of brewing coffee filled the air. He headed to his kitchen for a cup of coffee when he heard knocking. Ben paused and turned to his front door. Surely someone wouldn't be out this early. Maybe it was a chunk of snow falling from the roof. He pulled a coffee cup from the cupboard and heard it again. It was definitely a knock.

Ben hurried to the door. When he opened it, he was surprised to find Ike standing there.

"Look who's the early bird." Ben opened the door wider. "Come on in."

"Thanks. Do I smell coffee?" Ike stepped inside and removed his jacket. "I was out of coffee beans and I was sure I could find a cup here before we headed up to the worksite.

Ben cocked an eyebrow. Ike lived halfway between him and the store. It would have been just as easy for Ike to walk over there. Unless . . . Ben eyed the Amishman, whose smooth face proved he was still a bachelor. There was a shadow of worry in the man's eyes.

Unless this had to do with more than coffee.

Ben motioned to the dining room table, pushing to the side a pile of laundry he'd yet to put away.

He poured two cups. "Take anything?"

"Nope, just black."

Ben handed Ike his mug then added a teaspoon of sugar to his own.

"So the roads are pretty bad out there." Ike sipped his coffee. "There's been all types of accidents. You'd think people would understand that when it snows they have to slow down."

Ben sat across from Ike, brushing a few crumbs from the table onto the floor. "It's our hurried lives. We try to do too much, too fast and we end up paying for it." He nodded at Ike. "That's one thing your people have gotten right—taking the time to do things as they ought, in the time they need to take."

"Yeah, well, it was one of our own who was injured in one of those accidents."

Ben sat up straighter, leaning his elbow on the table. "Who?"

"You don't know him. It's a kid from back where we come from in Indiana. Not a kid, really—a man. The man Marianna planned on marrying."

The coffee cup in Ben's hand clunked onto the table, sloshing coffee over the side, but Ben paid it no mind.

"Mari . . . Marianna was engaged?"

Ben felt like someone had just sucker punched him in the kidneys. *I'm such a fool.*

"No, we don't have engagements like the Englisch. The easiest way to explain it was there was an understanding between them.

"And he's here?"

Ike nodded. "At my brother's home, all casted up with a broken leg."

Ben leaned back in his chair and slouched down. No wonder Marianna acted so distant yesterday. No wonder Mr. Sommer had given him that talk. Both needed to make sure he was out of the way so Marianna's old beau could step back into place.

Not that Ben ever had a slot on her dance card. He'd only wished for such a thing.

Ben took a sip from his coffee then set it down. He swallowed it, wondering why it suddenly tasted so bitter in his mouth.

Marianna walked to work, excited that her tracks were the first in the newly fallen snow. It glittered on the ground like tiny crystals reflecting the first rays of morning light. White snow stacked upon the dark green branches of the pine trees like a thick smearing of marshmallow cream.

She moved her booted feet with slow steps, amazed she'd lived so many years not knowing that such a beautiful place as West Kootenai existed. As she rounded the corner, turning onto the main road leading to the store, she could hear the sound of a river in the distance. A large creek—Boulder Creek she remembered being told—plunged down from the mountains. Unlike the smaller streams in the area, it hadn't frozen over and she guessed that it wouldn't. Instead, she imagined the water rushing down to Lake Koocanusa. So much power being absorbed into the expanse of the water, just like her breathed prayers escaped into the cold air around her.

God, show me. Help me.

She didn't know what she wanted to be shown. She didn't know what type of help she needed. Nothing made sense anymore. When she left Indiana she'd been certain of her feelings for Aaron. When she'd gotten off the train and returned to her parents' home, she'd been certain about that decision. But now? It was as if someone took a big, wooden spoon and mixed up her emotions. Thank goodness she had to work today. She needed to get away—to escape Aaron's fixed gaze. To put her hands to work so her mind wouldn't have too much time to think.

Entering the front door of the store, Edgar's smile greeted her first. His white beard looked fuller than she remembered, reminding her of the Santa decorations she'd seen in the windows of their Englisch neighbors back home.

"You feeling better?" She removed her jacket and brushed it off.

"As good as can be expected for an old man." Edgar pretended that answering her questions was bothersome, even though he had nothing better to do than wait for the next customer.

"It's quite a cold fall out there. Like nothing I've seen in Indiana." She hung her coat on the hook behind the counter and tucked her gloves into the pocket. Then she moved to the counter.

"Nothing unusual. Not like '96. Now that was a snowy year . . ."

"1896?" Marianna laughed, and he eyed her. Even though Edgar didn't smile at her joke, she noticed humor in his gaze.

"Haven't been around that long, but I've seen a lot of changes."

"Really? Like what?" She had baking to get done, but she also knew it meant a lot to Edgar for her to stop and talk. She could tell he appreciated it even if he never said so.

"Like the lake. It didn't used to be there, you know."

"Lake Koocanusa?" Marianna thought about the first time she'd driven over the high, long bridge that stretched from hillside to hillside with the lake far below.

"Everything changed when they put in the Libby Dam." Edgar sighed. "Sometimes I get homesick for how things used to be. My aunt and uncle's house is just under where the Koocanusa bridge now stands. My parents' house was two miles past that. When they put in the dam, they cleared off the mountainside. The Boulder Creek I knew changed too."

"You mean there used to be houses down there—where the lake is now?" Marianna straightened the stack of postcards on the counter, glancing at the captured images of the lake, mountains, and trees.

"There used to be a whole town. Stuff got moved up the mountain when they put the dam in. Other things just got covered over."

"That doesn't seem right." Marianna brushed a strand of hair back from her forehead. "Seems like things should stay the same."

"Nothing stays the same, darling." Edgar looked at her and winked, the hard edges on his face softening. "The older you get the more you'll know that. Even when we make it our goal to keep things the same"—Edgar nodded to her kapp—"life has a way of making changes for us. Our decisions and desires only go so far. Remember that."

"Yes, of course." Marianna nodded and then hurried toward the kitchen. Sarah, the other young Amish woman who worked there, hadn't arrived yet. Edgar's words replayed in Marianna's mind, yet before she had time to think about them, she paused at the threshold between the open kitchen and the dining room. Ben sat at the table closest to the kitchen and his eyes were on her, as if he expected her. No, more than that . . . as if he studied her. Without having to ask, she knew why he'd come.

He must have heard about Aaron.

Marianna paused and eyed the man who'd drawn her heart. If only she could be sure about her feelings for the handsome Englischman—about anything. Like water rushing over her, all she once knew lay buried under curling depths of emotion. Surfacing seemed impossible. Her steps paused. Her lips parted, but no words came.

He looked at her, and she saw in his eyes the same tenderness she'd first seen that night, months ago, when he played his guitar and sang at the restaurant. She could still remember how she'd felt hearing his music, how it had affected her when their eyes met. And yet . . .

Though she'd replayed that memory dozens of times, today she could no longer remember the tune.

CHAPTER NINE

en sat at the table, nursing a cup of coffee. All during the drive to take Ike to the worksite, and then the whole way back home, he'd told himself it didn't matter that an Amish man had arrived to sweep Marianna off her feet. That he'd probably been mistaken about her interest in him. The more he thought about it, he realized Marianna always tried to keep her distance. He'd been the one to approach, to talk with her. He'd been the one to wrap his arms around her as she held the guitar.

All during the drive back to his place, he told himself to give the woman time to figure out her own future. Even so, he'd showered, shaved, put on cologne, and dressed in his nicest jeans and shirt—without looking too dressed up—and put on his snow boots and headed out. He tried to pretend he'd come here because he hadn't had breakfast, but he knew better. Maybe that's what Ike had expected. He didn't seem surprised when Ben headed down the hill instead of staying at the worksite.

Now he watched Marianna cook up scrambled eggs and ham for him. She worked with an efficiency that she'd been trained to from birth. Her long skirt swished around her calves as she whisked the eggs in a bowl. Ben tried to convince himself he wasn't going against Mr. Sommer's wishes by being here, but he knew he was kidding himself.

Five minutes later Marianna approached, placed the plate before him, and refilled his coffee cup.

"Do you have a few minutes to sit? We haven't talked in a while."

Marianna nodded. "*Ja.*"

That surprised him. He hadn't expected her to agree.

She placed the coffee carafe on the table and then sat in the booth across from him. She glanced behind her, to where Edgar washed the front window. The store was empty of customers. She turned back to Ben.

"So, I hear that your friend was in an accident. Is he okay?" Ben added sugar to his coffee, stirring in slow circles.

Marianna shrugged and eyed him. She didn't seem shocked he knew about Aaron. News traveled quickly around these parts.

"He's okay, but not great. Aaron's leg is broken, just above the knee."

"Aaron, huh?"

She nodded. "Aaron Zook."

A good Amish name for a good Amish man.

"It's a bad break. He won't be able to do much for six weeks."

"Six *weeks?*" The words shot out before he could stop them. Ben looked down to his plate, feeling heat rise in his cheeks. He picked up his fork and cut off a chunk of his scrambled eggs. He took a big bite and inhaled. The still-hot egg burned his mouth. Ben swallowed fast, but it didn't help. The eggs burned all the way down his throat. Pain traveled with it, but it didn't compare to the pain Marianna's words caused.

The man she once loved—the man she'd planned on marry-ing—would be staying with her family for months. He'd be there, every day, close to Marianna. Close in a way Ben couldn't be.

He lifted his napkin to wipe his mouth, blowing air over his singed tongue and studying Marianna's face. Did she still love Aaron? Had she always?

Marianna sighed. "It shocked me too. I didn't even know he was coming. He's using my room, and I'll be sleeping with my little sisters. They may be small, but they sure take up a lot of space yet." The more Marianna spoke, the more she relaxed. Ben's shoulders relaxed too. He could tell from her wide-eyed gaze that she didn't want to talk about Aaron. She leaned forward more, as if saying, *I want to talk to you, not talk about him.*

Following her cue, he changed the subject. "I want to thank you. You know, for the quilt. I think of you when I use it."

"I'm glad." She offered a soft smile. "I enjoyed making it. It's my way of thanking you for—"

Ben raised his hands. "I know, you told me. I didn't say that to have you gush." He reached around and patted his back. "I have a big enough head as it is without your accolades. Time to change the subject again."

Laughter spilled from Marianna's lips, and the room seemed to brighten. "Okay, what is it we can discuss?"

He leaned forward, fiddling with the corner of his napkin. "Working on anymore quilts?"

She tilted her head down and eyed him under her lashes. "I thought we were going to change the subject."

"We did. Got it back off me and onto you. Or rather your handiwork."

"Well, I do have to make one for Annie. I've yet to start."

"If you need a ride down to Eureka, to the fabric store, well, I can give you a ride."

"I'll keep that in mind." Her finger ran up and down the crease where the wood planks of the tabletop joined together. She studied the wood as if it were a Michelangelo painting. From her expression, it was clear she was thinking about more than a ride to the fabric store. But what?

If only he could read her mind. Was she thinking about Aaron?

Ben chewed on his bottom lip. Should he ask the question that fogged up his mind, just like their warm breath fogged up the window beside the table?

"So you going to make a quilt for your friend? Aaron, right?"

"Yes."

Ben's heart sank. For all these weeks he'd considered the quilt a special gift, a token of her care, but if she made one for Aaron Zook too—

"Yes, his name is Aaron, but I have no plans on making a quilt for him." She paused and gazed at Ben, as if she wanted to say more.

"I better get back to work." Marianna rose and smoothed her apron. "And I'm glad yer enjoying that quilt, Ben. It has a special place in my heart."

With that, she turned and hurried toward the kitchen. He watched her and couldn't help but smile. He'd rather she'd confessed *he* had a special place in her heart, but he was satisfied with what she did say now. His appetite restored, he tucked into his breakfast.

He glanced down at his watch. He had work to do. He couldn't spend all day at the restaurant, sitting by the heat of the fire with a pretty Amish girl warming his heart.

So she'd once planned on marrying that Aaron Zook—he rose and left a generous tip—but what were her plans now? Surely, if she still loved Aaron, her special quilt would be draped over his lap instead of Ben's bed.

With a wave to Edgar, he headed out into the cold. The snowfall had stopped, and morning light turned the sky into a faded pink color—the same pink that had colored Marianna's cheeks when she saw him. He climbed in his truck and smiled.

She cared for him. Just as he cared for her. The problem was, neither could do a thing about the matter.

⁂

The morning crowd had been filled with familiar faces. Both Millie Arnold and Jebadiah Beiler had asked about Aaron. Others had asked too, and Marianna was surprised by how the news spread. Then again . . . it was news. In a small place like this, getting a new horse or a dog having a litter of puppies could stir conversation for a day or two. She supposed Aaron's accident was the biggest happening since the Carashes' barn fire and Charlie's accident before that.

The rest of the day went by as normal. She'd baked. She'd waited on customers in the restaurant. When her cookies were in the oven, she even took time to help Edgar stock the store shelves.

As she worked, Marianna couldn't believe how comfortable she'd become here working with the Englisch, serving them. They appreciated her hard work, and she found great satisfaction in seeing folks enjoy the special treats she baked. Like the weeks prior, this day continued on with no surprises. What did surprise her was seeing Ben again as the clock ticked closer to the time she got off. Seeing him enter the restaurant gave her a burst of energy as she helped Annie prepare the evening's dinner.

"Hey there." Ben approached the open door between the restaurant and the kitchen, leaning against the doorjamb.

Marianna eyed the stream of cream pouring into the potatoes. Her face was flush from spending the afternoon cooking, but her cheeks warmed even more upon hearing Ben's voice.

She glanced at him, feigning surprise. "Ben, hello." She placed the carton of cream on the counter and let a smile curl on her lips. "Yer a bit early for dinner." She took a deep breath in. "But it smells good, doesn't it?"

"I'm not here for dinner." Ben leaned his back against the refrigerator door. "I mean, I'll probably be back to eat later, but that's not why I stopped. The wind has picked up out there. It's miserably cold."

"You came here to give me a weather report?" Marianna picked up the hand masher and pressed in to the potatoes. Steam rose from the large pot, fogging the window and blocking the view.

"No, not quite. I came to see if you wanted a ride. I know you walk, and it's only a mile, but . . ."

As his voice trailed off, she turned to him.

"It's more than the cold. When the weather gets like this the roads are real slick. People don't slow down as they should."

Marianna pressed a hand against her hip. "Ben, I think you're worried about me. I better ride home with you or you're gonna be sneaking around my house tonight to see if I made it fine. And

Dat doesn't like sneaking much." She continued mashing but kept her eyes fixed on his.

He opened his mouth and laughter spilled forth. "That's one thing I like about you, Marianna. You say things how they are. There's no chance for a man to flirt with you . . . to try to make you see things my way."

"Flirting is nonsense." She waved a hand in the air. "All that acting and pretending. I already know about you, Ben. You're considerate—and determined. I'll ride with you."

"Okay then, thanks."

Marianna looked at him. "You're thanking me? I should thank you for your thoughtfulness." She took a cube of butter from the counter and dropped it in the pot. "And, truth be told, I wasn't looking forward to cold toes."

Thirty minutes later when she got off, Ben held her elbow as he led her down the front steps of the store. He was right, it was slippery out.

Ben's truck smelled like gasoline, wood shavings, and something sweaty, like dirty socks he'd shoved under the seat. Marianna climbed in and the wind shut the door behind her. The weather was picking up, and she didn't mind the smelly truck if it meant she'd stay out of the cold.

In the driver's seat Ben put on his seat belt and started the truck up. Tepid air blew from the vents.

"Thanks for the ride." She folded her arms in front of her, tucking her mittens under her arms. "I don't mind walking. Lately, it's been my best time for prayin', but I think that wind woulda blown me into the woods for good."

"No problem." He put the truck into gear and headed out. His tires slid as he pulled from the parking area onto the road—not that you could tell where one started and the other ended. All of it was white, icy.

"Gives me something to do. That's the hard part of cold nights like this. I've read two novels in the past week and wrote a new song—"

The truck slid and Marianna grabbed on the dash. "A song? Really?"

"Yeah, nothing special. It's, uh, never mind."

She looked to him and watched as he rubbed the back of his neck with his free hand. His cheeks looked red, and not from the cold.

Marianna couldn't help but laugh. "Ben Stone, did you write a love song?"

"No, not really . . . well, sort of."

"I want to hear it. Can you sing it?" The words were out before Marianna could stop them. For the Amish, playing musical instruments wasn't allowed and singing, other than their church's hymns, was also frowned upon. But at this moment she didn't care. Her curiosity got the best of her.

"Better not. I'm still working on it." He frowned. "I scribbled some notes." He glanced at her. "Maybe when I get it figured out. And have my guitar." He chuckled. "A guitar helps drown out my voice."

Marianna didn't mention that listening to him playing his guitar wouldn't be the wisest thing for her to do. Not that she wasn't allowed. She hadn't been baptized into the church yet. Even if she listened she wouldn't have to confess. It was something else. Even now, months after she'd listened to him play, tingles danced up her arms at the memory.

A small compact car passed, coming from the other direction.

Ben slowed and pulled to the side, allowing the car more room. Marianna was thankful for the distraction.

A few minutes later they pulled into Marianna's driveway. She placed her hand on the door handle. She'd like to invite him in but knew she couldn't. Aaron was inside. He was new to these parts. He wouldn't understand the friendships between the Englisch and Amish—especially between her and Ben.

Mem also wouldn't be pleased. Marianna bit her lower lip, remembering her mother's tears. She wondered again about the Englischman her mother once cared for but pushed that thought away as she turned to Ben.

"I would invite you in—"

Ben waved a hand. "No, don't worry about that. I just wanted to make sure you made it home okay. Besides those potatoes looked good. I have a hankering. I'm going to head back to the store."

"*Ja, gut.* Thank you, then." She opened the door, pushing hard against the wind. "See you soon."

Without another word she shut the door behind her and hurried to the house. As she got to the porch she turned and waved, but Ben's truck already headed back the way it had come.

Marianna stomped her feet on the door mat and then opened the door and hurried inside.

"Mari!" Ellie ran to her.

"Well, look here. See what the storm blew in." Dat smiled from his place near the fire. He sat in his favorite chair with *The Budget* in hand.

"Mari, you must be frozen." Mem hurried up, cupping Marianna's cheek with her hand. A puzzled expression filled her gaze when she felt warmth.

"Did you get a ride?" Mem's voice was just a whisper.

"*Ja*, a good Samaritan picked up me. And speaking of picking up . . ." Marianna pulled off her wool coat, hanging it by the hook near the front door, then bent down and swept Ellie into her arms.

Her mother didn't have to ask. Marianna could see her mother's disapproval from her narrowed gaze. Mem knew who the ride was from. For someone who'd first called Ben "harmless" when they arrived in Montana, Mem didn't seem to like him coming around any more. Not one bit.

Mem cleared her throat and looked to the sofa. Marianna turned, forcing a smile onto her lips. Part of her would rather be still driving around in an old, smelly truck with Ben than here with her family. With Aaron. But she couldn't let them know that.

Aaron sat on the sofa, his leg up on a wooden bench Dat had brought down from upstairs. An extra pillow Marianna didn't recognize propped up his leg. Something Mem stitched up today she supposed.

Charlie reclined on the floor, Marianna was so grateful his leg was healing, though she knew infection was the biggest worry now.

"So, how are our patients today?" Marianna moved to the living room. "Two bad legs, *ach*." She clucked her tongue. "What some people do yet to keep out of the cold."

She smiled, noticing the brightness in Aaron's eyes at seeing her. Back in Indiana that would have been enough for her to be walking on clouds all evening . . . but now? When did things change? *Why* did they have to? It should be easy to love Aaron, she'd done it for years.

He scooted up straighter, wincing. "*Ja, gut*. Not as much pain today. Wish I could be more useful."

"I bet it's hard."

"My leg doesn't hurt so much." Charlie patted it softly as if trying to prove his point. "Aaron's is much worse."

"Aaron read to Charlie, helped him with his homework." Mem called from the kitchen. "And he was a great extra set of arms with the baby. Don't know what I'd do without him here."

"So you arc making yerself useful then." Marianna pulled up a wooden chair and sat down next to him. "So have you drawn them any pictures yet?"

Aaron glanced up at her. "You remembered?"

"Are you kidding? Of course. I've always loved your sketches."

"You draw, Aaron?" Mem stepped from the kitchen, looking at him. "Didn't know that. You'll have to show us some of yer artwork. Or draw us something special."

"Best artist in Indiana." Marianna patted his hand. "Now Montana, too, I bet."

Aaron's eyes fixed on hers and his strong hand closed over hers. Marianna tilted her head, looking at him. Her heartbeat quickened and her pulse drummed in her neck. Even though Dat sat not ten feet away, reading his paper, Aaron didn't seem shy about this display of affection.

"Was work okay?" His voice held a note of concern.

"Yes, of course. Why do you ask?"

"Charlie told me about the Englischman on the train. How he tried to hurt you. It's a good thing yer dat was there."

"It wasn't like that. Not really. And things are different here." Even as she said the words Marianna remembered the man at the auction. He'd tried to hurt her too. That seemed like years ago, not months. The snow outside made it hard to remember summer had been here not too long ago, gracing the land with warmth, bathing it with sunshine.

"I don't like you working, Marianna. Doesn't seem right."

"Just helping the family." She tried to keep her tone light. "And if I'm going back to Indiana, I'll need funds for the fare." She didn't want to think about how she'd already wasted money on a ticket she didn't use.

"So you are coming back, then?" Aaron's light blue eyes focused on hers. Sweat beaded on his brow, and she wasn't sure if it was from the warmth of the fire or the pain. She resisted the urge to wipe it away.

"Well, I've always planned on going back in the spring."

"Is that still the plan?" There was urgency in his voice.

Marianna bit her lip, not sure what to say. She looked to her father, but he pretended to still be reading. The bouncing of his foot on the floor proved he wasn't focusing on the typed words. She doubted any news in *The Budget* could make him that nervous.

"I'm thinking about that. I imagine so, *ja*." She thought about the tension she felt on the train. The tightness in her chest over going back. "But spring is still a long time away."

"I'd like it if you did." Aaron leaned his head back against the couch cushions. For someone in a lot of pain he suddenly looked relaxed. And the way his eyes studied hers soothed her. It was as if an intimate cord draped between them, uniting them. Marianna crossed her arms in front of herself, for some reason feeling bare before him. She'd never known such a gaze. He did not look at her, but *into* her.

"You have to see the cabin."

She nodded and swallowed hard. It would be useless to speak. The words wouldn't make any sense if she tried.

She looked down at his hand, still wrapped around hers. His hands were strong from hard work, but gentle too. His long fingers enveloped hers and his thumb stroked the top of her hand. She closed her eyes for the briefest moment, reveling in Aaron's touch. When she opened them, her eyes met Aaron's and a thousand needle pricks stirred within her—so many she thought she'd jump from her skin.

With her hand in his, those feelings for Aaron she thought long buried came back with a warmth the fire behind her couldn't touch.

∽∾

"I wish you would have told me Aaron was coming, that's all I'm saying." Abe looked to his wife, who lay in bed next to him, curled to her side.

"I told you why I didn't," she whispered. "I thought it to be a nice surprise."

Abe sat with his back against the wall. Their lantern was set to low light and he had the Bible open on his lap.

"Not sure I needed to be surprised." The angry words dropped from his lips. "You made me look like a fool."

Ruth didn't comment, and Abe guessed it was best she didn't. If she said anything they'd continue deep into the night, the angry words building with each breath. They hadn't fought that way in years, but he'd never forget how things used to be when they first got married. She'd always try to justify her actions, his anger would build, and soon they'd both be shouting. Thankfully they'd mellowed over the years. By the time Ruth was pregnant with Marianna, they'd been happy. After the death of the girls they struggled with their loss. Sometimes together—more often alone. He saw something else in Ruth's gaze after that night that he didn't understand. Guilt. As if their daughters' deaths were her fault. If it was anyone's fault, it was his. He was the one who fell asleep before the crossing.

Abe hadn't seen Ruth's blameful look in a while, and he was thankful. That's why he knew he needed to drop this whole issue with Aaron's surprise visit. He let out a low breath, telling himself that wasn't what got him all riled up in the first place. It was Ben's question that made him angry.

Would non-Amish go to heaven? Didn't Ben know that wasn't for Abe to decide? Men could not decide the fate of other men. That was up to God alone.

Yet the more Abe thought, the more he realized what Ben was really asking: *"Am I good enough for your daughter?"* Ben loved God, that was clear. He cared for others. He read God's Word. Yet deep down in Abe's heart, the answer was "no."

Ben was not good enough for Marianna.

And that's what bothered him. Because by making this distinction, he was doing the judging.

He was setting himself up as God.

Chapter Ten

The next day at work Marianna was in the office, looking for more labels for their packages of bread when Annie looked up from her computer and cleared her throat. Marianna grabbed up the labels and turned, looking to Annie. She wore a long blonde ponytail like she always did, and though the wrinkles on her face hinted she was older, the youthful brightness in her eyes made her beautiful.

"Marianna, there's something I want to show you. I hope you won't be mad."

"Mad at you?" Marianna smiled. "I don't think that's possible. What is it?"

"Remember this summer at the auction? A friend of mine offered to take some photographs for me. She's building a Web site for my store and I wanted to post them online. She gave me the original prints to look through."

Marianna furrowed her brow. Whatever Annie talked about had to do with the computer. It meant nothing to her, so how could it make her mad? Marianna looked at the photos spread on the desk in front of Annie. There was a photo of the Miller's gas-powered ice cream maker. There were many photos of quilts. And one photo of three Amish girls sitting on a bench. From the back all you could see were their dresses and kapps.

"One of the things my friend found interesting was the interaction between the Amish and Englisch. She got some great shots." Annie held up a photo of an Amish girl, who Marianna recognized as one of the Shelter kids, handing an ice cream cone to a teenage boy with numerous tattoos and piercings on his face. "My friend's from Kalispell—not here. She didn't understand about Amish not liking to have their pictures taken, especially their faces . . ."

Marianna put her hands on the desk. Oh . . .

"Do ya have a photo of me?" She leaned forward, scanning her eyes across the desk.

"Yes, it's one of my favorites too." Annie reached into the envelope and pulled out a photo. "I wasn't going to use it on my Web site—you know, as a way to honor you."

Marianna took a step forward. "May I see?"

Annie held it up. "Yes, of course."

Marianna took the photograph from Annie's hands, and for the briefest second thought Annie had been mistaken. Studying it closer, Marianna realized the beautiful Amish girl in the photograph *was* her.

She tilted her head. She'd never seen herself in such a way. She'd never seen a photograph of herself and only glanced briefly at herself in the mirror to make sure her face was washed and her hair pinned up under her kapp.

In the photo her chin was lifted and her mouth open in laughter. She held three quilts and her smiling eyes were slightly closed. Ben stood next to her, his eyes fixed on her face. He wore a smile, but there was more than that. The way he looked at her.

Well, Marianna had never seen such a tender look. Not between her parents. Not from Aaron. Did he always look at her like that when she wasn't aware?

Marianna placed her hand on her chest and could feel it beating through her blue dress and black apron.

"It's a nice photo," she finally said, hoping Annie didn't hear the emotion in her voice.

"I like it too, but you can see your face. I know that's a problem."

"Well, I am in *rumspringa*. I suppose that out of all things having a photograph of myself can be my wild attempt at running around."

"Would you like that copy?" Annie looked up at her.

Marianna looked to the photo again, noticing the crowds of people in the background and the mountains in the distance.

"Yes, I would. I mean if I return to Indiana, I'd like something to remember this place by."

"You're returning to Indiana? Change your mind again?" Annie's wide eyes searched hers.

"No plans now, but you never know."

"I understand. I'm sure with that young man in your home . . . well, I bet it gets you wondering."

Marianna didn't know how to answer that. Instead she studied the photo of her and Ben again. It was the first photograph she'd ever owned and it was special, mostly because of the man she was with.

"Do you mind if I use it for the Web site, then?" Annie gathered the other photographs in a nice stack and returned them to the envelope. "I mean, since you are in your *rumspringa*."

Marianna laughed, her fast-beating heartbeat making her head light. "I don't mind. It's not like anyone from my Amish community will see. And if they do mention it, I'll know then they were using a computer." She clucked her tongue. "And we all know they ought not be doing that."

⁂

Marianna heard the jingle of the front door and stiffened. Her hand pressed the photograph in her pocket, and even though she'd only received it an hour ago she'd sneaked enough glances that the image of the captured faces burned into her mind.

Footsteps neared. Was it Ben returning? She'd been doing that all morning. Every time she heard the jingle of the front door bell—whether she worked in the kitchen, waited on a customer, or cleaned the dining room—her shoulders tensed, her movements paused.

"There she is . . ." Marianna recognized the voice and continued wiping off the table. It wasn't Ben's face, but her Uncle Ike's smiling face that greeted her as she turned.

"Hello. Come for lunch? Annie cooked up some Corn Bread Meat Pie from Aunt Ida's recipe." Marianna glanced to the kitchen and noticed Annie's gaze intent on them. Then Marianna looked closer and noticed it wasn't *them* Annie looked at, but Uncle Ike. Marianna tried to hide her smile. Was it possible? Did her boss have an interest in her uncle?

"Oh, wish I could. Annie *is* the best cook."

Ike looked to the kitchen and winked. Annie looked away, her cheeks reddening. Marianna covered her mouth with her hand. Sarah, her coworker, paused her work, whipping up cream in a bowl, and took note of the interaction too.

"Actually"—Uncle Ike turned back to Marianna—"I was on my way back to your folks' house. Yer dat made some wooden crutches for Aaron—to help him get around better. Was wondering if you had a lunch break and wanted to ride home with me? I'll have you back in an hour."

"That's kind of ya, but—" Marianna scrambled for an excuse.

"You should go," Annie called from the kitchen, wiping her sudsy hands on her jeans. Then with quickened steps she hurried into the dining area. "Things are slow enough. Sarah is almost finished with the peanut-butter pies."

Hearing her name, Sarah glanced up. "Almost done." She nodded her head and her white kapp bobbed up and down. "*Ja,* you should go home and check on Aaron."

Marianna folded her arms over her chest. It wasn't that she didn't want to go home. Sometimes Dat or Uncle Ike headed home for lunch in their buggy and she'd catch a ride. Nor was it that she didn't want to check on Aaron. It's just that everyone *wanted* her to go see him—that it was something a young woman in love with a young man should do. Romantic even. The more she played into that role, though, the more everyone would expect her to run to Indiana to get married as soon as the snow melted.

Yet with three sets of eyes on her, Marianna couldn't think of one good excuse. So without another word she took off the cooking apron that she wore over her black Amish apron and moved to the coat rack.

"Marianna?"

At Annie's call, she turned. "*Ja?*"

Annie approached with two loaves of bread in her hands, already packaged for sale.

"You can take this to your friend. Tell him you baked them this morning." Annie smiled, handing one of the loaves to

Marianna. Then she turned to Uncle Ike. "And I thought you'd enjoy one too. It's still warm. Your niece is a fine baker."

"Thank you." Ike smiled then lifted the bag to sniff. "Smells wonderful."

Marianna's jaw dropped as she watched. She'd been working here for months and hadn't seen this level of interest between these two before. *Have I been blind?*

But as she walked to the front door and followed Uncle Ike out to the buggy, she realized she'd been so focused on her own thoughts and worries, she hadn't been paying attention to anyone else.

"It's the way of pride," she could almost hear her bishop back home preaching in his singsong voice. *"If we're thinking more of ourselves than others, we're not living as the good Lord says we should."*

Marianna climbed into the buggy and grabbed a blanket from behind the seat, wrapping it over her legs. She'd had enough of herself. Of her thoughts. She needed to care for others as God would want her to, and leave the rest in His hands.

As the horse pulled the buggy down the road, the bread warmed her lap. Why hadn't she realized sooner that she needed to follow Annie's example of giving and caring for others, instead of being caught up in her own thoughts? How could she have missed it?

Annie cared for others through the store, through the kitchen, through conversation. It was a business, but so much more. The giving of warm bread to those down and disabled, not because they didn't have anything to eat, but because doing a little something proved care in big ways.

What would Aaron think? Would he take her offering as her showing him affection in hopes of soon becoming his bride?

And if he did, was that a bad thing? Marianna just wasn't sure. In a way she was eager to have Aaron try her bread. Eager to see the joy it brought to his gaze.

Who did she fool? The joy *she* brought to his gaze was what she enjoyed most.

CHAPTER ELEVEN

arianna hurried into the house, bread in hand. Uncle Ike tended to the horse, stating he'd be in soon. She stepped onto the doormat and stomped the snow off her feet. Her stomps stopped short when she noticed Aaron on the couch.

His leg was still propped up on pillows, but Ellie sat half on his lap and half on his chest. Josiah knelt on the floor with his chin resting on Aaron's chest. Trapper sat by Josiah's feet, and although he wagged his tail as Marianna entered, he didn't rise. Charlie sat there too, eyes focused on Aaron's sketchbook.

"*Die Katze!*" Josiah pointed to the sketchbook in Aaron's hand.

"*Katze!*" Ellie mimicked, meowing.

Hearing Marianna come in, Aaron glanced up, a smile spreading across his face. Then he turned back to the sketchbook.

"A cat? A cat might be hard to draw. Hmm." His hand set to work on a sketch.

"What's going on? Josiah shouldn't you be in school?" Marianna placed the loaf of bread on the kitchen table. She slipped off her coat, feeling warm, not only from the heat of the woodstove, but of the sight of Aaron with her siblings. She hadn't seen him with kids other than his own younger siblings, but the way her brothers and sister cuddled with him appeared natural, beautiful.

"Josiah begged to stay home from school yet. I supposed it would not hurt once." Mem stood at the top of the stairs. She descended, carrying a stack of clean dishtowels. Since it had gotten cold, their laundry had to be hung in the house to dry. Before Aaron arrived, Mem had hung it in the living room near the fire. Since his arrival, she'd been hauling it up to her room, where it hung until it finally dried.

"Aaron has been entertaining them all morn." Mem hurried into the kitchen. "He taught them a new song, and he read a story from one of Josiah's books. He—"

"But they're sitting on him, and he's only had surgery a few days ago. Ellie"—Marianna took a step forward and pointed to the floor in front of the sofa—"You should sit on the floor. Or I'll bring you a chair. You have to be careful. Give Aaron time to heal."

"I thank you for your concern, Mari, but she's not hurting a thing. They are helpin' to distract me. Keeps my mind off the pain."

"You sure?" Marianna picked up a kitchen chair by the chair back and carried it next to the sofa. "I don't want you to take longer to heal than necessary." She set the chair down next to Josiah and Charlie and sat, folding her hands on her lap. Worry caused a slight headache in her temples.

Aaron placed his sketchbook on his chest and reached for her hand, squeezing it. "I'm doing better today, and even more so now that you're here. Did I see you bring something in? Is that fresh bread I smell?"

"*Ja.*" She pulled her hand away and rose. "I made it this morning." Even as she said the words, she noticed his smile. A smile of appreciation. No, more than that. A smile of affection. She turned and stepped away, realizing Annie's plan had worked. The only thing was Aaron believed it to be *her* plan. She hurried to the kitchen.

"Thank you for coming home. It's a surprise," Aaron called from his place on the sofa.

She held the bagged bread to her chest and turned. "Yes, well, my uncle—"

From the cradle near the woodstove, Joy's cries split the air, interrupting Marianna's words. She put down the bread and hurried to her baby sister. She rewrapped Joy's blanket and then pulled the baby into her arms, breathing in the baby scent. Joy immediately stopped crying.

Marianna prepared to explain, when Uncle Ike entered with the crutches. He shut the door behind him and paused. His eyes scanned the living room, taking in the sight of her and Aaron with the children.

"Well, isn't this some sight. Aaron and Mari, you do look fine with all those children, if I say so myself." He held up the crutches, changing the subject as if his previous words had not just made both Marianna and Aaron's cheeks turn shades of red. "The wood's a little damp yet. I leaned them against a tree outside while I blanketed the horse, and they fell in the snow. Let them dry by the fire and I'll show you how to use them, Aaron. Mari can help." Uncle Ike winked.

Marianna didn't know what to say, but she refused to respond to her uncle. Instead she moved to the chair and sat by Aaron's side, cuddling Joy close.

"So what else did you draw?" She leaned forward and peered

at the sketchbook. "All the kids at school used to tell you the same thing, 'Draw this, draw that, Aaron.'"

"*Ja, ja,* I remember. I remember something else too." He picked up his pencil and started drawing a little kitten, curled next to the cat. "I remember out of everyone, you appreciated my drawings most. You always like to see what I'd sketched down at the pond or in the barn." His pencil stilled and he looked to Ellie, Josiah, Charlie, Joy, and then to her. "And yer uncle is right. Yer going to make a great mom some day, Marianna."

Uncle Ike dropped her back at work, and Marianna hurried into the general store. Even though the tip of her nose tingled with the cold, her cheeks stilled burned from her interaction with Aaron. It had warmed the pit of her stomach to see him like that, hair ruffled, with Ellie on his lap and Josiah and Charlie snuggled by his side. She blew out a long breath, as if to blow those thoughts aside for a time. She'd be useless at work if her mind stayed on Aaron's smile. The brightness of his blue eyes as he called out a greeting. The deep affection, as he told her she'd be a good mother. She'd tried to hold back her emotions, but hearing those words stirred something. The fire for a relationship with Aaron hadn't gone out completely. Every kind word, every caring look, was like a stick stirring the coals deep, sending off sparks and bringing to life what she'd thought had been extinguished.

She brushed the snow off her wool coat and pulled off the heavy bonnet she'd worn over her kapp. Hurrying to the coat-room, her steps stopped short when she heard voices coming from Annie's office.

"I'd love a job," a young woman was saying, "it's just that childcare—"

"Don't worry about that, dear." Annie's voice rung out like sleigh bells on a carriage ride. "I made a few calls yesterday and found some local ladies who volunteered to help with Kenzie. A few days here. A few days there. At no charge, of course. Just trying to be neighborly."

Marianna hung up her coat on the hook and then stomped her boots, releasing the snow in half melted clumps and letting them know of her presence.

"Marianna, is that you?" Annie called from the office.

"*Ja.*" She hurried to the office door and looked in. Jenny Avery sat there, her blonde hair pulled into a short ponytail. A thin hand attempted to quickly wipe away the tears on her cheek, but not quick enough.

"Jenny, hello. It's good to see you. I didn't mean to eavesdrop, but it sounds like you'll be working here, too, *ja?*"

Jenny nodded and shrugged. "Yes, I guess so, I mean childcare was my only problem." She turned to Annie. Her chin quivered slightly. "Thank you." She looked overwhelmed, but not in a bad way. "I can start tomorrow if you like."

"That would be great. I'll have Edgar train you at the cash register and next week Marianna can train you in the kitchen. Marianna would love an extra set of hands. It'll give her more time to work on new recipes, won't it, Marianna?"

"*Ja* . . . yes." Marianna smiled and glanced to Annie. They weren't so busy that they needed another set of hands. In comparison to the Amish way of working quickly and getting things done, they had plenty of time for their tasks. The way they often stopped and chatted with customers was proof enough of that.

Still, Annie had a heart of gold. She would make less profit for the store if it meant this young woman would be able to provide for her daughter.

"If you'd like I could show you around." Marianna motioned to the doorway.

Jenny nodded and rose, following.

Marianna walked out of the small back office and noticed Ben. He stood at the counter. Edgar was checking him out. Marianna paused and smiled. "You're back so soon?"

"My boss sent me down. I'm getting a sandwich for his lunch." Ben seemed to feel a need to explain.

"Do ya expect me to believe that? I think you enjoyed breakfast so much you've come back for lunch too," she chided.

Ben shrugged, paying for the lunch.

"I hope your boss enjoys it. Sarah does make good sandwiches." Then remembering that Jenny stood beside her, Marianna made the introduction.

"Nice to meet you, Jenny." He grinned. "I think you'll like working with Marianna. I'd work with her all day if I could."

Jenny laughed and turned to Marianna. "I think he likes you," she whispered.

"I like him, too." Marianna tried to play it off as a joke. "But if he shows up for dinner too, I'm going to be a little worried."

Ben smiled, adjusted his baseball cap, and sauntered out the door.

Marianna watched him go, feeling her stomach drop to her sturdy black shoes. How could she be so changeable? One moment she was sure she had feelings for Aaron, the next her heart was beating fast for Ben. Oh, what was wrong with her? She turned to Jenny and forced a smile.

"I do like Ben," she repeated. "As a friend, of course." She tried to act like he was any other customer. And the truth was, he had to be. If she let her feelings grow for anyone it should be the man sitting on the couch at home. Her first choice, the logical choice. There could be no other answer than that.

"Yes, I like him too. I've seen him around." Jenny's eyes held a wistful look. "Do you think someone like that would ever be interested in someone like me?"

Marianna didn't know what to say. She placed a soft hand on Jenny's arm. "Yes, Jenny. Of course. You're beautiful, sweet. What's not to like?"

It was true. And Marianna refused to give in to the pain that filled her at the words.

⚬◦⚬

"Hello, there!"

At Sarah's happy greeting, Marianna turned from where she was stocking the grocery shelves. Little Kenzie hurried into the store, followed by Mrs. Shelter with her own four-year-old daughter by her side.

"Look at you, Kenzie. Did you have fun playing at my house today?" Sarah bent down, smiling at the young girl.

"I's not go to your house. I went to her house." Kenzie turned and pointed a chubby finger to Sarah's little sister, Evelyn.

Sarah chuckled. "Yes, I know. Evelyn's my sister. It's my house too."

Kenzie looked up, wrinkled her nose and smiled, as if Sarah had just told her a funny joke.

Marianna laughed too.

Jenny, who'd been working behind the counter, hurried around and stretched out her arms to her daughter. "There's my girl. Did you have fun?"

Kenzie nodded. "I played with kitchens and we made cookies and I weared a kapp."

"Did you now?" Jenny ran her fingers through her daughter's reddish brown hair. "I bet that was fun."

"Mem, is that true?" Sarah asked Mrs. Shelter. Before getting an answer, she turned to Marianna, a soft giggle slipping through her lips. "I remember when I was her age. My Englisch friend and I played dress up. We traded clothes and my mother was so upset to see me wearing Englisch clothes."

"I can imagine." Marianna tried to picture herself putting on pants and a blouse. The idea was so foreign. She honestly didn't know if she'd choose another way to dress even if all Amish bishops told her she could.

"It was only a kapp. Kenzie looked cute. She wanted to be like the other girls." Mrs. Shelter shrugged. "I suppose I'm getting soft in my old age."

They chatted for a while, and then Mrs. Shelter left. The Shelters lived a half mile down from the store—an easy walk.

Jenny got her things together. She was only working a half day today. Marianna noticed she only had a light sweatshirt for a coat. If only she had her things from Indiana. She had an extra coat packed in her trunk and would be happy to share.

"It was great getting to know you both better." Jenny pulled her car keys out of her pocket with one hand and held Kenzie's red-mittened hand with the other. Just before she opened the door, she turned and paused. "And, Marianna, you'll have to tell me if Ben comes back for dinner. That'll be pretty funny if he does. It'll also be proof that he likes you as much as I think he does."

"Wait, Ben likes you . . . as in wants to court you?" Sarah's eyes widened. "But what about Aaron?"

"Who's Aaron?" Jenny walked back toward the other two.

Marianna looked from Jenny's face to Sarah's. How was she to explain all this? "Aaron is a friend from home. He's come for a visit and was in an accident. He'll be staying with my family for a while. And as for Ben"—she turned to Sarah—"you know the rules about becoming involved with the Englisch. I enjoy talking to him. He was the first person my family met when we arrived. He's a friend and nothing more."

"From the way he looked at you, he hopes you'll be more than friends." Jenny cocked an eyebrow. Marianna looked at her with a piercing gaze, but the young woman didn't get the hint.

"Is that true, Marianna? But what about Aaron?" Sarah asked.

Before Marianna could respond to Sarah's repeated question, Jenny placed a hand over her chest. "I doubt Aaron—whoever he is—could be as handsome as Ben."

Their words pressed against Marianna like invisible hands. She leaned against the drink cooler just to the right of the front door. She wasn't use to this. Amish women spoke in hints. They shared news between each other and never confronted.

"I . . . well, both men are just friends. Maybe . . . someday." Someday she'd put Ben out of her mind and focus on the man her community counted worthy of her heart.

Marianna heard footsteps coming from the kitchen area, and she turned to see Annie round the corner. From her expression, she'd overheard the conversation.

"Ladies, a girl never tells the secrets of her heart. I have to say I'm not surprised by all the attention Marianna's receiving. She's beautiful and kind. I'm amazed there are only two young men vying for her interest." Annie clapped her hands together as if signaling an end to the conversation. "But it was a good day, wasn't it? Just think, Jenny, soon you'll be in the kitchen. I think you'll enjoy it. Have a good night." Then with a wave to Kenzie Annie headed back into the kitchen.

Jenny nodded and headed out the door with Kenzie. Even after she left, Marianna stood frozen in place, staring at the floorboards. She wanted to say something—to explain to Sarah—but she guessed Sarah saw her true feelings for Ben on her face. Rumors were already circulating around Indiana that Marianna had stayed in Montana due to her interest in a handsome Englischer. No doubt the same rumors would soon find their way around West Kootenai, too.

Finally, not able to take the tension in her gut any longer, Marianna glanced at Sarah's face. The Amish woman stood there, her lips parted slightly as if preparing to say something. But before she did, she turned and strode away.

Marianna lowered her head and then turned, pressing her forehead against the cool glass of the drink case, as if that could bring some ease to her heart. She didn't know how this happened. Why things had to be difficult. She mourned losing the respect of her friends. What upright Amish woman would act such a way concerning two men?

She wanted to pray about it, pray for strength, but her shame blocked the words. She looked at the clock—she only had a few hours left of the workday. But leaving work wasn't going to help. She couldn't escape the problem, no matter how she longed to do so.

Half of it waited for her at home.

CHAPTER TWELVE

hy didn't she remember the answer sooner?

Marianna sat up in the small twin bed, trying to move as little as possible. Ellie still slept, her soft, breathy snores filling the room. Joy, too, was fast asleep in the cradle in the corner. She'd been a troublesome baby the first month, waking up throughout the night. After the second month Mem discovered Dat's loud snores woke the baby. Once they moved Joy into Ellie's room, the baby slept much better.

Marianna rose to full height and moved toward the small wooden trunk by the window. The trunk was an old thing Annie had in the back storeroom—something she gladly passed off when Marianna asked. It was just big enough for Marianna's private things, including her journal, the photograph she'd tucked inside it, and now the little book she'd bought at the West Kootenai store today. The book had caught her eye after Jenny left for the day. It had the simple title, *God's Promises for Uncertain Times*.

She'd flipped through the small book after she'd gotten off work and the words warmed her soul even better than the woodstove in the restaurant area warmed her body. It was filled with Scripture verses, nothing more, but they reminded her why she'd chosen to stay in Montana. It wasn't because she was fearful of going back to Indiana. It wasn't that she questioned her relationship with Aaron. And it wasn't because she wanted a relationship with Ben. She knew full well that wasn't possible. She'd met God in new ways in Montana. And as she'd prayed on the train for an answer, she'd opened her eyes to see her father's face.

God wanted her here, right where she was, for a purpose. She had to remember that. And she needed to keep in mind that her relationship with God was different here. Back home during uncertain times she'd let her fears carry her away. In Montana . . .

She'd discovered where to take those worries.

It wasn't as if everything changed overnight, or she had the answers immediately when she went to her Creator in prayer, but she did feel a difference. God was with her, even when she walked the cold wooded trails to and from work. *Especially* as she walked those trails. The cold air around her, the world muted by the snow, it all gave her the sense that she wasn't alone.

Marianna sat on the cool, wood floor. She leaned her back against the log wall and felt the cold air filtering through the glass window above her head, penetrating her nightdress, her sleeping handkerchief. There was just enough light from the moonlight to read the verses laid out one on each page.

"Psalm 25:5." She whispered the words out loud. "Guide me in your truth and teach me, for you are God my Savior, and my hope is in you all day long."

"Psalm 145:18. The Lord is near to all who call on him, to all who call on him in truth.'"

She paused. One word stood out in both verses. *Truth.* What was truth? For so long she thought she knew. She still believed the Amish way was right and good. She'd planned on following it without question. But now, the more time she spent in Montana, she knew truth existed in the Englisch world too. And if those she met believed in God, didn't they have His truth with them too?

Annie Johnson, Millie Arnold, Ben . . . They didn't just *claim* to believe in Jesus. They lived like they did.

"Marwi . . ." Ellie stirred and reached her hand Marianna's direction.

"Shh." Marianna scooted across the floor, back toward the bed.

Just seeing her, Ellie closed her eyes and smiled. How content it made the small girl to know her big sister was there. A soft smile filled Marianna's face. What a gift trust was.

She could give the same gift to God—be content in His presence. Just knowing He was there, that should be enough. It had to be enough. She couldn't imagine going through six weeks while Aaron healed with such battles raging in her soul. Leaving for Indiana—leaving both Ben and Aaron here—seemed a better option than that.

But trusting God had a purpose for all of this—that was the best plan of all.

Lord, help me to have peace. To be a good friend. To trust. I'll leave others opinions up to You . . . and while I'm at it, You can have my worries too.

Ellie's eyes fluttered open again, and Marianna stroked her hair that stuck out from her sleeping kerchief, knowing the one thing that would get Ellie back to sleep. She cleared her throat and started to sing Ellie's favorite song, her voice just above a whisper.

"Müde bin ich, geh' zu Ruh,
Schliesse meine Augen zu;
Vater lass die Augen dein,
Über meine Bette sein.

Ja, Jesus liebt mich,
Ja, Jesus liebt mich,
Ja, Jesus liebt mich;
Die Bibel sagt mir so."

Ellie drifted off to sleep somewhere before the chorus. Marianna's heart expanded in her chest and she sang it again, this time for herself. The Bible meant so much more to her now. Its truth filled her with warm hope.

"Tired am I, go now to rest,
And close my eyes;
Father, let Thine Eyes
Watch over my bed.

Yes, Jesus loves me,
Yes, Jesus loves me,
Yes, Jesus loves me,
The Bible tells me so."

❧

Dear Rebecca,

Thank you for your short note. It made me laugh at your description of the cows passing on news with their moos, and the horses their neighs. As fast as word about Aaron's accident and stay is traveling around the Indiana community, I wish we could blame it on the cows and horses. But I know some of the church ladies too well. They need no help in getting the word out!

*You ask how I'm doing with Aaron here—if I'm able
to sleep at night due to his closeness. I'm not sleeping as
well as I used to. Aaron's taken my room and I'm sharing
a bed with Ellie. For a small thing she sure takes up a
lot of room! Part of me is happy to have Aaron close.
It makes me consider more what it would be like to be
married to him. Another part of me feels like something
has been robbed. For so long my imagination has built
up what it would be like to live so closely with someone.
Reality isn't nearly as fanciful as my imagination. Is that
bad?*

*To answer your question, Aaron and I have not
talked about dating or marriage since he's been here.
Right now we're just concentrating on getting him better.
He's concerned about getting home and checking on his
house and herd. I don't blame him.*

*There is much more I want to tell you, but I can't
do it justice in a letter. Just know that I'm planning on
coming back to Indiana some day, and then I can tell you
face to face.*

*What I can tell you . . . I've found God in new
ways here. I feel so alive. Rebecca, I have a feeling you
would never look to the world again for happiness if you
experienced what my soul knows now.*

Love,
Marianna

CHAPTER THIRTEEN

*B*en drove down the mountain, his eyes focused on his headlights illuminating the road. This time of year the sky darkened at 5:00 p.m., and though it was only 9 o'clock it seemed like the middle of the night. He knew the way to Roy's place by heart. His first summer in Montana he'd spent weekends there—still trying to bridge his old life with his new one. After he'd returned to Montana to stay for good, he hadn't visited his old friend much. Yet he'd be welcome. Even more than a good friend, Roy had been a great business manager. Though Roy had sold his house in L.A. and bought a large place in Montana, he still had his finger in the business.

Ben pulled off the main road onto the long driveway. The tall iron gates were open. In Los Angeles, Roy couldn't give his address out. If he did, dozens of wannabe musicians would be lining up outside or ringing the doorbell all hours of the day and night. In Montana, all Roy had to fear was a black bear breaking in and getting into his trash. Montana was a great neutralizer. People were just people here, important or not.

He parked his old truck next to the shiny Suburban in the driveway and jumped out. The pavement had been cleared all the way to the front door, and Ben guessed the guy who did maintenance around Roy's house got paid more than most folks up in West Kootenai.

A front porch light lit the tall front door made of solid wood. Ben rung the doorbell, even though it wasn't necessary. From Roy's media room he had a camera on the front door. With one push of a button, Roy could open the door.

Sure enough, after five seconds the door swung open. Ben stepped inside, closed it behind him, and looked to the curved stairway that led up to the second story. There, looking down from the foyer balcony, Roy waited, a smile filling his face.

"So the prodigal son has come home. I was hoping when money was tight that you'd return." He chuckled. "You have too much promise as a musician to spend your time playing taxi driver." He motioned for Ben to join him, and Ben took the stairs two at a time.

For years Ben had found peace in doing simple tasks, delivering log furniture, driving the Amish, and working with his hands, but lately it hadn't satisfied. Things couldn't stay that way forever. If he ever hoped to marry—to provide for a family—he'd have to find something that paid better. Like a farmer being drawn back to the land, Ben returned to what he knew.

Roy squinted at his empty hands. "Did you bring your guitar?"

"Of course. It's in the truck. Do you want me to get it?"

"Maybe later. The night's still young. Come on in and make yourself comfortable." Roy patted his shoulder, as Ben expected he would. There was no prodding, no questioning. Being with Roy was easy. No matter how much time passed, once he and his old friend were together, they were both just themselves.

Ben followed Roy into the second floor media room. The

expansive space was bigger than the West Kootenai store. A theater screen filled one wall and six rows of leather couches faced it. On the far wall there was what appeared to be an ordinary door. What was behind it was more impressive than anything in the house—a complete recording studio that had been graced with the presence of many of music's most popular stars. Roy had a way of finding new talent, knowing deep down in his gut who was going to hit it big. A million musicians no doubt wanted what Ben had. The honor of knowing Roy, calling him a friend.

Roy moved to the stainless steel fridge in the small kitchen area behind the sofas. "Can I get you something to drink? A beer?"

Ben shook his head. "No beer for me, but I'll take a soda if you have it."

"That's right. You still sending out the letters?"

Ben nodded. "Every week. My old parole officer sends me an address of some kid who got caught with booze and I get to tell him or her Jason's story. I write it out."

"Sheesh, seems like you should just print up something on your computer, stick it in an envelope, and be done with it." Roy approached, a cold soda in his hand.

Ben accepted it and sat on the white leather. "I thought about that. Would be easier, take less time, but I think they'll pay more attention if they see it's written by hand. Besides, no letter turns out the same. I always pray and ask God to tell me what to say. I know He gives me the words. I can't bring Jason back, but maybe something I say will click."

Roy nodded, then took a long swig of his beer. He looked at Ben, but Ben could tell he wasn't interested in this conversation. Both of them knew why Ben had come—the only reason he'd return.

Roy sat on the next sofa over and kicked up his feet on the matching ottoman. "So what are you thinking? Ready to go on the road? I can get on the line and ring up some of your old gigs and fill out the calendar for most of the year."

"Actually, as tempting as that is, I'd like to stick around here. At least until spring. Do you think I can get some local gigs? Try out some new stuff."

"You've been writing?"

Ben nodded. "Got a few new songs." He looked away. He had a few that were decent and one . . . one Roy would really like. The thing was, Ben didn't know if he wanted to play that one for his friend. He pictured Marianna's face. Pictured her smile. He'd written it for her and his plan had been for her to hear it first.

Ben swallowed hard. Of course, things weren't turning out like he'd hoped. Marianna wouldn't listen to any of his music since it wasn't the Amish way. Then there was the matter of her friend from Indiana. Ben still didn't know what to think about that.

"I can get you some gigs around here. Some coffeehouse things, private parties. Won't make as much as a venue in Frisco or Vegas . . ."

"Yeah, I know."

Roy set down his beer on a side table and leaned forward, elbows on knees. "In that case, it must be a girl you're sticking around for."

Ben nodded and chuckled. He pressed his hand to his forehead. If Roy only knew. Roy wasn't the kind that had a new woman every weekend, but . . . well, Ben was sure Roy would be surprised to discover an Amish girl had captured Ben's heart.

"That's too bad, Carrie will be disappointed. Me too. I always thought you'd get together."

Ben tried to remember the last time he'd seen his former girl-friend—Roy's youngest daughter. It had been three years at least. She'd been sweet and pretty enough, but once he'd given his life to God . . . well, sweet and pretty weren't his main priorities.

"Yeah, I know. Things change, but it would be nice to see Carrie again some time."

Roy grinned and glanced at his watch. "Sometime may be sooner than you think. She went to a movie with a friend. A girl-friend, that is. She's still not dating anyone."

"She's here? In Kalispell?" The calm Ben had about coming exploded like a sleeping volcano, stirring to life in his gut. This was one thing he hadn't thought about—planned for. He doubted he'd fall for Carrie, like he'd done then. He doubted she'd even compare to Marianna in his eyes. Still, they had a history. She reminded him of how things used to be.

Stirring within was a passion he'd held at bay. Even though he'd recommitted his life and his body to God, the memories were still there. Memories that made his heartbeat quicken and his chest grow warm even now.

"She's been here a few months, but that's not why you came. Why don't you get your guitar and bring it into the studio? I wanna see if you still got what it takes, kid." Roy rose and rubbed his hands together. "And more than that, I always like a new proj-ect to dig my hands into."

Dear June-Sevenies,

It seems the older we get, the longer it takes for our letters to get around. We used to think we were busy with

school and chores but tending to homes and families—
and jobs like I have—seem to be more work, don't they?

Maybe we'll get back into schedule once the corn is
harvested, the silos are filled, and the fieldwork has come
to a close for all of you. Of course, here in Montana they
run by a different schedule. Outdoor logging has slowed,
but this just means the men have moved inside to their
workshops. Dat and Uncle Ike have been building log
homes. They took a break from that to make crutches for
Aaron.

Ja, ja, by now I'm sure all of you have heard of
Aaron's accident. Dat said it was published in The
Budget. He's mending on our sofa, and I do enjoy having
him around. I won't say no more than that. A lady never
confesses the secrets of her heart.

I wish I could describe what Montana is like. My
words fail greatly. Enclosed with my letter is a postcard
from the West Kootenai store. It's a good shot of the
mountains with snow, but the photo doesn't do the
area justice. Maybe next time 'round I'll ask Aaron to
sketch an image of the sky. I truly understand what
this Scripture means, "The heavens declare the glory
of God; the skies proclaim the work of his hands. Day
after day they pour forth speech; night after night they
display knowledge" (Psalm 19:1–2 NIV). The air is crisp
and bright. Some days when I walk to work I'm sure I
could reach out and tap it then watch it splinter into a
thousand pieces like fragile glass.

As for work, I like it greatly. There's another Amish
girl who's a friend and an Englischer, but I don't know

her too well. Jenny is not much older than me and has a daughter of age four. She seems to have many needs, like a good winter's coat, and I hope I can be of service. Did the Lord not say to help our neighbor? In these parts she'd qualify for that.

Sending all my love and soon-to-come Thanksgiving wishes,

Marianna

CHAPTER FOURTEEN

*J*enny brushed her blonde hair from her brow with the back of her hand. "I've always wondered what it was like—to grow up in a home like yours, with a mother and a father. Hearing laughter."

Marianna paused rolling out the dough for the biscuits and glanced over at Jenny. It was early morning and their first customer hadn't arrived yet.

The girl's statement was heartbreaking, but the way she said it—well, she spoke as simply as if she'd just told Marianna what she'd eaten for breakfast.

"There was no laughter in your home?"

"Sometimes, but not often." Jenny blew a puff of air up toward her bangs, blowing them out of her eyes. She wore her hair up in a scarf—Annie always demanded hair be tied back in the kitchen—but a few strands of hair had slipped out.

"That's why I'm trying to make things different with Kenzie. There was more shouting than anything—my folks arguing about things that happened years before. They divorced when I was ten. I don't think either of my parents knows what it means to forgive. Sometimes I wish I'd grown up Amish. I see the families that come in here. They care for each other. They smile . . ." She shrugged. "Like yours. I hope someday I'll have a family like that."

"You have to know that we're not perfect. It's harder for some than others, but we try to obey God by caring for others."

"And when someone does something wrong . . . do you just forgive? Does it come as easily as it seems?"

The way she said it, Marianna was sure Jenny thought of a specific thing. Did the young mom have someone she struggled to forgive? Kenzie's father perhaps, whoever he was.

"I wouldn't say 'just' forgive. It's a process. We confess our wrong. We try to understand the other's point of view."

"And your parents taught you that?" Jenny continued rolling out her dough, trying to get it into the shape and thickness Marianna had shown her.

Marianna had to think about that one. "Forgiveness wasn't something my parents talked about. It was something they lived. Or at least tried to. I can't really remember a time when I didn't know that's how I was supposed to act."

Marianna wanted to share more, but something inside kept her from opening up completely. And she knew what it was, much to her shame. She hated to admit it, but ever since Jenny had jabbered on about Ben in front of Sarah, she'd kept the young woman at arm's length. Oh, she'd been nice enough. She'd carried on conversations and helped train her to the best of her ability, but deep down Marianna held back. She replayed everything in her mind before she spoke, making sure she wasn't giving Jenny fuel to say more about her and Ben.

Jenny picked up the biscuit cutter and started cutting circles in the dough. "You may not know, but I've been trying to do that, to model myself after you, Sarah, and Annie. Even before I started working here."

"Really?" Marianna glanced at the young woman, and the wall she'd built around her heart crumbled slightly.

"Now don't get me wrong, I don't want to dress like you, but I try to smile when people talk to me, and after seeing you in the store speaking with such kindness to your younger siblings, I don't yell at Kenzie as much as I did."

Marianna didn't know what to say. Her heart warmed. Her hands stilled. She attempted to swallow down the shame, but it stuck in her throat. What if the situation were reversed? Would she have been willing to admit her faults so freely? Would she have been willing to look around for someone to model herself after and then work to do just that?

Marianna took some of the dirty pots to the sink and ran water to let them soak, and out of the corner of her eye she watched Jenny work. As she watched, her heart softened like butter in a skillet. Jenny had been raised in a home very different from her own. She most likely didn't understand how to hold back words or consider the feelings of others. It amazed Marianna that *she'd* been a model for someone. It made her want to do more for the young woman than just enough to prove oneself civil.

Jenny finished cutting the biscuits, lifted them off the breadboard, and placed them on the cookie sheet to bake. They looked pretty good. Jenny was a quick study.

"Like yesterday." Jenny situated the biscuits on the cookie sheet so they were just the right distance apart. "I noticed Kenzie had torn the hem of her new shirt. I'd just bought it. It made me mad, but I didn't yell like I would have before."

"Did you mend it?" Marianna turned back to her own dough. "I bet with a little mending it would be as good as new."

"Mending?" Jenny wrinkled her nose. "Like with a needle?"

"*Ja.* What do you usually do with torn clothes?"

Jenny shrugged. "Make Kenzie wear them that way. Either that or stuff them in the back of her closet."

Marianna nodded and smiled. This was a way she could help more. "If you like, I can help you with your mending. It's really not a big deal. If you bring a garment each day, I could show you during a slow time—I'm sure Annie wouldn't mind."

"You would do that?" Jenny's face brightened. "That's so nice of you!" Then her eyebrows peaked. "But I don't have a needle and stuff—"

"Don't worry. I have a small sewing box I could bring. In fact . . ." For a split second she'd been about to invite Jenny to the quilting circle. Then she remembered Jenny wasn't Amish. She smiled at herself, not believing she'd almost made that mistake. Perhaps because most of her life she'd only been around Amish. Or perhaps because she was starting to see people as people. Marianna bit her lip. She wished she could invite Jenny, but the truth was she'd never seen a non-Amish person at the quilting circle. It would be awkward for everyone.

"Were you going to say something?" Jenny slid her sheet of biscuits into the oven.

"Oh, I was just going to say that when Kenzie's a little older I can teach her some simple stitching. I've already been thinking about starting with Ellie in the next year or so. Mem started training me when I was that age." It wasn't what she'd wanted to say, but it was a good idea.

"That would be great. If you're around, that is." Even though they were the only two in the kitchen, Jenny leaned close and lowered her voice. "Everyone's saying you might not be around in the spring, you know . . . since you might be returning to Indiana with Aaron."

"Everyone's saying that?" Marianna folded her arms over her chest. Had Ben heard that too? If so, no wonder he'd been hanging around more lately—trying to get the facts for himself.

"Yes, well I haven't decided yet. And to tell you the truth I'm not going to worry about it. I'm gonna take one day at a time and jest enjoy my friends. I'm not committed to anyone, and I'm going to be thankful for those God has brought into my life." Marianna's heart settled as she said those words. She didn't need to worry. She needed to remember that God would show her His truth, and His timing.

"In that case, then, I have another request." Jenny lowered her head and looked at her feet. "Would ya show me how to cook a turkey? I'd like to make one for Kenzie and me."

"Of course." Marianna smiled. "I'd love to." Thank heaven for the way she'd been raised—now more than ever. It wasn't until she moved to Montana that she realized how blessed she was for her heritage.

Then again. It wasn't until she got here that she considered what it would be like to leave her Amish ways behind.

Aaron squinted as he stared out at the sun's reflection off the white snow. The brown of the tree trunks and deep green of the pine needles made the blue sky appear brighter.

It was like the Bible story he'd learned as a boy, when Jesus brought sight to a blind man. Aaron understood the wonder of it now, more than he ever had. Looking out the window for the first time in weeks was like having new sight, and even though his leg ached he didn't want to stop his staring.

From his place on the sofa, the view out the window had only given him glimpses of the tops of trees set against the gray sky. Today, sitting next to the window, a completely different world radiated outside.

His eyes scanned the panorama of snow, fields, mountains, trees. On a long branch that stretched over the barn two small finches danced and chattered, their song barely audible through the glass.

"Charlie, can you help me out?" Aaron turned to the boy who was hobbling out of the kitchen after sneaking yet another cookie from the tin.

Charlie glanced up, sheepish. "Sure."

"Could you fetch me my sketch pad? I left it in the top drawer of my dresser. And a pencil too?"

Charlie nodded and hurried to Aaron's room. Aaron could hear from the boy's quicker movements that his leg was healing. Aaron only wished he would mend soon as well.

Less than a minute later, Charlie emerged from the bedroom, sketchbook in hand. His eyes were fixed on the page in front of him. Aaron's heart quickened. He'd sketched the picture last night before he put the book away.

"Is this Marianna?" Charlie lifted his head and scrunched his nose, gazing at the sketch of a beautiful Amish woman sitting in a rocking chair before the woodstove.

Aaron reached out his hand.

"Oh, it's just a picture . . . no one in mind."

Charlie paused and shook his head. "I'd think you're fibbing yet. It is Mari. She always sits like that, and from her face it's easy to see it's her."

Aaron curled his fingers, giving Charlie the signal to bring the sketchbook closer. "Well, if I tell you it is, do ya promise to keep a secret?"

Charlie's eyes widened. "*Ja*, I won't tell." He handed over the book and pencil and then smiled. "Are you fancy on her?"

"Yes, Charlie, I am."

Charlie giggled. "You gonna marry her?"

"I'd like to. I'm gonna ask, but you promise not to tell anyone, right?"

Charlie bobbed his head. "I won't tell."

Then he looked out the window and pointed.

Aaron turned to look and saw that Marianna approached, her hands in her coat pockets, a smile on her face. She appeared to be enjoying the day. Aaron couldn't stop from smiling too.

"You gonna ask her now?"

"No. I'm going to wait until the time is right."

Charlie's brow furrowed. "I hope you don't take too long. I've never kept a secret more than a few days afore."

Aaron shook his head and sighed, and then turned his sketchbook to a fresh page and began sketching the trees. "You have to, Charlie. I'm depending on you. It's gonna take more than a few days. I guarantee that."

"But I don't understand, why don't you ask her now?" Charlie leaned his elbows on the window ledge. His breath fogged up the glass.

"Well, I . . ." Aaron rubbed his temples. He'd planned on

asking her quick like after he got here. He'd thought about it on the train ride over. He was going to spend time with her walking through the pines, and then he'd start giving her the letters he'd written over the months. They talked about his care more than he could speak. When he saw her response, well, then he'd know for sure. Then he'd be willing to risk his heart.

Now, of course, they couldn't go on walks. He couldn't even get all dressed nice for her. Even though he managed to wash up everyday, his hair stuck to his head and needed a good washing. But they *had* been spending time together. He smiled. Maybe he should start letting her read some of the letters anyhow. Charlie was right, why wait?

"You know. I can't tell you when it's going to happen, but it'll be before Christmas, for sure."

"Christmas!" Charlie sighed. "That's forever long."

Aaron chuckled. He'd make his intentions known long before Christmas. He just wasn't going to tell Charlie that. Let him think it would take longer. Aaron didn't want anyone to expect it coming as soon as it was.

Especially not Marianna.

CHAPTER FIFTEEN

arianna glanced up at her house. Two sets of eyes and two handsome faces watched her from the window. Both guys wore smiles. Large smiles, like they were waiting for something or had a secret they were eager to share.

She hurried up the steps and laughter poured from her as she stepped through the door. "Aaron, you're up!"

He sat in a chair by the window, his casted leg extended out in front of him. He had a proud and excited look on his face, like David's face the first time he hitched up the buggy alone.

"*Ja*, my leg's feeling better. Doesn't throb quite as much when I get up and hobble around."

Charlie stood by Aaron, his hand resting on Aaron's shoulder. His eyes were large and round, like Annie's cinnamon rolls.

"So what are you doing, Charlie?" One of his hands was bent behind his back. Did he have something in it? He had a secret, she could tell.

"You hiding something behind your back?" She took off her coat, hung it, then stepped forward and eyed him.

Charlie shrugged. "Jest another pencil. Uh, Aaron wanted to draw. I got an extra."

Marianna looked down at the page in front of Aaron with the beginning sketch of trees.

Something was up.

Aaron took the extra pencil from Charlie. "Yup, it's a beautiful day. I wanted to catch the light coming through the trees."

Marianna removed her boots. "Oh, okay." The lightness in her chest fell. She'd thought sure they had some type of surprise. "Where is everyone?" She tilted her head and listened for footsteps upstairs.

"David and Josiah ain't home from school yet. Mem and the little kids went to Carashes', down the road." Charlie leaned against Aaron as he talked. They were so comfortable with each other. "Said they needed to get out while the sun shined."

"That's a good idea." She sat down in a chair at the dining room table, waiting and watching. A minute passed and Aaron was still looking at the pencil and paper in his hands.

Something *was* up.

She straightened. "You going to finish that drawing?" Aaron glanced up, his cheeks slightly pink. "I was . . . but since you're here. Well, I was wondering if you could do me a favor."

"Sure. What is it?"

"I got washed up pretty good, but I've had a hard time with my hair. I can't bend down enough to wash it in the sink with this cast and . . ."

"You need me to wash your hair? Sure, I can do that." Marianna stood, trying to pretend her heart wasn't pounding in her chest. She looked around. The bathroom would be out of the question. There wouldn't be enough room for both of them and his cast. And the kitchen didn't seem right. She thought about the bedroom, but that didn't seem appropriate.

"Why don't you lie back on the couch and lay your head over the end. I can put a basin of water there." She moved to the screened-in back porch, where they kept their laundry supplies, and got the basin she and Mem used to wash small items. By the time she returned, Aaron had used the handmade wooden crutches Dat had made to hobble across the floor.

"I can help too!"

"Good idea." She smiled at Charlie, thankful he was here. If not . . . well, it would have been too easy to let her mind wander. To pretend this was their home—hers and Aaron's—and that she was caring for her husband.

"Charlie, why don't you run to the bathroom and get the shampoo and a towel."

Marianna filled the basin and heated the water on the wood-stove. When it had warmed enough, she set it on a chair that she'd pulled to the edge of the couch. Aaron lay on the couch on his back and hung his head over the end. He looked up at the ceiling and she knelt next to him.

"I've never done this before." She soaked a washcloth with water and then put it on his hair, squeezing.

"Me neither."

"Well, I've washed my siblings' hair . . .

"It's not really the same, is it?" His voice held a slight quiver.

No, it certainly wasn't.

After she wet his hair, she took the shampoo from Charlie and squeezed some in her hands. Then she worked it through Aaron's blond hair.

He let out a long sigh and closed his eyes.

"Tell me if I hurt you or pull your hair or anything." Her fingers scrubbed his scalp, then she worked through the ends of his hair. Touching him like this was more intimate than she'd expected. She liked being needed this way. What it would be like to be close to him in other ways? To sit by him, their legs and arms touching. To rest her head on his shoulder.

Charlie set the towel down and started playing with Trapper. He wasn't nearly as intrigued by this event as she was.

"That feels good." Aaron opened his eyes. "I appreciate it."

"Sure. It's *gut* to help. I'm not sure why I didn't think of it sooner."

After she finished shampooing, Marianna rinsed Aaron's hair. The warm water poured through his hair and down his temples. She dabbed his forehead with the dry towel to make sure the water wouldn't drip into his eyes. Satisfied his hair was clean, she pulled the basin away and wrapped the dry towel around his head. She rubbed his hair dry—and Aaron reached back. His hand covered hers.

"I can do that." He began to sit up.

"No, it's okay." She kept her hands there, enjoying his touch. "If you sit up you'll drip all over your clothes. I don't mind."

"All right." Aaron chuckled and removed his hand. "But I can comb my hair."

"Sure."

She finished drying his hair, and Aaron sat up. Just then the door opened, and Mem stepped in with Joy bundled in her arms and Ellie walking by her side. Mem looked from Marianna, to the towel in her hands, to Aaron's wet head, to the basin, and her brow furrowed.

"You're home early, Marianna."

"Yes, well, with Jenny's help we had all the baking done early. And good thing, because I was needed around here."

Aaron looked worried, but that look quickly disappeared as a smile spread across Mem's face.

"*Gut, gut.* You should be home more often. It'll be nice when you don't have to work away from home, don't you think?"

"Yes, of course." Marianna said what was expected, but she had to admit she enjoyed work. She loved baking and enjoyed the customers. She looked forward to spending more time with Jenny. Just helping her in small ways mattered.

Marianna rose to carry the basin out the front door to dump it. As she walked away from the sofa, she noticed Mem looking over her shoulder and smiling. Marianna glanced back. Were Charlie and Trapper doing something funny? No, that wasn't it. Mem's smile wasn't from humor, but rather joy.

Marianna saw the look of loving appreciation in Aaron's gaze as he watched her, and she couldn't help but smile too.

❧

Dear Journal,

Today I washed Aaron Zook's hair. We've yet to kiss, but in a way this seemed more intimate. He was appreciative, and I was glad I could help. It seems like he'll make a good husband for someone, some day. He doesn't take much for granted. Says thank you. That's different from other guys—guys I knew back home who sometimes treated their wives as slaves. Not all guys, but there were some. Seems because most Amish women don't work outside the home that thinking of them like that can come natural.

I have to say that I've enjoyed serving lately. I musta glanced at Aaron's clean hair a dozen or more times during the evening by lantern light. Makes me think of Jenny. She appreciates even the small things. She's said a little of what her life used to be like and it's hard to imagine. When most folks' lives are like yours, you forget others don't got it as good.

Makes me think of what I read in the Bible today. Annie's Bible was open on her desk, and I read it during my break. Jesus was saying it's better to serve than be served. Our Amish ancestors understood that. I knew it before with my head, but lately it's moving to my heart, dripping down like an icicle melting, filling me up in places love and understanding hasn't been before.

Enough of that. There was news at the store today. A newly wed couple moved to West Kootenai from Ohio. They are staying at a small cabin that belongs to a cousin. It seems like a hard time to come to Montana, but I suppose newly wed couples don't need to leave their place and brace the snow much. I think I've said enough about that. After washing Aaron's hair today I don't need my mind wandering down that path.

It's been doing too much wandering lately.

Abe Sommer sat at the edge of his bed looking at the Bible in his hand. His eyes blinked and he knew if he laid down he'd be asleep in less than a minute. Ruth sat up, scooted closer to him, and rubbed his shoulder with her hand.

"You can get up in the morning and read. You've had a long day." She yawned. "We all have."

Abe nodded, but he opened the Bible all the same. "I sleep better if I read God's words. And it gives me things to think about the day next."

"I'll read it for you if you'd like." She scooted up even more and swung her legs over so her feet touched the floor.

Abe's head jerked back. "You will?" He cocked his head and narrowed his gaze. Was this the same woman who told him he was going against their ancestors by not reading the Bible in German? Wasn't she the one who refused to talk to him for a whole day when he dared to mention a prayer meeting held down the street that was attended by both Amish and Englisch?

He handed the Bible to her, and she opened it to the book-marked section. She glanced down briefly and then looked back at him.

"I appreciate your help with the dinner dishes tonight, that was *gut* of you. I never thought I'd see the day."

"Jest trying to be a loving husband, that's all."

She placed a hand on her hip. "Some Amish man you are. If word gets out you'll get a tongue lashing for sure. They might even try to get you to wear an apron." She chuckled.

He smiled and placed a hand on hers. He held her gaze for a moment, wanting her to know that even though he appreciated her humor he was being serious. "I know I haven't always been the best husband, Ruth. Especially early on. I know that I was harsh even, and"—he lifted a finger and stroked her chin—"and it left you looking for love in other places."

Ruth's eyes widened and a small gasp escaped her lips. Pain cut through Abe's heart. He swore to himself long ago he'd never bring it up. He'd try to forget. But that had been impossible. And forgiving? Folks just expected that because a person was Amish it came natural-like. From the deepest part of him, he knew that wasn't the case.

"I forgive you, Ruth. For what happened then. And for not telling me you invited Aaron here. I know why. I know you don't want Marianna to make the same mistakes you did, and while we're both praying for her choice to be Aaron, I want you to know that if Marianna fails—if any of our children fail—it's not your fault. You've been the best mother anyone could imagine. You've been the best wife."

The tears came with a quiver of Ruth's chin. She sucked in a heavy breath, and she cried silently into her cupped hands. Abe didn't try to stop her. Just as he'd been holding inside all the pain and heartache for so long, she'd been too. She needed this. Just like he did.

He reached over and took the Bible from her lap and then lifted it so he could see the Scripture verses he had underlined.

A few minutes passed, and as her crying softened, he began to read the words that hadn't left his mind the last few days.

"Then Peter came to Jesus and asked, 'Lord, how many times shall I forgive my brother or sister who sins against me? Up to seven times?'

"Jesus answered, 'I tell you, not seven times, but seventy-seven times.' Therefore, the kingdom of heaven is like a king who wanted to settle accounts with his servants. As he began the settlement, a man who owed him ten thousand bags of gold was brought to him. Since he was not able to pay, the master ordered that he and his wife and his children and all that he had be sold to repay the debt . . ."

CHAPTER SIXTEEN

esterday's clear skies were just a memory. What sounded like a rumble echoed down from the mountains, sending a shiver down Marianna's spine. Earlier today—like yesterday—the sky had been clear, deceptive. Then, in less than an hour's time, a storm blew in. More than one customer said that's how it was. If you didn't like the weather in West Kootenai, just wait fifteen minutes.

"Sometimes the mountains roar when the big storms are coming," Edgar said. "The whipping of the pines on the snow-covered hills is like the mane of a beast shaking to life."

"That's some image." Marianna rubbed her arms trying to warm them. For the first time the woodstove in the dining area couldn't keep up.

"It'll be a good night to pop popcorn and make popcorn balls." Edgar sounded so wistful. "That's what my mother used to do on nights like this."

Marianna leaned against the front counter watching the wind whip the falling snow sideways. "In Indiana, Dat would read us stories under the lantern light. Sometimes—no make that most times—we'd drift off to the sound of his voice. Mem would let us get our blankets and pillows and sleep by the woodstove. If it was real bad, Dat and Mem would join us."

She thought back to those times. Considered how they'd bring their clothes down and dress by the woodstove, too, trying to keep warm. With Aaron around, Marianna couldn't do that. Instead, she dressed as fast as she could in the cold room upstairs and hurried down to warm herself.

Through a quarter inch of ice on the window, Marianna watched their last customer hurry out to the car.

"Think we'll close up shop early today." Annie rubbed her hands as she hurried from the back room, closing the flue on the fireplace. "No one's going to be out in this weather."

"Are you sure? What if someone comes and needs something? I can stay if you like." Marianna couldn't help but wonder about Ben. She hadn't seen him for almost a week, and Dat said he hadn't seen him around either. Had he left the area? Was he holed up in his cabin? Marianna hoped he wasn't staying away in order to stop the rumors about the two of them. And yet, it seemed like just the noble kind of thing he'd do.

Annie shook her head. "If it's an emergency, they all have my number. I'm just down the road."

Marianna hid her smile. She never imagined keeping the phone number of the store owner back home—not that she made many calls. It was just that folks around here were like an extended family, everyone taking care of each other. She imagined Annie had a few numbers she called when she needed help. Was Uncle Ike's number for the phone he kept in his shed one of those?

"Get your things, I'll drive you home." Annie hurried through the building, shutting off most of the lights as she did so.

Marianna didn't protest. She didn't like the idea of walking home in that weather.

They locked everything up in record time and hurried out to the car. Marianna noticed some of the drifts near the shed were waist-high already.

A few minutes later Annie's small car was chugging over the mountain road. The engine moaned as it plowed through the drifts.

When they pulled up to Marianna's house, lantern light glowed in the windows. Marianna could see her family gathered around the dining room table, including Uncle Ike. It was a bit early for dinner, but they were focused on something.

She put her hand on the car's door handle and turned to Annie. "Thank you so much for the ride. I appreciate it."

"No problem. I couldn't let you walk in the storm." Although Annie spoke to Marianna, her eyes were on the window.

"I suppose I'll just go home and feed my cats. Maybe eat some leftovers and watch a movie." She looked to Marianna, and for the first time Marianna considered her boss's life.

Annie lived alone. She didn't have any family in the area. No wonder she liked being at the store so much—these people, this community—they had become her family.

"Would you like to come in?" Marianna pulled her collar tighter to her chin. "Everyone's home. I'm sure Mem would love to visit. Ever since having Joy she hasn't been out much."

"Yes, sure." Annie didn't have to be asked twice. She drove her car farther up the driveway and turned off the engine. Before Marianna could open her door, Annie stepped outside, the wind whipping her long, blonde braid like an angry snake.

Marianna climbed from the car. She didn't need to worry

about closing it because the wind slammed it shut for her. Small bits of snow stung her face as she hurried to the house. Her hand held her bonnet, which she wore over her kapp. The wind blew hard enough to blow them both away.

They rushed through the door and let out heavy sighs, feeling the warmth of the house. Marianna wiped the cold wetness from her eyes, then looked to the table and saw that everyone had gathered around Aaron.

"Marianna, you should see these sketches." Uncle Ike motioned to her. "Annie, you too."

They both took off their coats and hurried to the table. How different things were from this time last year. Before, having an Englischwoman in their home would have been a big deal. Everyone would have been on edge, but having Annie here wasn't unusual. She was just another neighbor stopping in during the storm.

On the table were six sketches Aaron had drawn. They were all done in pencil, yet to Marianna they reminded her of some of the black and white photos they had hanging in the craft area of the store.

There were three landscape photos, two of the barn and one of the woodstove with Trapper sleeping curled in front of it. But it was the final sketch that took Marianna's breath away. It was her. Sitting in the rocking chair by the woodstove. Her hands were folded on her lap, and she looked at something in the distance, her smile joyful.

Sudden tears stung her eyes, partly because Aaron had captured her that way. She didn't remember him sitting there, watching her and sketching. He must have captured the image in his mind—in his heart—and later put it on the page.

The tears came for another reason too. The joy on her face reminded her of the smile in the photo with Ben. She'd tucked that photo away and refused to look at it. Seeing this sketch made her miss him in a way. It also made her realize how close Aaron watched her. How . . . how beautiful she looked in his gaze.

No one in the group mentioned that he'd captured an image of her face—something the Amish weren't supposed to do. Instead, they were enthralled by his talent.

She wiped her eyes and glanced up to see his face. He lifted his eyebrows. *Do you like it?* his gaze seemed to say.

She nodded, offered Aaron a smile, and then turned to Annie.

"I can't believe these." Annie sounded so excited. "Aaron, I have to have them for my store."

"Excuse me?" Aaron ran a hand down his cheek. "What do you mean? For folks to look at?"

"Look at? To buy!" She leaned closer and shook her head, as if not believing it.

"Nah, I don't think so. I wouldna even have shown everyone if Charlie hadn't told." Aaron sent a piercing gaze to the boy. "He's not so great at keeping secrets, but he'll get better. Won't you?"

Charlie nodded, his bangs swishing across his forehead.

"But, why wouldn't you want to sell them? These are wonderful."

Uncle Ike placed a hand on Annie's arm, as if trying to temper her excitement. "It's the Amish way. We don't produce art for show. We don't hang art. We dona like to draw attention to ourselves. That's why we dress as we do—all the same. It's a way to show that no one is better than another."

Annie's eyes focused on Ike, and she seemed to be listening, but Marianna could see by her tight-lipped smile she didn't agree.

"Yes, I know," Annie stated simply. "Yet it's possible for everyone to be on equal ground and still be unique, isn't it? Aaron's artwork is unique. It's a gift from God and he should use it. Wouldn't you hate it if you gave a special gift to someone only to later discover it was never used?" She paused and scanned the others but did not get an answer. Still, that didn't hinder her. "I have some old frames in back of my store I'd be happy to donate. We could free these and put them up for sale. It could help Aaron with some money. I'm sure, with the hospital bills—"

Dat raised his hand. "That's not needed. Our community takes care of its own. When one is in need, we all pitch in. From what I hear, Aaron's bills are already covered. Just like Charlie's bills."

"Yes, well"—Annie jutted out her chin—"can't he use a little money? He can't work with his injury. And if he wishes to"—Annie seemed to rethink what she'd been about to say—"I'm sure he'll need the money for his own home and for whatever his future plans may be."

"And I *would* like to give some to the Sommers."

Aaron's words startled Marianna. When she looked at him, she found him looking up into Annie's face.

"Do you think I could really make money?"

Annie nodded. "Yes. I'm not sure how much. I can price them at different amounts and see." She chuckled. "We'll start off high, of course."

Aaron nodded. "It sounds good, *ja*." Then he reached out and took the sketch of Marianna. "Except this one." His face grew serious. "I really should have shown Marianna first."

"I understand." Annie looked around the room, as if taking in the sight of the place, and perhaps also noticing for the first time the lack of wall art. Then she looked to Ike to see if he still disagreed. Ike didn't comment, but he looked away. He rose and moved into the kitchen to see if Mem needed any help with dinner.

Marianna noticed disappointment in Annie's face. She'd won the argument, and perhaps helped Aaron, but she did not win favor with Ike. And from the sadness in her eyes, Marianna wondered if Annie wished she hadn't pressed. Maybe she should have handled that different. If Amish men appreciated anything, it was being respected—especially in front of others.

Still, that wasn't her problem. Instead, Marianna's eyes drifted back to the sketch of herself. She wanted to say something to Aaron, to tell him that she wasn't upset that he'd drawn her, but she didn't know how. She glanced to his sketchbook. What else was inside? Were their sketches of Indiana? Of his cabin?

Then another thought came to her. After she'd left, Aaron and Naomi had gotten close for a time. Were there any sketches of Naomi?

Marianna's stomach turned. She placed a hand over it. *Don't be ridiculous. There's no reason for you to feel this way. You're not even sure how you feel about Aaron.*

That was true . . . so why did it bother her so to think of him with another?

CHAPTER SEVENTEEN

*B*en sat with his guitar in front of the microphone, yet he couldn't help but see the disappointment in Roy's eyes through the window, where Roy sat in the technician's room.

It had been a long few days. He and Roy had worked on getting Ben's career back on track. They made plans on where to go, who to talk to. Then Ben got out his guitar. He'd started with some of his old stuff, just to see if he still had it. Thankfully Roy thought he did.

"There's something different about your songs . . . or your singing. Maybe it's different about you," Roy said.

"What do you mean?"

"There's a maturity that wasn't there before—a depth. It's hard to explain."

Ben had to admit he enjoyed playing again, especially in a studio. To see appreciation in Roy's eyes. Yes, he'd enjoyed singing at small gigs, like at the restaurant at the West Kootenai store. The guests appreciated it, but it meant more in a way to see appreciation in the eyes of someone of Roy's caliber.

So now Roy's disappointment caused his fingers to stiffen and he fumbled with a few chords. Roy's smile faded as he listened to Ben's newest songs. And in the place of the excitement that had shone on his face . . .

A look of concern.

Roy took a breath. "Okay, the first song wasn't bad, but the other two . . ."

"Lame. I know." Ben's hand spread across the body of the guitar.

"Well, we have your old stuff. We can revisit that. We can also listen to some demo tapes, see if there's anything—"

Ben held up his hand. "Wait, wait."

"What? You're against demos now? There's some good song-writers, up-and-comers I've had my eyes on."

Ben ran his hand through his hair and the war raged inside him. Roy would love the special song he'd written. But . . . once anyone in West Kootenai heard the song, they'd know who he'd written it for. If Mr. Sommer had been worried enough to talk to Ben, many other folks no doubt would be talking too.

Ben sighed.

"Tell me, Ben. Talk to me. I'm not sure what you're thinking."

Ben lowered his head. Roy would love this song. And if Roy loved it, then they'd produce it. Once it was out, Ben would look like a fool. With Marianna's beau in the picture . . . he'd be a laughingstock. He'd be a fool to sing about the woman he wanted to be his wife.

Especially if she chose someone else.

Ben was just about to tell Roy that maybe they should start listening to demos when a strange stirring filled his heart, and then a voice filled his mind. Not an audible voice, but a deep knowing:

Who gave you the inspiration?

Ben knew the answer. God did. Ben couldn't put two syllables together on his own. And if God wanted him to sing it . . . he supposed it would be worth looking like a fool.

"Okay, okay." Ben spoke into the mic. "I have another song."

"Title?" Roy leaned back in his chair and folded his hands behind his neck, as if preparing not to be impressed.

"Ever' Day of My Life."

"Sounds like . . . well, ever' other song out there."

"Might be." Ben pulled his guitar into the right position. "Or maybe not." Then without waiting for Roy's response he began.

> Entered my cabin, all warm from the fire,
> Muscles were achin', worn out n' tired
> From hard work like granddaddy did—
> Ever' day of his life.

Looking through the glass window Ben could see Roy wasn't impressed so far. Probably thought it was too Brad Paisley and not enough George Strait, but he didn't care. Ben closed his eyes . . . and pictured Marianna.

> Got my cabin deep in the woods
> But need somethin' more to call it all good
> To fill the aching hole in my life—
> Cuz every warm cabin
> Needs a good wife.

> You're nothing alone, you're everything together
> Aches all fade when someone helps you weather
> the hard times,

Come fill my heart, come fill my life—
Every warm cabin
Needs a good wife.

My granddaddy told me, "If you wanna be whole,
Son, find a good woman who fills up your soul.
Whose smile brings sunshine, whose laughter rings
    true—
'Cuz son, life ain't nothin' 'til you do."

Then came the day I looked in your eyes,
I knew granddad's words were heartfelt and wise.
Your smile, your laughter proved my grandad knew
A thing or two about life.

Your gray eyes a'dreamin', your smile so warm
Could melt all the ice from the cold winter's storm,
And by the March thaw, my soul came to life
When I asked gray-eyed girl to be called my wife.

You settled my heart, you warmed up my life
The day you agreed to be called my wife.

You said:
We're nothing alone, We're everything together
Aches all fade when someone helps you weather
The hard times,
I'll enter your heart, I'll enter your life
Every warm cabin
Needs a good wife.

Baby,
We're nothing alone, we're everything together
Aches all fade when someone helps you weather

The hard times,
You entered my heart, you entered my life
Every warm cabin
Needs a good wife.

Got a warm cabin, got a good life,
Got all I need
Ever' day with my wife.

Ben finished the last chords and opened his eyes. Instead of sitting, reclined, Roy stood, his hands pressed against the glass.

"That's it."

Ben cocked his head.

"Yes!" Roy punched his fist into the air.

"So?"

"So I think I need to make some calls. We'll do some shows and maybe Monday we can capture that."

"Uh . . ." Ben cleared his throat. "Monday night I have a prayer meeting. I'd really like to be there."

Roy nodded his head slowly, as if trying to take in the news. "Okay. We'll have to look at our schedule. See what we can do. Can you play it again? I'd—"

Just then the door opened. A woman with dark hair walked in, and Ben's heart jumped to his throat. *Carrie.* She was beautiful, just as he remembered. Tall and thin, with a heart-shaped face and long, dark hair that fell over her shoulders.

"Hey, Dad, am I interrupting?"

Ben watched as she looked through the glass and paused. With two steps she entered the studio door, swinging it wide. "No way. Ben! My dad told me you came by."

Ben lowered his guitar to the stand, then he opened his arms for the hug he expected.

Carrie crossed the studio in three long strides and nearly fell into his arms. She'd always been affectionate—something he used to appreciate. She pulled him close and laughter spilled from her. Ben buried his face in her neck, and with the scent of her a hundred memories came back.

Carrie pulled back, taking his face in her hands. "I should be horribly mad at you, disappearing into the woods like that. I thought for sure when I saw you you'd be sporting a beard and a lumberjack's plaid shirt."

Then she dropped her hands and stepped back, eyeing him. Though her hands no longer held him, her gaze did. She still cared. He could tell from her soft smile. Did he make a mistake letting her go?

The answer was immediate.

No, he'd done the right thing. His relationship with Carrie had been anything but pure, and years ago she'd chided him for his newfound faith. She'd tried to bring him down, drawn him back. Her beauty couldn't make up for the fact she refused to commit her life to God.

"Well, I do have a red, plaid shirt." Ben chuckled. "That shirt is in the wash, but I shaved just for your dad."

She laughed and gave his arm a soft punch, then she stood back and crossed her arms over her chest, giving him a sour look. "I was so upset when I came back the other night and Dad said you'd been here but didn't wait around for me. You should have just stayed the night. You never know how the roads are."

He shrugged. "I made it home fine."

"Yes, well, I'm afraid tonight we're not giving you a choice.

It's a blizzard out there. I was out in the stalls with my horses and barely made it back. Thankfully Dad keeps all the lights on. I had to take a hot shower just to get warm." She curled a strand of damp, dark hair around her finger. "You have to stay. We won't take no for an answer."

Ben nodded but didn't answer. *Lord, keep me strong.*

Ben looked around. Roy had left the control room and now stood in the doorway to the studio. He wore a smile, no doubt happy they were hitting it off. More than once Roy had told Ben he wanted a good guy like him for his little girl. When Ben explained he wasn't as much good as forgiven, Roy didn't seem to care. He'd seen enough creeps to know what he did—and didn't— want for his daughter.

"Good idea." Roy pointed a finger at Ben. "And while you're here, we should just plan on recording tomorrow. I have some ideas I want to run by you. But Ben, you need to play the song one more time for Carrie." Roy wrapped an arm around his daughter's shoulders. "Honey, you need to hear this song. I think you'll like it." Roy winked at Ben. "It's about a good wife . . . something I know you want to be some day."

<hr />

Aaron looked at the one sketch out of six he hadn't given to Annie. He could have throttled Charlie for bringing it up—the one of Marianna.

"You should see how Aaron draws," Charlie had said. "He made Marianna so real that it looks like you could talk to her."

He'd had no choice but to show everyone the sketch of Marianna, and just so they didn't think he'd only drawn her he'd pulled out the landscape sketches he'd done. Good thing he'd had those. Even better thing they didn't know he had more of Marianna than anything else.

Opening up his sketchbook, he glanced through the sketches he'd done of her over the last year or so. There was one of her holding an apple pie at church. Another of her watching the children play at the barn raising.

Aaron remembered that day. She'd blushed as he'd approached. Her eyes had been wide, shining with loving appreciation. Was that only six months ago? It seemed years had passed since Marianna left.

He looked at the last sketch he'd drawn of Marianna, from when she was still in Indiana. She was looking through the train window. Her chin tilted up, showing her determination. Yet her eyes had been wide with worry, fear even.

Aaron's heart ached. He missed her. He missed *that* girl. Something about Marianna was different now. At first he'd been excited to see her newfound joy, but with it had come other changes. She seemed so independent, striding off to work each day. And in the evenings she talked about her coworkers and customers as if they were friends. And the way she'd invited the Englischwoman in tonight . . . no one seemed bothered by it.

His chest tightened. He could hear his mother's concerns playing over and over. Unfortunately . . . she was right.

Aaron closed the sketchbook, and then opened the small cardboard box he'd brought in his suitcase. Inside were twenty letters. He'd been faithful to write a few times a week. Well, except for the weeks he'd been so involved with Naomi. He'd planned on giving the letters to Marianna once he got here, but now he wasn't sure.

He opened the box and reached to the bottom, pulling out the first letter he'd written.

⁂

Dear Marianna,

I cannot believe I have to write you. I cannot believe you're not at the house down the road. Seeing you leaving on that train was something like a bad dream. Unfortunately it wasn't something I could wake up from.

This wasn't how I had planned things. During the months I'd worked on the house, the story in my mind went so much different. I suppose I shouldn't have kept that story to myself. Maybe I shoulda let you in on it sooner. Maybe things would be different now.

I'm not sure if I should tell you this, but as the driver took us away we stopped for fuel. We saw Levi there. He was sitting in his car staring at the train tracks. He musta still been there since the train went by. He didn't see us, and I'm glad for that. He was leaning over the steering wheel crying as hard as that time his horse accidentally trampled on his new pup. Maybe this time— like the last time—he realized he was partly at fault. Everyone round town is talking about how his straying was one of the things that forced your folks to head out. Maybe they thought that being close to Levi would be a temptation for your brothers. The way I see it, a person's gonna do what they're gonna do. Just like you and I are determined to follow the ways of our ancestors and get

*baptized into the church, I think some folks are gonna
leave no matter what we do or say.*

    *But enough of that. I didn't pick up this paper
to share all my observations on life. Instead there's a
simpler message I want to share. I love you. I have for
years. I shoulda done a better job showing that love,
telling of that love, instead of building it with wood. Even
now I wish I would have told you more clearer. I wished
I woulda heard it from your mouth.*

    *Even as I write this, I doubt I'll put this letter in the
post. For when I express my truer feelings, I'd like to look
into your eyes. Maybe I'll hold this back until you return
to Indiana. Maybe I'll hold it until I know it's time for
you to be mine again.*

    Love,
    Aaron

Aaron blushed as he read his own words. How naïve he had been.
Did he really think that this move wouldn't change her? Did he
really think she would be the same the day she returned as the
day she left?

He held the envelope in his fingers. Half of him told him
to give it to her—tomorrow even. And then they'd have time to
talk. The other half weighed down those noble thoughts. What
if, instead of drawing them together, it pushed them apart. If he
pushed too hard or moved too fast, she'd run away. Or she'd close
up and not let him know her true feelings.

A pain stirred in his gut when he realized it was possible that he'd leave without her—head back to Indiana alone once he was all healed up. She didn't need him—not really. Not with the satisfaction she found in her family, the community, even her work.

Aaron tucked the envelope in his sketchbook. He'd decide tomorrow. Tears filled his eyes and after a few minutes he realized his leg ached. The pain consumed his limb and his whole body tensed because of it. He looked to the bottle of pain pills but couldn't get himself to take one. He didn't want to be weak. He refused to become addicted.

Aaron put his things in the dresser and then lay in bed, realizing his heart ached too. The pain wasn't as sharp as his leg but there all the same.

His mind tried to think through how things would work out now, but no path he traveled down seemed as good as it would have been before the Sommer family had left. Aaron turned to his side and punched his pillow. The truth was, nothing would ever be like he'd planned. Things had changed. She'd changed. Even if he took her back to Indiana now, Marianna would always have the memories here. She'd understand more of what the world outside their community was like.

And that kind of knowledge never led to good.

CHAPTER EIGHTEEN

*S*unday morning dawned, and with it Marianna's anticipation of a slow-paced day. Their community only had church every other week, and this was an off day.
She snuggled closer to Ellie and pulled the covers up tight under her chin. It must be earlier than she thought. It was still cold, which meant Dat hadn't been downstairs to get the fire going yet.

Marianna looked to the cradle and saw that Joy wasn't there. Marianna had heard her baby sister crying in the night and barely remembered her mother coming in to get her to nurse. Mem probably kept Joy in bed with her to keep her warm.

She waited for a while, expecting to hear the stove lids rattle downstairs and Mem humming as she started breakfast. As Marianna lay there, she thought about the day ahead. She looked forward to sitting by the fire, hearing news from Aaron about folks back home, and maybe even playing with quilt blocks. She still needed to design a quilt and get to sewing it for Annie. Instead of getting a ride to Eureka, she'd purchased quilt squares from the craft room at work and now had to try to figure something out with those. It wasn't that she wouldn't have enjoyed spending the day with Ben. She would, and that was the problem. It also would have been a problem because everyone—Dat, Mem, Aaron—would have protested her doing such a thing. Perhaps they thought if she just stayed away from Ben, it will solve everything. That it would snuff out all the emotions in her heart.

Marianna listened to Ellie's soft breathing. Last night things warmed up again after dinner. Uncle Ike and Annie were restored to friendly terms before the night was over. The most humorous part came when Uncle Ike gave Annie a ride home. Her little car had trouble getting out of the driveway. The horse did better by far, especially with the sleigh tracks Uncle Ike had attached to his buggy. That's how the Amish did things in the winter around here, she'd learned. It reminded her of the old storybooks she'd read as a child.

It was romantic to see her uncle remind Annie to bundle up before heading out, and Annie didn't seem put out by all the attention. Not in the least.

Marianna's stomach growled, and not willing to wait any longer, she dressed and tiptoed downstairs, hoping to start breakfast before everyone woke. But as she stepped off the last stair, she turned and noticed Aaron already dressed and standing by the fire, preparing to get it going. By his side sat Trapper. Ever since Aaron arrived, the dog had decided Aaron needed his companionship at night.

Aaron put wood in the stove and then crumbled a few sheets of newsprint, setting it inside. He looked tired. And something else . . . worried, maybe?

"Are you okay?" She hurried to the small jar on the side table for a match. "The pain didn't keep you up all night, did it?"

"Nah." Aaron rubbed his leg above the cast. "Pain is pain. Just woke up early, that's all."

"I hope the bed's comfortable." She approached and bent down to pet Trapper. *She* used to be his favorite.

"*Ja, ja.*" Aaron looked up at her. "I wasn't complaining. In fact, I'm still sorry I took your room. This isn't how I planned things."

Marianna glanced up at him, meeting his blue eyes, seeing his embarrassment. She sort of liked this Aaron. She'd always looked up to the Aaron who took charge, took matters into his own hands, provided, planned. But now, with Aaron not able to do much more than light a fire once in a while, Marianna saw again the tender boy she remembered from childhood. And his finger-combed hair added to the allure.

She wanted to know this Aaron better. Wanted to understand what had changed since she'd last seen him on the platform of the train station, standing strong and brave.

If only she could sit next to him and ask about what things had been like after she'd left. Not only things in their community. More than that. Things with his heart. His cabin. Naomi. How intimate had they been? Had it been more than friendship?

Instead, she moved toward the kitchen, and then paused, calling back over her shoulder. "Do you like your eggs scrambled or fried? I could do either."

When he didn't answer, she turned.

He got the stove going and then closed the door. Hopping on one foot, he moved to the sofa, sinking into it with a weariness she didn't understand.

Then she noticed a sketchbook on the floor. And on top of it what looked to be a letter. Her eyes zeroed in on it.

"Did someone from home write?"

Aaron studied her for a moment, then reached down and slipped the envelope into his book. "Oh, no. I wrote something. Nothing really."

A letter? To Naomi? Her heart sank. "If you'd like, I can take it with me to work tomorrow and mail it out."

Aaron nodded and then cleared his throat. "Fried."

She tilted her head. "Excuse me?"

"I like my eggs fried, if you don't mind."

"No, of course not. That's how I like mine too."

She turned back again and hurried to the kitchen. What was the letter about? Of course he'd written Naomi. It only made sense. That was probably why he didn't want her to mail it—to see it. And if it *was* a letter to Levi's old girlfriend . . . what did it say?

Aaron squirmed. From the look on his face, he had something important to talk to her about. She just wished he would come out with it already. If he kept this up he'd get her kapp strings all in a bunch as her mind spun with thoughts and worries.

She didn't understand men. Aaron Zook might be talented at drawing, but he didn't hide his feelings well. Why didn't she realize that sooner? Maybe because back at home he'd been surrounded by what he knew best, doing what he did best.

And here . . . he seemed all out of sorts. She didn't blame him. It took time to get used to a new place, new ways. Plus, there was the injury.

He had gotten used to having her around more. He hadn't seemed to mind one bit—until today. Was he nervous because he wished he was with someone else?

Marianna bit her lip. If he didn't come out with it soon, she was going to scream.

Marianna sat on the floor in front of the fire, her legs crossed and her skirt tucked around her. She started laying out the small snippets of fabric she'd bought at the store. She looked down at her gray dress with the colored fabric patterns spread over it. The reds, oranges, and yellows made her smile.

She placed a few more squares on her lap. What it would feel like to wear colors such as these? With a swoop of her hand she brushed them away, as if they were covered with ants.

How could she let her mind wander so?

"You're working on a quilt?" Aaron leaned close, looking down.

"Well, I'm just playing with these now . . . I'd like to start one soon though."

"If you'd like some help I can sketch something for you."

"Really?" Marianna sat up straighter.

"My mem used to have me design quilts for her all the time."

Marianna tightened her lips, holding back the giggle that threatened to break through. "*Ja?* I did not know that. I've always admired your mem's quilts." Everyone admired Mrs. Zook's quilts for their color and style, and not once had she confessed that her oldest son was the designer of the patterns.

Marianna looked up at Aaron. Thankfully after breakfast his attitude had changed. He smiled now. Whatever had been the problem did not seem to matter any longer. Maybe he'd just been tired or in pain. At least, she hoped that was the cause.

"So, what would you like your quilt set to look like?" He motioned for her to bring the swatches of fabric closer.

"Well, I'd like to make it for a queen bed. I'd like to do a colorful pattern too, but not just a plain design."

"Do you have graph paper? And a pencil?"

Mem must have heard them talking. "I have some." A few minutes later she returned with both.

Aaron leaned down and picked up some quilt squares, running them through his fingers. "I have an idea. You can do a colorful, yet simple boxed pattern in the border of the quilt, then we can have a wide border . . . and you could trace the hands of the members of your family and stitch around those." He glanced over to the children at the table with a smile.

The kids were still there, supposedly eating their breakfast. Yet Josiah complained he dropped his eggs and Trapper gobbled them up. David and Charlie talked about the snow barn they wanted to build, and Ellie cried because she had something in her eye. No wonder Aaron's first idea had to do with the children.

Marianna watched Aaron sketch his idea. Tears filled her eyes as she imagined Dat, Mem, her young siblings, even baby Joy. That would be so sweet, but—

"Oh, that won't work. What about Levi?" Marianna's heart ached to think that their family quilt wouldn't include her older brother. "Also, there are my sisters, Marilyn and Joanna . . ." She shook her head. "Besides I was going to make this quilt to sell. I need the money."

Aaron nodded but didn't respond. His lowered eyebrows and slightly downturned lip reflected his disappointment.

"But some day I'd love to make a quilt like that. Some day when I have a family of my own . . ."

"Or it would make a perfect wedding quilt." He erased the smaller handprints in the border, replacing them with just two different sizes—like the hands of a husband and wife.

Marianna looked up into his eyes and smiled. "I love that idea, but I need to make a quilt for Annie first."

"*Ja.* I understand." Aaron nodded and then turned to a new page. "Can you hand me the rest of those swatches?" Was it just her imagination or had his cheeks brightened to a soft rosy color?

Marianna nodded as he handled them, studying their texture and their color. He laid some out, using his cast as a display board. A few times Marianna was surprised by the colors he put next to each other, but as he continued to lay out the pieces an image began to form. As she sat there, it wasn't just blues and browns and yellows and whites. She could almost see the landscape out the window.

"I see it!" She scooted over, pointing to the quilt squares. "You're creating borders . . . landscape borders. Blue for the sky. White for a thin layer of clouds. A wide strip of dark green for the mountains, with bits of yellow mixed in for the larch trees. Then white for the snow at the bottom." She turned to him and his eyes were bright.

"You do see it." He smiled. Then, as if satisfied with his work, he leaned back against the pillow, folding his hands behind the back of his head.

"If you get the fabric, I can help you cut it out."

"That is not necessary." She chuckled. "Besides, it's not really manly work."

"I know, but I can't do much. And if it will help you . . ."

She nodded. "*Denke.*"

"Besides." He held in a grin, but she could see hints of it by the way his lips curled up slightly on the corners. "When you finish this, you can get started on the next one."

"Next one?"

He turned back the graph paper to the quick sketch of the wedding quilt.

Aaron set down the paper and rubbed his leg just above his cast. Marianna studied his face and noticed hope in his eyes. If he was in pain, one couldn't tell from his gaze.

"Well, Aaron, I have to say that's not a bad idea." She smiled.

Dear Journal,

I don't know what's gotten into me. The way I talk, you'd think I've already decided that I'm going to be marrying Aaron Zook in the spring. The problem is, my words are leading him to believe that too. Like today. I was innocently working on a quilt when he suggested I make a wedding quilt next. I agreed with him! Why? Do I want to break his heart more than necessary?

Then again, it's not that I've decided to refuse Aaron's advances either. I have to admit I enjoy being with him. I've known him for many years and I've seen him as hardworking, kind, stubborn at times, but strong. There are other parts of him I'm discovering too. When no one is looking, the gentle, artistic part of Aaron comes out. He is also good with children, and he's thankful for a good meal. He's dedicated to our Amish ways and takes interest in the feelings of others.

Look at me. There I go again. You'd think I was interviewing the poor man for consideration of my future husband!

I'm still not sure if I'll be going back in the spring. I feel as scattered as all of those fabric pieces laid out on the floor. If only I could piece my life together and make sense of it too!

CHAPTER NINETEEN

en awoke at 10 a.m. and realized he missed church. It turned out that Roy couldn't get the song out of his mind and they did a pre-recording last night—just so Roy could get a jump on production, since Ben planned on going back to West Kootenai for a few days.

Carrie had watched movies in the media room, waiting for them to finish. When they finally emerged from the recording studio, she was curled up in a ball on the leather sofa, fast asleep. In the old days Ben would have picked her up and carried her to her bed. Then he most likely would have stayed. This time he went to her room, found a blanket, brought it down, and laid it over her. She hadn't budged.

"I'm sorry I didn't treasure you as I should have," he whispered to her sleeping form. "I'm sorry I took from you what belonged to your future husband."

His heart ached. Though he wasn't the only one Carrie had been with, he took what did not belong to him. After giving his life to Christ, changing his physical relationships had been the hardest part. Stopping drinking hadn't been a problem. The parties he didn't even miss. But there were many nights he'd lain at home, alone in his cabin, and wished he had someone there, sleeping next to him. He missed feeling desired. Missed the intimacy.

Ben brushed his hair back from his forehead. *Get those thoughts out of your mind, Stone.* He was different now. God had made him different.

He rose from the bed and sighed. If only, when God washed away his sins He'd washed away his memories too. Why couldn't things work that way?

He found his way to the adjoining bathroom and noticed someone had slipped in through the hallway door and left him a set of Roy's clothes. They were a size too big, and not really his style, but he was thankful for them.

Downstairs he found Carrie sipping on coffee, staring out at the open field behind the house. The ocean of white snow appeared to have waves rising and falling near the fence posts.

Ben poured himself a cup of coffee. He leaned against the counter. What it would be like to live in such a place? This open kitchen with tall windows made the little window in his cabin's kitchen seem like a porter's hole on a ship.

"Sorry we didn't get a chance to talk last night. Your dad was pretty excited about one of my songs. He was on me like a wet tick in a watermelon patch. I couldn't shake him off."

Carrie laughed. "He gets that way sometimes, but it means the song has promise, and after listening I have to agree it's good."

"You were listening?" Heat rose to his face. He lifted his mug and took a sip from his coffee, hoping to hide his worry from Carrie.

"Yes, I confess. I snuck in the back so you wouldn't see. My dad gave me the angry eye, but he didn't kick me out. He knows how musicians get when their music is still in progress. They don't like folks listening in. But it was great—a beautiful song. I can almost picture the music video now. You should be proud."

Ben nodded and a knot tightened in his throat. It had been so long since someone called him a musician. And to have such kind words said about his song. It surprised him, actually, how much it meant to hear her say those things. In West Kootenai he'd gotten used to just being Ben, and he thought he liked it that way. He enjoyed being like everyone else.

Yet Carrie's appreciation and respect when she talked about his music—well, he hadn't realized how much that mattered. He shouldn't compare Carrie with Marianna, but her words watered a part of his soul that had nearly dried up. It made no sense why he'd fallen for a woman who wasn't even allowed to listen to music, let alone show her appreciation for it.

What is it about Marianna that makes me care for her so?

Carrie eyed him, and Ben guessed what she was thinking. She was about to ask him why he ended up living in the woods. He moved to the table, sitting opposite of her, and launched into his own questions before she had a chance to ask. Not that he had anything to hide—just that he didn't know how to explain.

"So, what brought you back up here to Montana? I mean, last time we were together—uh, last time I heard from you, you were enjoying L.A."

"Enjoying it a little too much." She sighed. "Ended up in rehab. Isn't that just part of the lifestyles of the rich and famous? Part of the gig?"

Ben coughed, nearly choking on the sip of coffee he'd been taking. "What . . . I never thought—"

"You never thought I had a problem? Yeah, most people didn't. I drank to mask my loneliness. It's tough having everything and no one to share it with."

Heaviness weighed on him, as if the large ceiling beams overhead pressed down on his shoulders. He was part of the reason Carrie had been lonely. Even when they were together, he'd taken everything for himself and given little back. Of course, to the public—to her dad—he'd always acted like a good guy. He'd treated her like a lady and opened doors for her. He'd bought her gifts and always bragged about her to his friends. Yet, deep down, he did that more as a show than because it came from his heart. She must have known it too. She'd been better off without him. Who wanted to be with someone who didn't love you with all his heart?

"I'm so sorry."

At his whispered apology, Carrie shrugged, then wiped the corners of her eyes. "Thanks, it was hard, but it ended up being good. One of the directors at the clinic had worked up here at a ranch for teen girls before. Once I got cleaned up, he told me about it. I volunteer there nearly every day. In fact, that first night you showed up that's where I was—with some of those teen girls. They earn points for good behavior and got to pick a special outing. We went to a movie and then got some pie."

As she smiled at him, Ben had an odd sensation that he was talking to a stranger. Oh, she looked like Carrie, but the way she talked—this wasn't the Carrie he'd known.

"Wow, I don't know what to say."

"From the look in your eyes, it would be, 'What happened to the old Carrie?'" She chuckled.

"Yeah, that's what I was thinking."

Carrie rose and carried her coffee mug to the kitchen. "She's gone, hopefully for good. Well, some of her. I do still know how to make some mean pancakes if you're hungry."

"Starved."

Carrie smiled. "Great, and after I whip them up I want to hear about you, especially about the girl in the song."

Ben watched as Carrie made breakfast, and they talked about old friends and how they were doing. Most of Ben's old music buddies were living the same wild life. A life Ben didn't miss.

When they finally sat down to eat, Ben knew he wasn't going to get out of her questions this time.

"So, tell me about this young woman. You know, the one in the song."

Ben took a small pile of pancakes and put them on his plate, covering them with syrup. "Who says there's a girl? Maybe I just made it up. If everyone had to be in love before they wrote a love song, then we'd be hurting for some good music."

Carrie took a big bite of her pancakes. She cocked one eyebrow, and he could tell she didn't buy it.

"If you're a good Christian boy, like my dad says you are, I don't think you should be lying like this." She smirked.

Ben nearly choked on his pancakes. Then he took a large drink from his orange juice, washing it down. "Okay, there is someone. She moved here from Indiana this spring. She—" Ben considered telling Carrie she worked at Kootenai Kraft and Grocery, but then he changed his mind. Driving up there—deep into the mountains—and checking her out was just the type of thing Carrie would do.

"Really, an Indiana girl? Is she a musician too?"

"No." The memory pierced his mind of the one time Marianna held his guitar but he pushed it away. "She works a little. She quilts. She has younger siblings and helps her mom with that. And . . . she makes the best pies and cookies."

"So basically she's a young Betty Crocker." Carrie placed her fork on her plate and wiped her mouth. "That really doesn't seem like your type. Let me guess. Does she wear a skirt and pearls while she cooks?"

Ben frowned at Carrie's harsh laugh. Clearly, she was bothered by what he'd said. Maybe because Marianna was everything Carrie wasn't.

"So, why did they move here? I mean West Kootenai of all places."

Ben opened his mouth, his mind racing. Heat rose to his cheeks. "Um, just for adventure. Doesn't everyone want to live in Montana? Experience the Wild West?" Once the words were out he wanted to take them back. Why had he lied?

Because, his mind tried to convince him, it would take so much time to go into it all, to talk about Levi and his influence on the kids . . . about all that had happened.

Carrie narrowed her gaze studying him.

What had gotten into him? *Why can't I just come out and say that Marianna's Amish?* In West Kootenai the Amish were their friends and neighbors. They were highly respected. But here . . . Ben swallowed hard. He was protecting Marianna, he supposed. Protecting her privacy, heading off any smart-aleck comments Carrie would make.

Ben rose and picked up his empty plate. "Hey, I'd love to stick around and talk about my love interest, but I really should head to the studio and get to work before your dad gets up. There's a bridge he wants me to work on, and I've already been a sloth."

Carrie nodded and looked away, but not before he saw the hurt in her eyes. She thought he didn't trust her with knowing more about Marianna. And the truth was, he didn't. Carrie was sweet now, but he'd seen another side of her.

And there was no way he would risk setting that side loose on Marianna.

CHAPTER TWENTY

*A*s she swept the floor for the second time that morning, Marianna couldn't help but appreciate Aaron's four sketches hanging over the back wall, behind the cash register. Like Annie promised, she'd framed them, and they looked good enough to hang in an art gallery—not that Marianna had ever been in a gallery. She just supposed that Aaron's sketches looked as good as any she'd find there.

Marianna studied them, and her eyes widened. Annie asked a few hundred dollars each for them. A sticker on the front read *Amish Art*. She didn't how art was valued, but it seemed like a lot. That would help with Aaron's train ticket home and whatever he still needed back at his house—

She pushed the thought aside. She'd been working hard not to think about where she stood with all that—him returning to Indiana, her going with him or staying.

"Marianna, could I ask you for a favor?" Annie usually looked refreshed on Mondays, but not today.

"Sure, although since this is a job, and you pay me—I don't think it's a favor, rather another item on my to-do list." She smiled.

"Actually, it's a little of both. A favor *and* something on your to-do list." Annie moved to the rack that held the bread, pulled off a fresh loaf and a package of cookies, and placed them on the counter near the front register.

"Jenny called, and Kenzie's sick. I could hear Kenzie coughing in the background. Jenny won't be coming in today."

Marianna continued to sweep chunks of mud off the floor near the front door. Boots usually came in caked with ice, snow, and mud, which fell off in clumps. The snow and ice melted, leaving only clumps of dried mud.

Annie scooted past Marianna and pulled a half-gallon of milk from the refrigerator case. "I was wondering if you wouldn't mind going over to their house for the day?"

"To deliver groceries?"

"Yeah, and just to give Jenny a break. She sounded exhausted. Maybe watch Kenzie for a while so Jenny can get a nap. Edgar's out sick today, too, but I called Sarah, and she can come in to take your shift. I'll pay you as normal."

"*Ja, ja,* I can do it, but you can't pay me."

"Yes, I can. It's going on your time card. Work is work and your time is time." Annie brushed her long, blonde ponytail from her shoulder.

Marianna didn't argue. She could use the money—it was true—especially since Dat had extra expenses now with another mouth to feed. Aaron had been faithful to give her parents some money, which they didn't expect and almost didn't take, but Marianna could see a difference in the way they lived with Aaron there. Mem cooked bigger meals, of more expensive food—all of which they had to buy since they'd left their storehouse back in Indiana. Mem washed everything more often too. Every day Mem strung laundry upstairs to dry. On days Mem washed sheets and blankets, they filled the living room.

Marianna shook her head. Would Mem ever relax? Amish women considered slothfulness the greatest sin. It was bad enough when someone from the community came for a visit, but to have Aaron in her home . . . she doubted Mem ever sat.

"If you double-bag those groceries to take to her, it'll work better." Marianna pointed to the grocery sacks. "I don't want the snow soggying up the bag as I walk."

"Walk? Oh no, I should've mentioned, I've called Ben. He was out delivering furniture today and doesn't mind swinging by to give you a ride."

She should refuse. Jenny didn't live more than a mile away. But she pressed her lips tight and didn't say a word. The truth was, she'd like a ride, not because she was getting lazy, but because Ben hadn't been far from her thoughts. When he wasn't around, she missed him.

As if her thoughts had been a beacon, drawing him in, the door opened and Ben strode in. He was looking at his boots, stomping them on the doormat as he entered. When he glanced up he almost jumped back, seeing her there.

"Marianna." Her name escaped like a breath from his lips.

"*Ja*, you seem surprised."

He studied her for a moment. "I'm not surprised, but I'd just forgotten."

"Really? What did you forget?"

"How beautiful you are." As soon as the words were out of his mouth his jaw dropped, as if he didn't believe he'd just said them.

Marianna's stomach did a flip. She didn't know how to respond to that. "Well, I forgot how much mud your boots bring in." She wagged the broom at him. "Couldn't you have come barefoot? It would've saved me time from cleaning up such a mess." She laughed.

Ben nodded but the shocked look he wore transformed into one of sadness, and for a split second she thought he would cry.

"What's wrong?" Worry filled her. She hadn't heard why he'd left town and suddenly hoped it wasn't a serious problem. Had he lost someone he loved? Or maybe they'd been injured. "Are you okay? Everything's all right, isn't it?"

"Everything's all right, but I'm not." He pressed his hand to his forehead as if trying to figure out how to explain. "I've just been sticking my foot in my mouth lately. Saying what I shouldn't. Not saying what I should."

Marianna glanced down at his boots. "Well, in that case I hope you like the taste of mud, because if you put that foot in, that's what you're gonna get."

Laughter spurt from Ben's mouth and he shook his head, then he eyed her. "I've never met another woman like you, Marianna Sommer. Your manner of dress is plain, but inside you're anything but. That kapp and apron can't hide how special you are."

A smile lifted her lips, then she pushed it back down. No one in her community said such things to each other. Yet she did like it. She especially liked that Ben was saying those things—which made matters even worse.

She put the broom back behind the counter and grabbed her coat from the hook. "Will you do me a favor? Would you grab those bags of groceries? This special girl needs to run back to the kitchen and get a pumpkin pie I have cooling on the rack."

Ten minutes later they were pulling into the driveway of a small single wide trailer. Ben's mood had lightened, but Marianna could still see from his eyes that something wasn't right.

"You coming in to say hello to Jenny and Kenzie?"

Ben shook his head. "Nah, not today. I have to get this delivery up the road, but tell Kenzie I said hi and hope she's getting better." He paused, as if something just occurred to him. "Actually "—he reached for the door—"I should help you carry that up."

He grabbed the bag of groceries from the seat between them and got out of the truck. Marianna took the pie and followed. As they approached, she saw the curtain next to the door flutter back into place, as if someone had been looking out, watching them.

Then, just as they climbed the steps, Jenny opened the door and stepped out. "Hey there. Annie said you were coming." She forced a smile. "Thanks so much." Her feet were bare and she wore a pair of sweatpants and a sweatshirt. She had to be freezing. Marianna was shivering, and she wore a thick coat and a bonnet over her cap.

Ben approached with the bag. "I can carry this inside if you'd like."

Jenny reached for the bag. "I can get it. No problem." She took it from his hands. "Thanks for giving Marianna a ride, that was nice of you." Puffs of frosty air escaped Jenny's mouth as she spoke.

"Okay then." Ben looked back at Marianna, then headed to his truck. "I do have to get to work anyway."

Marianna turned and watched him leave. It was only after the truck pulled out of the driveway that Jenny opened the door again.

"Sorry about that. Kenzie's been sick, and I haven't had much time to clean up lately. I didn't want Ben to see the house like this."

"I'm sure it's fine. I have five younger siblings at home. I know what it's like."

Jenny nodded as she stepped inside. "That's what I figured." She motioned for Marianna to follow, and she hurried in. It was warmer than outside, but not the same warmth as when walking in the door at home. There weren't the wonderful smells of her mother's cooking, either.

"Excuse the mess," Jenny muttered once again before shutting the door.

Marianna glanced around. The noise of the television assaulted her first. How could people put up with that? She stepped over shoes strewn about, noted a small jacket on the floor, along with toys and dirty paper plates. Was this how all Englisch lived? She couldn't imagine Annie living like such. Annie always seemed tidy at work—but then, so did Jenny.

"Sorry it's a little messy around here, Kenzie's been sick and I haven't been feeling well either," Jenny said yet another time.

As if proving her mother right, Kenzie's small cough sounded across the room. Marianna followed the sound to the small girl stretched out, lying on her stomach and watching what appeared to be some type of children's program on the small television. She wore a thin night dress and her bare feet were lifted in the air, swinging to the tune playing for the dancing, fuzzy puppets. Scattered around the couch were various toys, including a Bible storybook that was open, and from the look of it, had some additional help from Kenzie coloring its pages.

"No problem. I can help if you like. I know how life with little ones can be."

A half-dozen empty soda cans littered the counter between the living room and kitchen. Jenny pushed them aside and put the sack of groceries in their place. Marianna's eyes scanned the rest of the counter, looking for a spot to place the pie. It was covered with dirty dishes.

Following her gaze, Jenny pointed to a small dining room table. "Just find a spot on there. Wow, that pie looks good."

"I made it this morning. Maybe next week I'll teach you how to make one."

"Yeah." Jenny nodded, her short ponytail bobbing. "I'd like that."

Marianna pushed a ketchup bottle to the side and piled a few plates on top of each other to make room for the pie. She tried not to look around at the mess, and instead focused on Jenny's face, remembering why she was here.

Jenny forced a smile. "You said there are kids around your house. I know you live with your parents, but are any of them yours?"

"Oh no." Marianna laughed. "Not my children, my brothers and sisters. I have five younger siblings and one older—but the older one lives in Indiana still."

"Wow, that's a ton."

Marianna nodded, taking off her coat and hanging it on a chair back. Then she stepped over a newspaper that had been trampled on. "*Ja, ja,* I suppose." She didn't tell Jenny that her family was small by some Amish standards. The young woman appeared to be having enough trouble with just one child.

"Well, what can I do?" Marianna clasped her hands together. The wind outside rattled the windows, and she resisted the urge to rub her hands together. A shiver moved up her spine and she tried to ignore it but couldn't keep her shoulders from trembling.

"It's chilly in here, I know. This place isn't very well insulated and it cost a few hundred dollars last month just to keep from freezing."

"I'm warm enough, but do you have warmer clothes for Kenzie? That might help her feel better."

Jenny glanced behind her and yawned. "Yeah, she does look cold, and she hasn't eaten all morning. I bet she's hungry too."

"Cereal!" The young girl clapped her hands. Kenzie's eyes were still focused on the television, but it was clear she knew what was going on.

"Tell you what." Marianna moved toward the small girl, sitting at the end of the couch near her feet. "Why don't you get some rest and I'll take care of things here. Kenzie and I will have some fun, won't we?"

Kenzie nodded, even though her eyes stayed focused on the television screen.

Jenny yawned again and moved down the hall to the back room. "Thanks, Marianna. I owe you one."

∞

The first thing Marianna did was to get Kenzie into warm clothes. The second, turn off the television.

Kenzie folded her arms over her chest, and her bottom lip popped out. "Hey, I was watching that."

"I know, but don't you want to help me make lunch?" Marianna stretched out her hand.

Kenzie shrugged. "I dunno how to cook."

"Well, that's perfect. I'll show you."

Marianna led Kenzie to the kitchen and opened the refrigerator. There were only a few items inside. She checked the cupboard and noticed there wasn't much there. In fact there were more groceries in the bag than there were in Jenny's kitchen. Marianna put the food away and then turned to Kenzie. "How about a piece of pumpkin pie?"

"We're going to cook pie?" Kenzie clapped.

"Actually, no. The pie is already made. In fact, I changed my mind. Why don't we cook another day. I'll bring over some special things."

Kenzie wrinkled her nose, and Marianna could see her disappointment.

She cut Kenzie a piece of pie and poured her some milk. Now . . . how to turn cleaning into a game? As she thought about it, something stirred inside her. Cleaning could happen another day too. What Kenzie would appreciate most was just time—time without the television on. Time to have Marianna's complete attention.

"Kenzie, do you have any favorite games? Or toys? I thought we could play something while your mom slept."

"Barbies?" Kenzie put down her fork and rushed to the small room just off the living room. She returned a minute later with two dolls in questionable attire. Marianna tried to ignore that for now. As she held the plastic figure in her hand she thought how different it was from the dolls she had as a child—the dolls Ellie had. Amish dolls wore simple dress and had no faces painted on their wooden bodies because Amish parents didn't want their children to have a "graven image."

"Hi, I'm Barbie." Kenzie spoke in a squeaky voice as her doll bounced on the table. "What's your name?"

Marianna did the same with her doll, making it look like it was walking on those strangely shaped pointy toes. "I'm Marianna."

"Hi, Marianna. You're a little Marianna just like the big Marianna."

"Yes, I suppose I am."

"Marianna." Kenzie cocked her head. "Why do you wear that Easter hat on your head?"

Marianna held in her chuckle. She supposed Kenzie's doll was talking to the big Marianna now.

"Well, it's called a kapp, and every woman in my family wears one."

"Is it to keep your head warm? To keep the snow from falling on your hair?"

"No." She patted her kapp. "It's pretty thin material. It doesn't really keep my head warm." How could she explain that the kapp was a prayer veil? They were supposed to "pray without ceasing" and "wear a covering on their head when they prayed"—hence, the kapp.

"It's to make God happy." Hopefully, that would suffice.

Instead of seeming satisfied, Kenzie scowled. "My mama doesn't wear one of those. Does that mean she makes God mad?" Kenzie put down her doll and looked at Marianna. From the serious look on her face, this conversation was no longer play.

"No, of course not."

"Mama says we need to love Jesus to go to heaven. Do I need to tell Mama we need a kapp like that too?" Kenzie pointed. "A hat that doesn't keep you warm?"

Marianna studied the little girl's face, and suddenly all she'd been taught seemed to shatter around her feet. Because she knew what she had to answer.

"No, you can love Jesus and not wear a kapp."

All her life she'd been told her people were God's chosen people, that following their ways was right and God was pleased by the way they lived. But did that mean that folks like Jenny or Kenzie had no way of pleasing God? Was the most she could ever offer them a few hours' break and a piece of pie? But nothing to help with their eternal life?

If they believed in Jesus, like Jenny had told Kenzie, wasn't that enough?

Marianna's mind seemed as numb and heavy as the wet snow outside. She put down the doll. She no longer felt like playing.

"Hey, Kenzie." Marianna held out her hand. "I have an idea. Instead of playing dolls, why don't we read some stories for a while."

"My Bible book?" Kenzie set her doll by the piece of pie and hurried to the living room, nearly tripping over an abandoned shoe.

"Yes, your Bible book." Marianna rose and followed. What stories did Kenzie's book hold inside? She had a feeling there was more truth in those pages than she'd heard from the bishops—mainly teachings on dress, and buggies, and traditions.

Marianna sat on the couch and Kenzie snuggled on her lap. A peace she hadn't experienced in a while moved from her chest to her limbs. Maybe Marianna hadn't come to Montana just to help her parents.

Maybe she was here to reach out to those unlike her too.

CHAPTER TWENTY-ONE

en walked into the prayer meeting, his heart heavy. It still troubled him that he hadn't been bold enough to tell Carrie that Marianna was Amish. And coming back to West Kootenai—to the simple way of life—made him realize what he'd been missing.

Oh, he'd enjoyed being in the studio. He'd enjoyed dreaming with Roy, and brainstorming together to make his songs better.

But he'd missed this. He'd missed . . .

Home. If only he could hold on to how he felt here while he was with Roy. But it wasn't easy. Sometimes . . . he felt like he changed when he was with Roy. Like he was giving up some part of himself to become successful.

Ben sighed as he stomped the snow from his boots. It wasn't that he'd done anything wrong. It wasn't that he planned on going the wrong direction, to live the wrong type of life again. He understood the path—and its dangers. He'd been there—accustomed to the crowds, the praise, the fans. He'd had Carrie at his side and spent just as much time at her apartment as his. He remembered all too well what it was to strive for more and more, to try to do better every time. He'd wanted to reach the next level—only to find out that once he got there, that too gave him no satisfaction.

Over the weekend he'd recorded his new song, and a few old ones he'd written that Roy wanted to give new life. Was he making the right decision? God gave him a gift—but was he using it in the right way? If he wanted to care and provide for a wife, he'd have to do more than drive people around and deliver furniture. The thing was, if Marianna didn't fit in the Englisch world of West Kootenai, Montana, there was no way she'd fit in L.A., in a world of tour buses and recording studios.

Yes, he was making changes to get what he wanted. He just wasn't sure that what he wanted would fit with the changes he was making.

"Ben, good to see you." Ike approached and placed a hand on Ben's shoulder. "Heard you were out of town a few days. I was wondering if you would make it tonight." Ike ran a hand down his smooth cheek, and Ben wondered why the man had never been married. Maybe he should talk to Ike about that.

"I couldn't miss it. This is where I get fueled up for the week." Ben removed his ball cap and his jacket. "I did have a little work to do down in Kalispell, but nothing that would keep me away. I'd drive across the state for this. I need it. I need folks' prayers tonight."

Ike nodded.

"Well, Ben, it sounds like you've come to the right place."

Susan Carash reached her hand out for his coat. "Give me that snowy thing. I'll hang it in the closet. Would you like some coffee? It's decaf."

"Got any of the real stuff? After this I'm going to be up for a while." Ben strode into the living room and took a seat on the empty sofa.

"I can make some. Got work to do?" Susan closed the door to the coat closet.

"Yeah, you could say that. More like just fiddling with my guitar." Roy wanted a few more songs. He'd convinced Ben to just play around—to see what would come out. Ben told him he would, and that he'd return to Kalispell in a few days.

As Ben watched the other folks show up and greet each other, his mind was on Roy's statement that one more new song would finish off the project. Ben had tried to think of something on the drive up to West Kootenai, but there was no inspiration.

Then, right before he got to the Carashes' house, he'd driven by the Sommers' place. A single lantern had hung in the living room, casting a soft glow through the windows. His stomach knotted as Ben pictured Aaron sitting in there with Marianna by his side. Even now the lump was still lodged in his throat, and he wished the coffee would come so he could swallow it down.

Then, as softly as the snow falling on the window, words had come to him as he drove: "Sometimes light only shows me what I'm missing out on . . ."

But by the time he'd parked in the Carashes' driveway, he'd already nixed that idea. Light to him was God showing him how things truly were. It was darkness that hid things. Hid the truth. He didn't like the idea of casting light in a negative way.

More people piled in the house, all of them folks Ben knew. In addition to members of the Community Church he attended down the road, some Amish friends attended. Three families, with members of all ages, piled into the house—their cheeks especially rosy from the ride over. Some horses pulled buggies, others sleds. The men were the last to enter. They'd been outside tending to their horses in the new barn that the community had put up for the family.

Ben remembered the fear in the Amish folks' faces when they first started coming to the prayer meetings. Not only were they assembling with Englischers, but the Englischers were praying aloud—something not encouraged by the Amish. Thankfully the Amish continued to come back, hungry for the interaction. Hungry for the connection with God. The cold winter outside the door and windows might be harsh, but warmth and love filled the room.

"Maybe the light's showing what I need to see," the words played through Ben's mind. *"It's not what I'm missing, but what's not to be."*

He opened his Bible on his lap and pulled a pen from his flannel shirt pocket, writing down the words on an old church bulletin. Yeah, those words made more sense. They worked—not for his heart, but for the song. At least it would give him something to play around with later.

In addition to two sofas, numerous dining room chairs and folding chairs circled the room. Sarah Shelter, Marianna's coworker, approached and sat in the chair closest to him.

"Ben, good to see you. We've been missing you around the store."

"We?" He tucked his pen back in his pocket and closed his paper inside the Bible.

"Me, the cinnamon rolls, and your favorite scrambled eggs." Sarah chuckled.

"Yes, well, I've been working in Kalispell."

"Good to know. Marianna's been asking." Sarah's eyes narrowed. She studied his face as if waiting for a response. Ben did his best to hide his emotions.

"Yes, well, she's probably worried about anyone out there driving on those roads—with what happened to her friend Aaron."

"*Ja*, I'm glad he's all right. Someone like Aaron is just who Marianna needs."

Sarah opened her own Bible on her lap and flipped through the pages. From the look in her eye it was clear she was trying to protect her friend. He would have laughed out loud if the room weren't already quieting for their time of prayer. How could Sarah think it was right for an Amish family to sneak out like this—to meet with the Englisch and pray with them—and yet also believe that an Amish girl and Englischman falling in love was bad?

"Welcome, everyone. It's great to have you tonight. We can get started," Devon Carash began. "Let's start by asking God to bring to mind those who need prayer. You don't need to state their need. You don't even need to say their names aloud, but if you know someone who needs your prayers—your friendship— would you raise your hand?"

Hands went up around the room. Some shot up like arrows, others tentative. Ben looked down at his Bible cover, considering all those with needs. Then, as he glanced up, a face formed in his mind's eye. It wasn't who he expected. Instead of Marianna . . . he saw Carrie's face.

Ben raised his hand. Devon looked to him and nodded, and he lowered it.

As heads bowed to pray, Ben rested his face in his hands. His shoulders shook, and he pressed his fingertips into his forehead. Was he being sucked back into that relationship again? Carrie was beautiful, no doubt. She had everything going for her—her father's money and her own personal drive. In Los Angeles she was never without friends, and while he liked that she volunteered to help with girls—something didn't seem right. Even volunteering didn't take up all of her day. Surely she didn't spend the rest of her time just hanging out with her dad.

So why is she really here? The question rose in his mind unbidden. He pushed away those thoughts and submitted himself to the fact that God wanted him to pray for her.

She's looking for something or waiting for something. Ben wasn't sure which.

As he thought about that, and as Devon began to pray for all the unspoken requests, Ben replayed the moments with Carrie in his mind. She'd been overjoyed to see him. She'd wanted to talk with him, cook for him. She'd smiled when she saw him, and talked with him—but what he saw in her eyes wasn't attraction—well, at least not completely. It was safety. She felt safe with him there.

Were there other things in her life that she felt were out of control and unsafe? Ben prayed there weren't.

Then, as they continued to pray, Marianna's face came to his mind. Compassion moved from his heart to his lips. How hard it would be to explore a new relationship with God and be confronted with so many duties, so many questions about where life was headed. She must be confused. She *was* confused. She'd told him that—or had she? Maybe he'd just seen it in her eyes.

He prayed for Marianna too. In silence. Other people prayed their prayers out loud. They prayed for children and parents and neighbors and friends. Still others read Scripture verses aloud, and as they did, God's Word burrowed deep into Ben's soul. One woman sang a song of praise, and though it wasn't professional, it was beautiful.

As the prayer meeting started winding down, a still small voice stirred:

Just be a friend.

It seemed too simple, but the words repeated.

They both need a friend.

It wasn't until he was putting on his coat, preparing to head into the cold night, that Ben realized he hadn't prayed for what he'd planned on praying for. He hadn't prayed for his career. He hadn't prayed for God to make him strong. He hadn't prayed for a song.

But that was okay. God knew his needs.

He didn't need to worry about who Marianna would choose. He didn't need to worry if Carrie would ask more of him than he wanted to give.

He'd be a friend and leave the results up to God.

Dear Journal,

I got scared today, real scared. It happened after I'd already gotten home. Jenny had been gracious enough to give me a ride home. She seemed rested and happy after her nap. I was able to clean up the house some, which I'm sure was a help, but mostly I just spent time with Kenzie.

When Jenny dropped me off, I would have invited her in to visit, but Kenzie had fallen asleep in her car seat, and Jenny said she needed to get her home. The fear came when I walked into Mem and Dat's home. They were just sitting down to chicken and dumplings, one of Mem's favorite dishes to make for Dat. The boys had built a tower of blocks that I almost kicked over by accident when I entered the door. The house was warm and clean. There was laughter. Baby Joy was sitting on Mem's lap smiling, capturing everyone's attention. Aaron greeted me as I sat next to him with a squeeze on my hand. And then, as we bowed for silent prayer, fear splashed over my soul like a bucket full of ice water. I realized then that if things hadn't changed so drastically I never would have understood what I had. More than that, I never would have understood what others didn't have.

Not once in my life before my move had I ever been in an Englisch person's home, except for our neighbor down the road to use her phone. And for the most part that home had been exactly like ours. The same style. Clean and tidy. Sure, there were colored curtains and patterned dresses hanging on the line. There was a phone and electric lights and art hanging on the wall, but the difference wasn't alarming.

Yet being with Jenny today made me realize even more that the world is not like we know it. Sure, we hear stories. Our parents tell us what could happen, how we could end up if we leave our Amish ways, but I don't even think they understand. Jenny's not much older than me. She has a child. She has little money. Her house is cold. I shiver as I write those words. Not because I'm cold—although the woodstove downstairs is dying out and the draft

*is sure to come soon—but because I wonder how
many Jennys are out there. I worry there is no one
to care for them.*

*Tears are coming now and I can't explain it.
All I wanted to do was marry Aaron Zook and live
a simple life. Nothing about my life is simple now.
Nothing will ever be simple again. For the rest of my
days I'll never forget walking through those doors,
seeing the empty cupboards. I'll never forget the stab
of my heart when Kenzie asked if God thought her
mama was bad because she didn't wear a kapp.*

*What if I'd never come here? I dragged my
feet but still I came. What if I leave? Will anyone
understand if I try to tell them? Or will they protect
their ears as they gather their families close and
keep the Englisch world far away.*

*I wonder what Levi sees. My brother has lived
in the Englisch world longer than me. When
I talked to him about just wanting to marry
Aaron and make a home, what had he been
thinking? Did he wish he could take me by the
hand and show me what I didn't yet know? Or
did he secretly wish he could return to the place of
innocence? Did he envy me?*

*This makes me think of my own siblings.
David's nearly thirteen, and before I know it the
other kids will be at their rumspringa too. Will
they, like me, already have their minds set on the
Amish way or like Levi will they feel like they never
belonged and leave all they know?*

I can't decide what I'd rather have for them. Would I rather have them only hold memories of the Amish world deep inside? Or would I rather have them know—know and understand heartache, cold, and pain? Do I want them to meet a Jenny and a Kenzie and understand the world in new ways? Understand God in a new way? I'm not quite sure.

What does Aaron think of it all? At dinner as I shared about my day, I saw him squirm in his seat. Does he worry about me spending too much time with people not our own? Maybe it was just the pain in his leg that made him fidgety, but for some reason I do not think Aaron would do well in the same situation as I faced today. In fact, I don't know what he'd think of Jenny, a woman with a baby with no husband around. My gut aches now, something else to add to my tears. It aches because the knowing makes me realize that even though reading Bible stories to one child is a start, there are far too many cupboards sitting empty this night.

CHAPTER TWENTY-TWO

limbing the store's back set of stairs that Ben had finished building a little over a month before the snow started to fall, Marianna pulled a set of keys out of her pocket, lifting them to the porch light.

As she moved the key to the handle, the door popped open. Marianna jumped back.

"Marianna, come outta the cold, wouldja?" Sarah called in her familiar lilt.

"What are you doing? I thought I was on the first shift."

"*Ja, ja*"—Sarah wiped her hands on her apron—"but I got me a ride. Jenny found me shivering, walking in the cold, and brought me in. Maybe we shoulda gone hunting the snow drifts for you too."

"Jenny?" Marianna scanned the dining room, then the kitchen. "Is she here? Is she already at work?"

"Oh no. Today's the day Kenzie was going to stay with her grandmother in Eureka. Jenny had to drive her there before work."

Marianna clucked her tongue. "That's a long drive in bad weather. Surely she could have called and changed the date."

"That's what I thought." Sarah moved back to the kitchen where she was hand-shaping donuts to be fried. "But she's canceled twice already and felt bad."

Marianna thought of the fresh snow she'd walked on. Unplowed. Untouched. She also thought about Jenny's compact car and the tires that were as bald as baby Joy's smooth head.

The numbness of Marianna's nose from her walk suddenly didn't matter. Even though she wasn't a fearful person, the hairs on the back of her neck stood on end.

Jenny's in trouble. Call for help.

The words came with the rapid beating of her heart.

Without a word to Sarah, Marianna hurried to the store phone, picked it up, and dialed. She dialed the only phone number she'd memorized. The only one she knew to call.

"Hello."

Hearing Ben's groggy voice caused her to smile, even though what she was calling for wasn't anything to smile about.

"Ben, I'm so sorry. I hope I didn't wake you."

"Mari, it's fine. I was up—well, after I heard the phone I was up. What's wrong? Are you okay?"

"Yes, I'm fine. I'm at work. It's Jenny and Kenzie. I'm worried about them. I—" She went on to explain Jenny's plan to drive to Eureka this morning. "The roads are covered with fresh snow, and the drive toward the bridge is always so bad." Marianna placed a hand on her heart. "I know people drive these roads all the time, but I can't explain it. As soon as I heard she'd be on that horrible road, I had to call you. I can't explain why, I just knew. It's like no matter how I tried, I wasn't gonna be able to think of another thing. That sounds strange, *ja*, but that's what it feels like inside— God trying to get my attention."

"She might be fine, but I'll go check. You were right in calling me, Mari. That nudge is the Holy Spirit. It's God-in-us pointing out things we need to pay attention to."

"I'm sorry, Ben. Sorry to bother you, to wake you." She looked over her shoulder and for the first time realized Sarah stood there, mouth agape. Sheepishly Marianna curled the cord of the phone around her finger and looked to Sarah's eyes, guessing why her friend was so surprised. First, Marianna was talking on the phone so naturally . . . and to an Englischman. Second, knowing his phone number by heart. Third, talking about God like this. Marianna looked back to the phone, pretending to be interested in the numbered buttons on the front panel.

"Like I said, don't worry about it. I'm heading out now. I'll call you and let you know what I find."

"*Ja, denke.* Thank you so much." She returned the handset to the phone's cradle.

"What was that about?"

Marianna turned. Sarah stood at the counter by the front register stacking the pennies in the small cup. The note on the cup said, "Take one, leave one." Oh, if only she could take her words back—at least what she'd said about God. She never would have said them if she'd known Sarah stood right there. No one that she knew—not even a bishop—would be so bold as to tell someone that God was directing her or him to do such a thing. That a stirring inside was actually God's prodding. The natural question to ask was, "Why you and not anyone else?"

She'd learned every day of her life that all Amish were the same. To say that God spoke to you in a way that He didn't speak to the others would be a sure way to set yourself apart—which no Amish person ever wanted to do.

Marianna took a deep breath and placed a hand over her heart, wishing she could calm the wild beating. The thing was, the feeling remained. It had eased after she'd called Ben, but it hadn't gone away.

"I just thought it would be a good idea that Ben drive down the hill. Just to check to make sure Jenny made it down the road all right."

With a swipe of her finger, Sarah knocked over the cup of pennies, scattering them. "I heard that, but what did you mean about feeling like God wanted you to call Ben?"

Marianna shrugged. "I, well, I can't explain." She sucked in a deep breath and thought about how Ben interacted with folks— Englisch and Amish alike—with boldness. More than once she'd heard fearless words come out of his mouth, even though the look in his eye told her he was worried about how his words would be taken.

But Sarah was Amish. Marianna knew how she would respond. Still, she had to say something. Had to try. It was as if the stirring within wouldn't let up on this, either.

Marianna took a deep breath. "Well, I've been reading a Bible—an English Bible. And the more I read, the more I under-stand that God wants us to have a relationship with Him that extends even beyond Sundays. It's not that I'm saying that I know better than our ancestors. Their faith was strong, I know. So many gave their lives for their beliefs, but sometimes I wonder if we spend too much time focusing on the rules rather than the One who gave them. And just now . . ." She turned and pointed to the phone. "As strange as it seems, I feel as if God wanted me to be worried about Jenny. He wanted me to call Ben and ask him to check."

There, she'd said it. Now she waited. Had she lost a friend?

"An English Bible?" Sarah cocked her head. "Really?"

Marianna took a step toward her. "I know it's not German but I understand it better, and for some reason I have a feeling since God went to the trouble of speaking His message to people, and getting them to write it down, that He wants us to understand."

Sarah nodded but didn't say another word. She just turned and walked away, hurrying to the kitchen with eager steps, as if putting Marianna quickly behind her would put this nonsense behind her too.

Marianna didn't know what else to do but to follow Sarah into the kitchen and get to work. Part of her was angry with herself for not watching her words. She was used to talking that way with Ben. The words just spilled out. But she had to remember there were others who didn't understand, just as she previously hadn't understood.

She looked at the list that Annie had left for them. Banana bread. Peanut butter pies. Whole wheat bread. From the looks of Sarah's measuring and mixing, she was already busy on the whole wheat. Marianna decided to make the pie crusts. They were the most time consuming, and Sarah liked them least.

She was getting the shortening from the pantry when Sarah turned to her. It wasn't anger in her friend's gaze, or even confusion. Instead Marianna saw excitement there. Maybe even joy. Marianna's footsteps stopped short.

"I have to tell you something. I can't keep it inside any longer."

"*Ja?*" Marianna continued to the counter and placed the shortening on it, then went to the drawer for a measuring spoon.

"I've been praying about this, Marianna. Praying for someone to talk to. Someone who would understand. My parents and

I have been reading an English Bible too. I'm the oldest at home now. My older siblings are gone and married. And sometimes the three of us, Dat, Mem, and me will read it together at night after the little kids have gone to bed."

Marianna's jaw dropped.

"There's something else too." Sarah stepped nearer and took Marianna's hands. She leaned close to her face and her eyes sparkled as if she were about to reveal the hiding place of a buried treasure.

"On Monday nights there is a prayer meeting. It's down the road from your place at the Carashes' house. My family has gone nearly every week since September, and we've worried your folks can hear our horse and buggy when we pass. There are some Amish families who attend, but mostly Englisch. We read God's Word together and pray. We pray a lot. We pray out loud."

Praying out load? With the Englisch? Marianna's mind tried to comprehend what her friend was saying. "But—but that's not allowed." The words sputtered from her lips.

Sarah cocked an eyebrow. "Well, is an English Bible allowed?"

Marianna moved to the shelf with flour. She pulled down a Tupperware container and put it on her workspace. "No, I suppose not."

Sarah didn't say anything else. She went back to making the bread. Marianna set to work on the pie crusts, her mind racing. Part of her hated to hear Sarah was sneaking out, doing that. If it ever got out to the Amish community, it would be another bit of gossip to share.

And the fact that all this was going on right down the road. She could imagine what people would say about that. Pretty soon folks would be saying *her* family was sneaking out to go to prayer meetings too—then she wouldn't be able to marry Aaron Zook if her life depended on it.

As she worked, she thought about Sarah's family. Why had they started reading the English Bible?

Thirty minutes passed, and she began rolling out the dough into perfect circles. Many emotions had coursed through her during those thirty minutes: worry, excitement, confusion, curiosity. Another emotion stirred in her too. Desire. Was there more to God? Could she go deeper with Him? What would it be like to pray aloud to God in a room filled with other folks? Would she experience even more of God? If so . . .

She wanted that.

Was it even possible to get more of God? His love draped over her, especially when she prayed or read the Bible. How could more fit? But maybe there was more room.

Who else was at the prayer meeting? What had she been missing? Did Ben go? Her Uncle Ike? Sarah had said Amish *families*, which must mean more than one other family. She rolled the dough and in her mind's eye she clicked through the names of the Amish in the community.

Who else hid a truth they should be shouting from the top of the snow-covered pines outside the window?

Marianna was going to ask more questions, but Edgar showed up with customers trailing him—the familiar early birds like Millie, and Jebadiah, and Uncle Ike who were always looking for a fresh cinnamon roll, coffee, and conversation. And as she poured each one a cup of coffee she studied their faces. *How about you? Do you go? If I happened to make my way down the road, would I see you there?*

Ben drove, amazed by how much his truck slid even though he had snow tires and he'd filled the truck bed with bags of sand for more traction. Marianna was right to be worried. No one should be out on these roads. Ben made it nearly to the bridge. Should he follow the road all the way to Eureka—?

Wait. What was that? A spot of red light and movement in the ditch on the side of the road. Ben slowed his truck to a crawl and angled the headlights onto the car.

His heart pounded. It was Jenny's car. She stood behind the vehicle, clad in only a thin jacket. She held a large stick in her hand. As his truck neared, she dropped the stick and started waving her arms.

Ben parked and, leaving his truck running, climbed out and hurried toward her.

"Jenny, you okay? Where's Kenzie? Is she inside the car?"

Jenny's eyes were wide, and she had a far-off look in her gaze. "Ben, is that you?"

"Yes." He pulled her red hands into his grasp.

"Kenzie's in the car." Jenny blinked as if she still wasn't sure she trusted what she saw.

"What are you doing?"

"The exhaust pipe. It was under the snow, but I needed to keep the car running to keep Kenzie warm. I had to clear it, otherwise that exhaust would have filled the car and killed us."

"Smart girl, but you don't need to worry about that now. I'll give you a ride home and we'll figure out how to get your car out after this storm."

Jenny nodded and then sobs shook her shoulders. "Oh, Ben."

She nearly fell into his arms. "I was so worried. I was almost out of gas. I was afraid no one would find us."

Ben wrapped his arms around Jenny's shivering form. An urge came over him to protect her. To see that she was warm. To make sure she stayed safe.

"It's okay. You and Kenzie don't have to worry any longer. God was watching after you. Now let's get you someplace warm . . . and then we can talk about how I ended up here. I think you'll like the story."

Dear Journal,

You'll never believe what happened today. God used me to save the lives of two people. I can't tell you what it felt like when Ben walked through the door with Jenny, shivering and crying, and a sleeping Kenzie in his arms.

We wrapped them up in blankets and then warmed them by the fire. Annie cooked them a huge breakfast, three times as much as they could possibly eat. Millie called a tow truck and told Jenny she would pay for her car to be pulled out of the ditch—as soon as the storm let up, of course. I was busy waiting on customers, but I couldn't help looking at the mother and daughter. I couldn't help but to think about what could have happened if I hadn't paid attention to that feeling deep in my gut. They could have froze. They could have died. I'd like to think that if I wouldn't have paid attention that God would have alerted someone else, but I'm not sure. I suppose I'll never know.

After the lunch crowd left, Annie offered to drive Jenny home, but before she left, Jenny gave me a huge hug. "Ben told me how you listened to God, Marianna. How you called Him. Makes me wish I were Amish too in order to know God like that," she said to me.

I was trying to explain that being Amish had little to do with that when a customer interrupted, needing a quick order to go. By the time I'd finished helping the woman, Jenny was already gone. I'd carried around the knowing all day though—and it's with me even now. The knowing that God maybe wants to show me Himself in ways I hadn't known before. That's good, because I'm wanting to be shown.

CHAPTER TWENTY-THREE

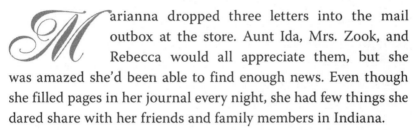

arianna dropped three letters into the mail outbox at the store. Aunt Ida, Mrs. Zook, and Rebecca would all appreciate them, but she was amazed she'd been able to find enough news. Even though she filled pages in her journal every night, she had few things she dared share with her friends and family members in Indiana.

To Mrs. Zook, she'd written about Aaron's care and how he seemed to be healing. To Aunt Ida, she'd written about the quilt Aaron helped her design. To Rebecca, she shared about the mountains, the snow, and family life. With each, she'd held back what she wanted to talk about most—her struggles over caring for Aaron and Ben, each for different and unique reasons. She also didn't share about her new friendship with Jenny and how her heart went out to the young mom. She didn't mention much about working in the store and the community of people she considered friends. She wished she could have mentioned her conversation with Sarah and how Amish families here were seeking God in new ways.

More than anything she would have loved to talk about how God was changing her heart, and how His love made her look beyond how folks dressed or whether or not they were Amish, and rather focus on their needs.

She'd discovered the hard way that the news in her letters was spread beyond the folks it was intended for. It was as if those at home shared what news they'd heard as soon as a letter carried it in. Maybe because everyone was curious about the family who went off west. She supposed the same thing could be true of anywhere, for she heard the same type of chatter within the walls of the store. Thankfully she could fill her journal with the things she could reveal no place else. The experiences challenged her as consistently as the falling snow outside.

The mailman entered, stomping his feet on the door mat. Marianna heard Edgar filling him in on Jenny's experiences.

"That's amazing Ben found her in time. I've heard of cars getting stuck like that before. It hasn't been a good experience." Their voices carried through the store.

"You're telling me." Edgar's gruff words were filled with emotion. "And with that little one . . . seems that coulda turned out to be mighty tragic."

"How did Ben know to go looking?"

Marianna couldn't help but smile to hear them spreading the gossip the same way the women at the sewing circles did.

"He said Marianna called him, all worried. Those people must have a way of knowing . . ."

Her smiled faded. She considered talking to Edgar about that. It wasn't just about being Amish. It was listening to that urging deep inside that could only be God. It was something she was just learning, and something she'd pay more attention to in the future.

"Marianna."

She turned from slicing tomatoes for the salads to find Annie approaching.

"I got a call from Jenny. She went to town because she hurt her arm when her car slid off the road. The doctor wants to do some X-rays on her wrist. She has an appointment with the X-ray tech in an hour. Poor thing, sounds exhausted. I was wondering if you'd like to go down and help with Kenzie again? That little girl does love you. Jenny says she can't stop talking about how you played dolls with her."

Marianna paused. "I can, but—"

"I know it might be hard to watch a child in town, but the library's open. Maybe you can take her there for a while. Read some books. I can give you money for lunch too."

"Well, of course, but the problem is . . . I have no way to get to Eureka."

"Oh, I should have mentioned that." Annie looked behind her. "I've already gotten you a ride."

Marianna followed Annie's gaze and spotted Ben in the dining room, filling up his thermos with coffee.

"*Ja*, I see." Marianna placed the knife on the cutting board. Her shoulders tensed. *Lord, is this You? Do You keep putting me with Ben, to spend time with him?*

"If you need me in Eureka, and if you don't need me here, I'd love to help." Marianna dropped her hands and clasped her palms together.

After putting the tomatoes away, she washed her hands and then smoothed her dark blue skirt over her hips. She wanted to look at Ben, to see the appreciation in his eyes again. It had been hard to forget that he told her she was beautiful. And that's why she didn't dare look. To look at him, to see the care in his gaze, would just make matters worst.

Ben didn't see her as Amish. He saw her as *her*, and she'd never experienced that before. Back in Indiana when she was around the Englisch, their awkwardness was obvious. People didn't know how to talk to her. Some stared while others refused to meet her gaze. Even around the other Amish in her community, Marianna was watched and judged by how well she stuck to their ways. But with Ben . . . she sometimes forgot she wore her kapp. She guessed that if one day she showed up in slacks and a blouse, he'd treat her no different. Ben saw *her*. It was something Marianna didn't realize she'd been missing in life until she had it.

She moved past him, still without looking at him, but that didn't mean she didn't feel his presence. Didn't breathe in the scent of his cologne.

Marianna moved to the coat room and grabbed her heavy, black wool coat, carrying it to the front door. Ben waited there. He motioned to her, and as she approached he took the coat, holding it as she slipped her arms in. Then he watched as she buttoned the top button.

She followed him to his truck and got inside, not realizing until she sat that she'd been holding her breath. The truck's cab was no warmer than the outside. Finally warm air blew from the dashboard.

They were quiet as they rode along. A song played from the stereo, and Ben hummed. As they reached the long hill that dropped down toward the lake, he must have remembered that Amish weren't supposed to listen to music like that and he turned it off.

"I hope you don't mind, but I have some questions about your Amish ways." He cleared his throat and glanced at her, but his look wasn't fast enough. She caught the sparkle of his blue eyes.

"Okay, although the way you say that gives me a fright."

He laughed, and the sound of it filled the cab. "You have to help me understand, why do you people do it? I'm not talking about the simple dress, I understand about not wanting to put emphasis on your clothes, but what about technology? I've driven the Amish to town and they come home to dark, cold homes. It takes time to light the lanterns and build a fire. Wouldn't it be easier to just flip a switch and be done with it?"

"Modern technology weakens the family and brings temptation and vanity." The words came out of Marianna's mouth as easily as if she recited the alphabet. She talked more about why it was important to follow the ways of their ancestors—to not be prideful in thinking they had a new or better way. "If our way was good enough for my great-great-grandfather, who lived one hundred years ago, it should be good enough for me. I should be content."

Ben nodded. She could tell he wasn't trying to build a case for why they should do things a different way, but rather he listened to understand. As they neared the bottom of the hill, approaching Lake Koocanusa, the bumping of the truck smoothed as the dirt and gravel road turned into asphalt that had been cleared of snow. Up ahead, the bridge crossed the lake. Marianna's breath pulled from her as she eyed the modern marvel that stretched across the expanse. In the distance, high mountain peaks jutted into the sky.

"And *rumspringa*? I've heard a little about it. One Amish family I drove had a teenage daughter. When we'd get to town, she'd take off her Amish dress and underneath she'd have on jeans and a T-shirt. Her parents never made a comment."

"*Rumspringa* is sort of like this bridge. Amish youth go through a time that stretches between childhood and adulthood.

From age sixteen to around nineteen or so, they can test the world. Usually they find there is nothing worth leaving everything they've known and believed."

"Nothing? Is it only things that draw them away—cars, televisions, parties?"

"That's part of it. But it's also people." They began to cross the bridge, Marianna's stomach dropped. She turned her gaze away from the water and stared at the dashboard, not knowing if it was the height of the bridge, or the closeness of Ben, that gave her the uneasy sensation.

"People?" Ben glanced at her only briefly and then turned his gaze back to the road.

"*Ja*, if they fall in love with someone who is not Amish. Or with someone who left the Amish. It's a great temptation. It's not the technology that draws them—in fact, the matters of the world frighten some. Instead, it's the matters of the heart."

"Matters of the heart. I like that. It sounds simple and sweet."

Marianna nodded, but as she did her gut tightened. There was nothing simple and sweet about her feelings for Ben. There was excitement and interest and . . . desire. Things that should never be.

"So do you know anyone who's done that?"

"*Ja*, a number of people. Mostly older siblings of my friends. Some have come back. Some I've seen around town and such in their Englisch dress. We really don't speak. And . . . well, my friend Naomi had planned on leaving. She was going to leave for my brother. He's left the Amish. I'm not sure if you knew that."

"Your Uncle Ike mentioned it. He'd tried to contact Levi—that's his name, right?"

"Yes, Levi."

"Your uncle's tried to contact him to see if he wanted to come here and work. But from what Ike said, Levi wrote a letter and declined. He claimed your father worried about his influence on the younger boys, and Levi said it would be too heartbreaking to live near family and not see them."

Marianna nodded. How strange that this Englischer could know so much about her family. What else had Uncle Ike told them? Marianna wiped her hands over her dress, suddenly feeling exposed.

Neither spoke for a moment and then Marianna turned to Ben, studying his profile. "Sometimes I still can't believe Levi has left. It must have been hard for him."

"I'm sure it was, but considering all the obstacles, I think staying is just as difficult. It takes courage to be an Amish in this world."

"I'm not sure about that. Not if it's all you've ever known." Her hand tightened on the door handle.

"But you do know more now, don't you? I mean living here . . . and with some of the folks you've met."

"Yes, Ben, I know more." She leaned forward, eager to see the buildings of Eureka looming ahead, but they still had a while to go yet.

He glanced at her, and she could see from the look in his eyes what he wanted to ask—he wanted to know if she'd ever considered leaving. But he pressed his lips together and focused on the road. She was glad for his silence, but she honestly didn't know how she'd answer. Would she lie and tell him the thought had never occurred to her? Would she admit it? No, she couldn't do that. To confess the idea had crossed her mind would bring more questions. She didn't want to have to say that he was the reason—the only one. Him knowing would make things harder than they already were.

Protection for her heart showed itself as the silence that filled the air between them, yet like the homes and buildings that had been covered by the lake, there was more hidden inside, down deep.

∞

By the time Marianna and Ben arrived at the hospital, it was clear Kenzie had had enough sitting still. As they walked into the small exam room, the little girl rushed toward Marianna, arms wide. She wrapped them around Marianna's legs, pressing her cheek against her skirt. Marianna chuckled as she patted the young girl's head and then turned to Jenny.

"How ya doing there?"

"Oh, okay I guess." Jenny sat on the examination table with her sore arm pulled tight against her body. "They're going to do an X-ray, but the machine wasn't working right. They got a guy up from Kalispell and he's fixing it." She looked to Ben, smiled, and then turned back to Marianna. "Thanks for coming. I tried to entertain Kenzie, but it wasn't working well."

Marianna glanced around noticing a few rubber gloves that had been blown up to balloons. A paper cup, a few depression sticks, and a dozen tissues were scattered on the floor.

"No problem. We'll go out for a walk," Ben said.

Jenny wrinkled her nose. "Well, okay, but Kenzie only brought a sweatshirt."

"Or we can go to the library," Marianna improvised. "Kenzie likes books."

"Yeah!" Kenzie punched her arms into the air above her head.

With a small wave they were out the door, and five minutes later they were walking into the small library. Ben had tucked Kenzie inside his coat, and she giggled telling Marianna they looked like a two-headed monster.

Marianna was thankful when they stepped inside the front doors. Warmth enveloped her. She'd rarely visited the library in Indiana. She didn't appreciate all the stares. She couldn't pick up a book from the shelf without people going out of their way to walk by her and see what the Amish girl was reading.

This small library seemed more comfortable, more inviting. She noticed the children's area straight ahead beyond the checkout counter and headed that direction. She stopped short though when she realized Ben didn't follow. Looking back she saw he stood in place as if his feet were frozen to the ground. Kenzie babbled about something, but Ben wasn't paying attention. Instead he focused on the line at the checkout counter. There were three teen girls in line with a few books each and a beautiful woman standing with them, checking something on her phone. As Marianna watched, the woman glanced up, met Ben's gaze, and then squealed and hurried toward him. Even though Marianna couldn't hear their conversation, she could tell the woman asked about Kenzie. Ben pointed out the window toward the clinic, no doubt telling her about Jenny.

Marianna couldn't hear them as they continued to talk, but Kenzie's voice was clear. "Down, down. I want Marianna!"

Ben unzipped his coat and let her down. Kenzie raced her direction. She should have taken the girl's hand, turned around, and walked to the book area. Instead, she kept her eyes on the woman, waiting to see her reaction.

Yes, there, she saw it. Noticing Marianna's Amish dress the woman's eyes widened and then she forced a smile. Marianna smiled back and then ushered Kenzie into the children's area.

"Find a *gut* book, *ja*?" She pointed to some easy readers, hoping Kenzie didn't notice the quiver in her voice. Kenzie found a few books that interested her, and Marianna sat on a small reading bench—with her back to Ben—and pulled Kenzie on her lap. She tried to ignore the feeling that someone—or two people to be exact—were staring at her, their eyes boring through her kapp.

She was nearly through the second book, reading it aloud to Kenzie, when Marianna heard footsteps approach. A hand rested on her shoulder. She turned, looking up to Ben's face. The woman stood next to him. Her hand clung on Ben's elbow as if holding onto a lifeline, afraid he'd slip through her grasp.

"Marianna, I wanted to introduce you to one of my old friends, Carrie."

"Old in number of years we've known each other, not in age." The woman chuckled, and Marianna gazed up at her. And as their eyes met, the woman's head jerked back—then her eyes narrowed.

"Hello, *gut* to meet you, Carrie." Marianna smiled, unsure about the woman's reaction. She held Kenzie closer, a shield protecting her from the piercing look.

"Yes, Marianna, it's nice to meet you too. And I have to say you have the most amazing gray eyes."

◦◦◦

Ben felt Carrie's hand tighten around his elbow.

"Beautiful gray eyes." She turned to him. "Just like your song."

"Song?"

At her question, Ben straightened his shoulders and stepped out of Carrie's grasp. He walked to the bookshelf, pretending he hadn't heard Marianna.

"Kenzie, do you want to help me find Dr. Seuss? His books are always a favorite."

"My mama's at the doctor," Kenzie said. "She's got an owie on her hand."

Carrie laughed, but the laugh was tight, as if it caught in her throat. "I don't think Ben's talking about a real doctor, silly. Haven't you heard of Dr. Seuss before?" Then she cleared her throat.

Ben looked back and noticed her narrowed gaze. Her stare was a mix of anger and pain. He knew what Carrie was thinking. She had everything—and Ben had instead been attracted to this . . . this simple Amish girl?

"Look for the shelves with the letter *S*, Ben." Carrie pointed.

He nodded and turned back, noticing Kenzie had already pulled a few other books from the shelf.

Ben's stomach churned as he pulled out *Cat in the Hat* and *Green Eggs and Ham*. Kenzie would enjoy them, but had Marianna ever read those books before? Not that Dr. Seuss was literature. What other books had Marianna missed out on? What artists hadn't she heard of? She obviously had never heard a Josh Grobin song and had no idea who Celine Dion was. She'd never watched *Star Wars* or *Lord of the Rings*. Seeing Marianna side by side with Carrie showed him everything Marianna lacked, but it also made him appreciate her more. She wasn't worried about getting her nails done or hair highlighted. She found more interest in cooking a good meal, or helping a friend, like she had for the second time in a week.

"So, Marianna, you don't happen to be from Indiana, do you?" Carrie raised her voice, paying no attention to the fact they were in a library. A few other patrons from around the room turned and stared.

"Yes, how did you know?"

"Well, Ben used to be my boyfriend, but he told me he's interested in a woman who moved here from Indiana. I assumed that was you. So do you like him too? Can you like him? Or would that be a sin to you?" Carrie placed a hand on her hip.

"Mari." Ben rose and strode over to her. "You don't have to answer that."

Marianna turned to him, her eyes wide and full of questions. He saw something else too.

Tears.

"I believe I'll keep the answer to that question to myself, but it was nice meeting you." Marianna rose and touched her kapp, then pulled her fingers away as if she'd touched something hot. "I better help out Kenzie. I'll let you and Ben get back to visiting." She offered Carrie a thin hand. "It was *gut* to meet you."

Carrie took Marianna's hand and shook it. Then she smiled. "It was *gut* to meet you too."

Marianna hurried over to where Kenzie had nearly cleared a shelf of books. "Oh, Kenzie, no."

Ben didn't look back. Instead he fixed his gaze on Carrie. "You didn't have to treat her that way."

"What way?" Carrie patted her head as if patting a kapp.

"She's a good woman."

"I bet she is. Aren't all Amish *gut?*"

Before he could stop himself, Ben grabbed Carrie's arm and pulled her toward the front door.

"Ouch, that pinches!" She hissed the words at him.

The teen girls were just finishing checking out and they eyed Ben.

He led Carrie outside. A cold wind hit Ben's face and he released Carrie's arm.

She zipped up her jacket and put her hood on.

"Are you crazy?"

"I'm sorry. I didn't mean to hurt you."

"I'm not talking about that." The wind blew strands of Carrie's hair in her face and she quickly brushed it away. "I'm talking about *her*."

"What's wrong with her? Nothing. There is nothing wrong with Marianna. She's good, she's pure."

Carrie opened her mouth wide and her face turned red. "Is that what it is? You got what you wanted out of me and then you want som—" She seemed to choke on the words. "Someone *pure* to be your wife?" Carrie crossed her arms over her chest.

"It's not like that." Ben's heart grew heavy as if someone had filled it with concrete.

She didn't seem to be listening and pulled her keys out of her jacket pocket. "I have to get the girls back to the ranch." She moved to the door.

"Carrie. Did you hear me? I said it's not like that. I didn't mean it that way." Ben reached out and took her hand, gentler this time. Carrie paused, but she didn't look back.

"You can say what you want to say, Ben." Pain laced her words. "But I know what I am, Ben, and no matter where I go or what good I do, I can't forget that." Her hand pulled away from his and reached for the door. "The memories won't let me forget."

Ben watched her walk back inside, her shoulders slumped as if she carried the weight of those memories on them. Pain stabbed his heart again. Over the years he'd battled this very thing. He'd changed, but the changes came only after he'd caused people he cared about a world of pain. Jason was dead. Carrie, a shell of the woman she could have been. God had forgiven him, but like Carrie, Ben hadn't forgotten. Each memory waited only a heartbeat away, whether he liked it or not.

As he stood there, in the cold, trying to get his composure, the door opened and three teen girls exited, followed by Carrie. All four of them looked straight ahead not acknowledging him as they passed. He guessed he deserved that. He also guessed those young women would get an earful from Carrie on the way home.

Taking in a breath of cold air, Ben walked back to where Marianna held Kenzie on her lap, reading. He sat on the bench next to them, and Kenzie hardly stirred, so engrossed was she in the story. Marianna glanced up and then returned to reading. Ben felt a tear come to his eye at the look she gave him. He expected her to be hurt by the way Carrie had acted. Instead, he noticed light, happiness coming from her eyes. If he would have guessed what she was thinking, he would have guessed it was this: "So you told her you liked me . . . that is *gut*."

The thing was, he wished she didn't know. He had a feeling when Roy found out about his feelings for Marianna, it would be seen as anything but good. Roy didn't like his musicians to be distracted. He wanted their attention on the music first. More than that, Roy was all about image. How would it look for one of his star musicians to be courting an Amish girl? The media would have a heyday with that. He could almost imagine one of David Letterman's top ten lists: "Ten Reasons a Rock Singer Needs an Amish Girlfriend."

Ben could date a wild woman, someone immersed in the party and drug scene, and no one would think twice about it. But a woman who wore a prayer kapp and apron? Who didn't use makeup or electricity, let alone technology?

Oh yeah. Roy would love having to explain *that* one without making Ben look like some kind of moron. Ben sighed.

Maybe Carrie wouldn't tell.

Marianna didn't notice she was humming until she looked up from folding a pile of Joy's diapers and saw Mem's, Dat's, and Aaron's eyes on her.

"I'm sorry. I didn't realize . . ." She lowered her head and went back to work.

"The store plays music." Mem spoke to Aaron, her voice hinting of apology. "It's not like she has a choice."

Marianna didn't tell Mem that it wasn't in the store, but in Ben's truck that she'd heard the song. And as they rode home together, and she listened to the music, she couldn't help but wonder what *her* song was like—the one Carrie claimed Ben wrote about her.

After their visit to the library, they'd returned to the clinic where they found out the doctor had determined Jenny's wrist wasn't broken. It just had a bad sprain. Still, he didn't want Jenny to use it for a week at least. Because of that, Jenny asked to stay at her mom's house in town. Thankfully her mom had agreed.

The ride home was peaceful—as if the interaction with Carrie at the library never happened. Even though Marianna wanted to ask Ben about his relationship with Carrie, Marianna talked about her grandparents instead. Both Dat and Mem were close to the youngest in their families, and her grandparents on both sides had died long ago. Aunt Ida was the closest relative, and Marianna considered her relationship with Aunt Ida as what one with a grandmother would be like.

He'd also asked about *demut*—humility. That was such a deeply rooted value for the Amish. . . . She'd done her best to explain. Yet even as they spoke, Marianna could tell that wasn't what he wanted to talk about. Had he wanted to talk about Carrie? Had he wanted to explain? Or what about the song? If only she'd had the nerve to prod him about that.

"Marianna, did Dat tell you I got a letter from Levi today?"

Charlie's voice interrupted her thoughts and he approached with an envelope.

"Levi? Really? Can I read it?" She took the envelope from her brother's hands, then looked at the three faces watching her. None of them seemed happy about the letter or thrilled about the fact she'd been excited about it. Should she have handed it back and pretended she wasn't interested? That was far from the truth. She'd been waiting to hear from Levi, excited to discover what her older brother was up to.

Ignoring her parents and Aaron, she looked to Charlie. "Do you mind if I read it?"

Charlie shrugged. "No, go ahead."

That was all the encouragement Mariana needed. She opened the envelope and pulled the letter out.

꧁꧂

Dear Charlie,

*Thank you so much for your note. I'm excited to hear
that you're doing better and will probably be going back
to school soon. I'm sorry that you had to face such a long
recovery, but I have no doubt, little brother, that when
this is all over your leg will be as good as new.*

*I'm glad that you got bored and decided to write me
a letter, but I'm not so happy that you're worried about
me, and worried that I might not go to heaven. I will tell
you that I still believe in God even though I don't want
to live the Amish way. Being Amish isn't what gets you
there. Maybe ask Dat or Mem to talk to you about that.*

Marianna drummed her fingers on her lips as she read,
knowing all eyes were on her. She paused. Would Charlie ask? If
so, what would her parents say?

She didn't know.

She kept reading.

*Things are the same in Indiana. I'm still working at
the factory. I'm saving up money. I'd like to find a small
home. I won't lie and say I don't miss the family. It would
be good to see everyone, even though I doubt that would
be possible anytime soon.*

*The only thing I cling to is the fact that Marianna
might be coming back. There are all types of opinions on
what folks around here think of that. I hear about them*

from some of my Amish friends who are brave enough to talk to me. Most believe she'll return with Aaron Zook. I can't be certain but I hope that's the case. Aaron's a good man, and even though I've left the Amish, he's exactly the type of husband I want for our sister. Can you take care of her, brother, since I'm not around to do it?

I best be going now. Write soon and tell me if you find any more bear tracks. Although by this time I'll bet that those bears are all snug away, waiting for spring. Perhaps many of us are like those bears. Hunkering down, hiding from the elements, waiting for spring and new life in our hearts.

Love,
Levi

Marianna pushed out a soft breath. She missed him so much. He was bossy and had always gotten her into trouble as kids. He'd slacked on his chores and begged her to help him catch up so he wouldn't get in trouble.

But oh! How she missed him.

Marianna's chest welled with emotion, and she realized she'd help him stack a cord of wood in the dead of winter if it meant they'd be able to spend the day together. It was odd how those memories didn't leave, but somehow the years passed, turning from ones of frustration to fondness. Then to longing.

"Do you miss him, too, Marianna?"

She looked at Charlie and saw tears in his eyes.

"Yes, I do. Very much. It just is not the same without him

here." She folded up the letter and tucked it back in the envelope, handing it back to Charlie.

"He used to help Dat a lot." Charlie took the envelope from her. "I used to imagine myself as big as Levi being able to do that stuff."

"You'll be that big soon. Yer growing every day."

"*Ja*." Charlie nodded. "I am, but I don't want to be like him so much any more. He made Mem cry a lot. He made Dat sad too. All of us sad." Her brother lowered his head. "I dunno why he'd want to go with the Englisch."

"Yes, I know he's caused pain, but he's still Levi. He still loves God. He . . ." Marianna didn't know how to explain. She lifted her head and looked around. Even though all their eyes weren't on her, she sensed everyone waited to see what she was going to say. "There are many people who love God, maybe even Englisch too. But yer right. Losing Levi hurt us all very much."

Marianna wanted to say more. She wanted to tell Charlie about how her Englisch friends had encouraged her to seek God in different ways, but now was not the time. There were things she still hoped to talk to Dat about, and Mem. Maybe even Aaron. She wanted to tell him about how her love for God had grown and how she understood God's love for her better than she ever had.

"I jest don't understand how he could leave." Charlie rose and shrugged his shoulders. "I never want to hurt someone like that or make them cry."

Marianna nodded and then turned to Aaron. His eyes were on *The Budget* newspaper spread open in his lap, but she could tell he listened. She bit her lip and curled one of her kapp strings around her finger. Aaron would be so upset if he knew how much she enjoyed being with Ben. She told herself she'd continue to pray for God's direction . . . and she'd just be friends with them both.

If that was possible.

As if feeling her gaze on him, Aaron lifted his head, his eyes meeting hers. His eyes held questions, as if he wondered what she thought about Levi. There was something else too.

Guilt. What she knew—but no one else did—was how close Aaron had gotten to Naomi after Marianne left. Her friends from her circle letter had written and said they'd seen Aaron and Naomi "together" at Clara's wedding. What did that mean? Talk of Levi obviously stirred his memories. What did those memories hold—fondness, closeness, love?

"Anyone want Carmel Pie?" Marianna rose, and a chorus of excited voices answered her.

She hurried to the kitchen before Aaron could see the tears coming to her eyes. If he and Naomi had been that close publicly, what had things been like when they were alone? Aaron had confessed kissing Naomi before, and he claimed that was all that happened. But could she be sure?

Marianna pulled plates from the open cupboard and then began cutting the pie she'd made at work and had brought home for the family. It was easier to work, to serve, than to think about such things. Still the thoughts wouldn't release.

"I jest don't understand how he could leave."

Being only a boy, Charlie didn't understand. Before coming to Montana, she hadn't understood who would want to leave the Amish either.

Levi told her he felt pushed—like he never belonged. Marianna had never felt that way, but she did understand what it was like to be pulled.

Don't think of that, jest focus on being a friend.

After getting all the pieces of pie onto plates, she carried two into the kitchen, serving Dat and Aaron first.

"Looks delicious, *denke*." Dat grinned.

"*Denke*, Marianna." Aaron took the plate, and his hand touched hers as he did so. "It'll be good to see Levi again when we return. I think it'll give him encouragement, maybe help remind him why family's so important."

When *we* return? Did Aaron really think that? Or maybe— she studied his face—yes, he was just hoping. His smile was filled with questions.

Marianna returned to the kitchen. A sudden urge to see her brother, to embrace him, overwhelmed her.

When we *return.*

She didn't know why but she liked the sound of that. And after all, they could return as friends. That's what she wanted, for now.

And later? Marianna didn't know. She didn't want to bring her family pain, and in the long run only one path would ensure she wouldn't. But could she do it?

Could she walk away from the Englischman whose friendship had been one of Montana's greatest gifts to her?

Dear Levi,

I know it's been far too long since I've written. I've been busy, yes, but it's no excuse. Perhaps I haven't written because doing so would mean I have yet again a need to confess that I was wrong. Are you surprised?

Most likely not! Older brothers are used to younger sisters doing as they ought not.

I'll start by saying that Charlie let me read the letter you wrote to him. I'm not sure what he wrote to you, but there is something we agree on. After reading God's Word for myself, I've discovered I agree with you. One does not have to be Amish to go to heaven. 'Tis a good thing. There are many more folks in this world different from us yet the same. One does have to believe in Jesus, though, to live for Him and love Him. But of course you know that.

While I do think we've chosen a right and good way to live, and even though I have no plans to leave myself, I've met good Christian folk here in Montana. People who love each other, care for each other, and do as Jesus told us we ought. They do not dress plain, yet I rarely see pride. They use electricity, yet still take time to focus on what matters. Not that I believe all Englisch are like this. But the men and women I've been able to know here are different from us by lifestyle, but same by heart.

And that's what I want to tell you, brother. Even if you do not choose to live the plain way, do not turn yer back upon God. Though those in our community have shunned you, He has not. Find yerself an English Bible, read the words. You will find hope there. And when you are feeling lonely because yer family is so far away, I pray our Jesus will be with you. Know my thoughts are with you too.

Whew, it's gut to have this off my chest. It's gut to tell you the words I've been thinking. I'm mighty needy to know what you've been thinking and doing lately, so when you have time I'd love to read a note from you. Have you seen any of our old friends? Are you still working the same job at the factory or did they put you in another position? Do you live in the same place with the other guys who've left the Amish? Has anyone new joined you?

Fer myself I've been helping Mem and spending time with Aaron. I've gotten to know him better here. It has been nice. I'm working on a quilt, stitching by the light of the lantern at night. I'm selling it to my boss—an Englisch lady who is kind. I've been helping a friend too. An Englisch woman about my age with a daughter. She has no husband yet others in the community help her get by.

If you have any needs of yerself please let me know. I realize I am far. I know I haven't been as loving to ya in the past as I could, but I do care. I do treasure you as my brother, and even though I'll always hope you return to the Amish way, I understand more now than I ever could before.

I'd blow kisses your way, but I'm sure they'd freeze on the way. It's mighty cold outside, makes Indiana weather seem mild. But I am sending warm thoughts—something that's useful on every chilly day.

Love your sister,
Marianna

CHAPTER TWENTY-FOUR

*"I*s Mari here?"

Ben entered the Kootenai Kraft and Grocery, CD in hand. He'd recorded it last time he'd been at Roy's, and Ben was eager to share it with the person he wanted to hear it first. The person he'd written the song about.

Annie stood behind the counter and leaned against it. "Well, good morning to you too."

"Sorry, Annie." He leaned over the counter and gave Annie a quick hug. "There's something I want Mari to listen to."

"Music?" Annie cocked an eyebrow and bristled up like an old mother hen.

"Just one song." He let the breath release—the one he realized he'd been holding. He'd hardly slept all night. Instead, he'd been up thinking about their day together and how much he enjoyed having Marianna by his side. He also realized that if his song was going to be released soon, he wanted her to hear it first.

"Ben, I've been meaning to talk to you." Annie's usual smile was gone. Her blonde lashes fluttered closed for a brief second.

"What is it? Do you have more steps for me to build? Or need me to make a run to town?" He chuckled. What was the look she gave him about? No matter, nothing could get him down today.

"No, son." Annie let out a long sigh. "It's Marianna."

He leaned his weight against the counter. "Is she okay, did something happen—?"

"Not unless you call falling in love a sickness." There was no humor in her tone.

"I'm sorry, Annie. I don't understand."

"You should. I've seen the way you look at her—the way she looks at you."

Ben ran a hand down his cheek. He supposed there was no hiding their attraction.

"She's Amish, and I suppose I can be partly to blame for letting this happen. For throwing you together—asking you to give her rides. But yesterday I heard folks talking, and it made me realize I wasn't taking this as serious as I should." Annie's words were hardly more than a whisper. "I've lived in these parts a long time. I've seen this happen before. Hearts get broken. Folks that were friendly, turn. I, as much as anyone, know things are different here. The community is different." She settled onto the stool next to the cash register, where Edgar usually sat. "I know the Amish and Englisch usually don't mix like they do here, but there are invisible walls. There are some lines you just can't cross."

He fought to keep the anger from his tone. "So I can be friends with an Amish person, but I can't fall in love?"

"You know what'll happen. People don't turn Amish, but the Amish . . ." She tilted up her head and looked out the window to where a large four-wheel-drive truck drove down the road half-speed. The snow was picking up.

Ben didn't need her to finish. "You're worried about her leaving?" He dug his hands deep in his pocket. "Really, Annie, you're concerned about that? I know it's her tradition—the way she was raised—but she'll still be walking with God, even if she doesn't wear a kapp. I've seen the change in her, haven't you? I see peace in her eyes where there was pain before."

"I'm not worried about her leaving. Everyone has a choice, their own life to live. I'm worried about her being led away. Think about it, Ben. Do you want to be the cause of a split in her family? Of her battle with her faith? Of the struggle whether to wear a kapp or not? It sounds like minor issues, but to these people it's everything."

"So what do you want me to do? Do you want me to walk away? It's not just me. I see her feelings when I look in her eyes." He pulled his stocking cap from his head, smacking it across his leg. "Do you think I wanted it to be this way? Don't you think I've struggled? I've asked God to take away these feelings. I've argued with Him, told Him it would have been easier if I hadn't fallen in love with an Amish girl. If it could be anyone else . . ."

Ben leaned forward on the counter, hiding his face in his hands. If Annie saw how he felt about Marianna, no doubt everyone did else too. That's why Marianna's dat had that talk with him. And it probably was why some of the other Amish families he used to drive stopped using his services.

"Annie . . ." His voice sounded dry, hoarse. Maybe because all the moisture pooled near his eyes. "What am I supposed to do?"

"You have to back off. You need to let time tell the matters of the heart. You need to allow Marianna to come to you instead of drawing her away. Love will come in God's time. I know, because I had to learn all that years ago, when I fell in love."

"But . . . you're single."

Annie took Aaron's hand. "Uh-huh."

"That doesn't help."

"I know, son." Annie squeezed his hand. "But you have to let her go. This has to be Marianna's decision. She's got to choose her own path. Let God lead her. He has the perfect plan for her—for you—you've got to trust Him with that."

He hated this. It was tearing him apart. But he knew Annie was right. "I have to let her go."

"Walk away, Ben. Only then will you really know." Annie reached over and patted his hand. "If she comes to you, if she follows, then—son—you know it's meant to be."

<hr />

As she neared the house after work the next day, Marianna couldn't help but notice the front curtain flutter.

She entered the house and inhaled. The moist air smelled of laundry. A line hung from the second post on the stairway, leading up to the bedrooms. The other end was connected to a hook her father had placed in the wall by the dining room. Unlike their house back in Indiana, this house had no basement for laundry to dry and on blanket and sheet wash day there was not even room upstairs.

Without even looking, Marianna knew hers and Mem's dresses were drip-drying over the bathtub. She pushed a cool, damp sheet aside and stepped through, as if stepping through a theater curtain.

"Marianna, hurry. Dat might come. This is surely a *gut* surprise!" Charlie's voice rang out. A sea of faces greeted her—Mem, her siblings, and Mr. and Mrs. Carash from down the road with their three kids. Aaron had moved from his place on the couch to one of the dining room chairs that had been pulled into the living room. The bench that Dat and Mem kept at the end of their bed had been brought downstairs and topped with a pillow, and that's where Aaron's leg rested, his pink toes poking out from the end of the cast. Meeting her gaze, he smiled. She offered a quick glance, then her eyes moved to the stairway where Ben walked down with Ellie cradled in his arm. *What is he doing here?*

Her Uncle Ike descended behind him, and a smile filled her uncle's face.

"Mari!" Ellie waved a piece of paper in her hand.

Marianna's heart leapt in her chest, and she didn't know what surprised her more—that Ben was here or that Aaron's gaze upon her was amused—as if he considered her wide-eyed reaction as funny.

"Ellie colored a picture for your dat's birthday," Ben explained. "Or at least that's what I guessed she said when she dragged me upstairs with her. I had to get Ike to help translate. I'm still not great at deciphering Pennsylvania Dutch. But it is a good gift for the party."

"Dat's birthday. Of course." How could she have forgotten? She'd talked to Dat this morning and hadn't said anything about his birthday before heading off to work. Had Mem mentioned something about this party? She thought so, but she couldn't remember. Her mind had been on other things.

Besides, even if she'd remembered there was a birthday cel-ebration today, she would not have thought of this. Their usual celebrations involved a nice dinner followed by cake and one simple present at most. This . . . surprise party, with sheets hang-ing across the room and Englisch friends . . . This was not typical.

In fact, she'd never heard of it being done. She'd have to ask Mem about it later. Why had she chosen such a way?

"Wow, look at that." Marianna unbuttoned her coat and moved to the stairs. *"Darf ich es mal sehen?"*

Ellie lifted the page for her to look at. In the hand that rested on Ben's shoulder, Marianna also noticed Ellie still had the stub of a red crayon in her grasp.

"Let's get that and put it away before you accidentally write on the wall again." Marianna chuckled and took the crayon from Ellie.

"Good idea." Ben winked. "I missed that, but I bet I would've been called back to help clean up the scribble."

Marianna placed a balled fist on her hip. "You better believe it, mister," she said, mimicking Annie. Then, remembering she had an audience, Marianna stepped back. "It's good to see you." She touched his arm. "It seems like every time I see you as of late you have a little girl in your arms."

"Maybe I'm practicing." Ben smiled. "Making sure I know what to do when I'm blessed with my own family some day."

With the noise of many voices, Marianna hoped no one had heard what Ben said. She also hoped no one in the room noted the red she could feel rising to her cheeks. Especially Aaron.

"Speaking of being blessed, have you met Aaron? He's a friend from home." Marianna turned back to Aaron and sent a quick smile.

In spite of the smile, Ben seemed stiff, uneasy. "Yes, your mem introduced us."

"Ja, of course." Before she could worry about that any more, David's voice called above the noise.

"He's here. Quiet. Everyone behind the sheets."

The room turned silent. Even Ellie held a finger over her lips. Her eyes were wide. Her small button nose wrinkled.

They listened to the sound of Dat's booted feet coming up the front porch steps. Then his stomping as he knocked snow off his boots. Finally the door opened.

"Anyone home? It's awful quiet." He pushed the sheet to the side, stopped in his tracks, and threw his head back, laughter bursting from his chest.

"Surprise!" A chorus rang out. Voices began again, raised in excited chatter, and Ellie pushed against Ben's chest, wanting down. He set her on the ground and she ran over to Dat, arms wide. With a smile, Dat swept her up, accepting the birthday wishes and kisses.

"I'm surprised you're here." Marianna didn't know what else to say to Ben.

"Yes, well, I was driving home from work tonight when I saw your uncle walking down the road. Seems his horse twisted his leg on a slippery ice patch yesterday and he didn't want to take a chance with the sled." Ben laughed. "Personally, I believe Ike just wanted a ride. When we got here, we needed someplace to park my truck so your dat wouldn't know. We parked it down at the Carashes' house and Ike invited them too. I'm not sure it's what your mem had in mind."

Marianna brushed a stray strand of hair behind her ear, and though she wasn't about to look, she was sure Aaron's eyes were on her. She also noticed out the window that more people were arriving—Amish friends she guessed Mem had invited. The Shelters, the Peachy family, and a few others from their church.

Marianna looked to Mem. There was a pinched look around her eyes. *What would her Amish friends think of the Englischers here?*

"So, Marianna." Ben touched her arm and she stiffened. Heat rose on her neck—probably because of Aaron's steady gaze fixed on that spot. "Hmm?"

"I was looking on the Internet and I saw Annie's new Web site. There was a wonderful picture . . . of you, of us."

"Yes, I know. I gave her permission to use it." She swallowed down a lump that formed in her throat. Oh, why had she ever said yes?

"I love it. I asked Annie for a copy and she said she gave you one too."

The door opened and the other Amish families began filtering in.

"She did." Marianna looked to his eyes. "I have it around here somewhere, I'm not sure where I put it." From the hurt on Ben's face, he believed her.

"Oh, yes, I know that Amish don't believe in photos of themselves. I should be glad you didn't burn it." He forced a smile, but Marianna wasn't fooled. Her heart ached to see she hurt him, but as the other families entered and scanned the room she noticed disapproval on their faces then they saw her standing near Ben.

"I like it. I . . ." Ben let out a sigh. "It's good to know I'll always have it, in case you do return home."

Marianna didn't answer, instead she took a step back. "I should go. I need to introduce our company to Aaron."

"Yes, of course." Ben nodded. "Sorry for keeping you so long."

Marianna hurried to Sarah, trying to focus on making introductions. She could tell by the look on Sarah's face she thought Aaron to be handsome. And he was. If she ever told Aaron that things were not to work out between them, there'd be a long line of Amish women that would set their sights on such a man.

Marianna didn't like that thought at all.

More guests arrived and the mood in the room changed. Ben had been around the Sommer family often. They laughed and joked in his presence—or at least they had before he started letting his feelings for Marianna show. After they talked about the photograph, Marianna retreated, moved closer to Aaron. She sat in the chair next to him, and Ben's stomach sank and pooled on the floor between his feet.

Neither Aaron or Marianna spoke to each other—she was busy talking with the other guests—but it was clear they felt comfortable in each other's presence. The casualness of their years as friends tied them together, like an invisible clothesline wrapping around their bodies, tethering them.

She sat only inches away from Aaron, yet her body seemed relaxed. Even as Aaron scanned the room, smiling at the introductions, his focus was on her. Every few minutes he gazed at her from the corner of his eyes. It wasn't a possessive look, but an eager one—as if Aaron watched to see if she had a need he could help with. Ben's stomach ached when he saw that.

Someone offered him a piece of cake, but he couldn't think of taking a bite. His throat was tight, his stomach clenched. Aaron had what *he* wanted—a closeness with Marianna, a history, a common lifestyle.

Hope for a future.

And that's what bothered him—no, was driving him crazy. Though Marianna seemed interested in him, she *fit* when it came to Aaron. Their care for each other went beyond attraction. It came from years of spending time together, of sharing common dreams and memories. Aaron knew what Marianna had been like as a girl. He no doubt remembered some of her brightest—and even most embarrassing—moments. Aaron knew her. The real her.

Another emotion that Ben hadn't faced in a while bubbled up inside him, mixing with the jealousy: embarrassment. The emotion trickled down from his head to his heart. *What a fool.*

Marianna was interested in him because he was different. She might even think him handsome, but now . . . now he saw it. She'd never seriously consider a relationship with him. Not when there was someone like Aaron around. Someone good and handsome. Someone she wouldn't have to sacrifice her community, her lifestyle, and her right standing before God for.

Let her go.

It made sense, but could he do it? Could he say good-bye? And if he did . . . would she follow?

Ben swallowed hard. *Lord, You know what this could mean. Life without Marianna.*

But maybe that's what God wanted. Roy had been asking Ben to commit to his music. Traveling back and forth to West Kootenai wasn't working. Being here, seeing this—her reaction— Ben knew the right thing to do.

As much as it broke his heart, he needed to allow Marianna to live the life already laid out for her.

It was time to say good-bye.

⁂

Aaron could hear upstairs that the children were still stirring after an exciting time at the birthday party, and that wasn't a happy sound. He wished he could go away. Be alone. He'd give anything to just be in his cabin in Indiana. To see the work of his hands. To remind himself he'd been strong once—not weak like now. To feel as if he hadn't been betrayed.

A lantern flickered on the nightstand, and Aaron glanced down at the image he'd sketched of the shadowed mountains outside the window bathed in moonlight. The sketch was emotionless. Meaningless, random lines connecting together couldn't portray all he felt inside. He started scribbling on the pad, digging his pencil deeper into the paper until finally the lead broke. As a deep darkness absorbed the landscape outside the window, anger bubbled up inside him.

How could Ike invite Ben to the party? And how dare Ben behave as he had? As the party wound down, Marianna walked to the door, saying good-bye to many. Some of the Englischers hugged each other, but the Amish kept their distance. The only affection their community ever shared was the offering of the holy kiss at church services.

Yet as Ben prepared to leave, he wrapped his arms around Marianna. Aaron had waited for her to stiffen, to back away. Instead, she stepped into his embrace as if she'd been waiting for it all night. And then, instead of a quick hug like all the others, Ben held on, nearly burying his face in her neck. He held Marianna as if he owned her. He held her as if he didn't want to let go. And Marianna hadn't moved.

It was only as Ben pulled away that she released her grasp.

Aaron lifted the pencil and snapped it in two. If it wasn't for this cast, he would have shown that Englischer Ben Stone what he thought about that.

Of course, the cast wasn't going to stay on forever.

Dear June-Sevenies,

I've never experienced a fall like a Montana one. Looking around, I tried to consider what object I'd include in the package yet. Would it be the snow that glittered like diamonds. Nein, that would melt before the postman was able to pick it up. Would it be the large moon that hung in the sky—golden and round—unlike any I'd seen in Indiana? I could do that but folks around here would complain. I finally decided on some yellow needles. No, not sewing needles, but rather those of the larch tree. They are trees that disguise themselves as evergreens all year until fall. It's then they turn golden and then needles drop. I picked them up off the forest floor, so who knows what creatures walked over them. A bear? A wolf? It's possible for both.

Dat's birthday was yesterday and we invited many friends. There is good Amish folk here and we enjoy them much. I still miss some of the old faces yet.

Aaron is still recovering from his accident and getting around better than before. He's been drawing sketches and we hope to sell them in the general store. Some folks have mentioned their interest.

I enjoy work and have new friends too. Ain't much else to share. Think warm thoughts of me cause I'll need them during this coming winter. May each of you enjoy a lovely Thanksgiving dinner with family. Know this year one of the things I'm thankful for is you.

Love,
Marianna

CHAPTER TWENTY-FIVE

oonlight filtered through the windows. Marianna crept down the stairs as quietly as she could, stepping over the third step from the bottom— the one that tended to squeak. She'd lain in bed for the last hour trying to decide if she was brave enough to sneak down to get Dat's Bible and read it by the light of the moon. There were too many thoughts, longings, desires stirring within her. She couldn't get her mind off of Ben's arms around her. She couldn't release the words he'd whispered in her ear.

She'd tried writing a circle letter, hoping that would get her mind off things. It hadn't. She'd kept more inside than she'd been able to share. She wanted to share about Annie, Jenny, Kenzie, and even mention Ben's music, but none back east would understand her relationships with her Englisch friends. As she finished the letter, Marianna knew deep down what she needed. She needed to center her mind on God alone.

She needed peace.

Even as she tiptoed down the steps, bright light from the full moon reflected off the blanket of snow outside, bathing the house in a yellow glow. She reached the bottom step, then hurried toward the dining room. The squeak of a chair behind her paused her stride. Marianna's heart leapt into her throat. She turned, expecting to see her father sitting by the woodstove and reading as he'd done of late. Instead, she saw Aaron.

As she turned, he glanced up at her and then looked away. He was dressed in the same clothes he'd been wearing at the party. His shoulders were slumped. His arms rested on his thighs and his head dropped in defeat. In pain.

"Aaron, are you okay?" She hurried over to him, kneeling beside his casted leg. "Do you have pain pills? Need water? Is there anything I can bring you?"

"It's not my leg, Marianna." His words were drawn out, as if they carried pain too. "I mean, it hurts, but that's not the problem."

He looked at her again, this time his gaze searched hers, held it. Mostly his eyes spoke of heartbreak. Without him saying a word she knew the problem.

"I am so stupid. Jest a fool."

Marianna's brow scrunched up. "Aaron, no. Don't say that."

"You said you came back because you wanted to be with your family a little longer." A sharp laugh escaped his lips. "But it's not your family you wanted to stay for."

Marianna moved her hand to his. He pulled back, brushing her away. He sat in silence, clearly expecting an answer. Marianna didn't want to give Aaron the true answer but knew she had to.

"You're right," she finally whispered. "I'm so sorry. It wasn't my family . . ." She bit her lip, urging herself to continue. "I was concerned about my family, ja. Mem with a new baby. Charlie with the accident. But why I stayed was . . . God."

His head darted up and he lifted a hand, brushing his blond bangs back from his forehead. "I'm not joking, Mari. How could you—"

"I'm not either," she said in a loud whisper. "I see things different since I've been here. It's something I've wanted to talk to you about. I see God different. I just felt He didn't want me to go back. Not yet."

Aaron wiped his eyes with his palm. "I can't believe this. You care for this Englischman, and then you lie to me and tell me that God wanted you to stay. Does God talk to you, Marianna? That sounds strange to me. Who are you? He doesn't talk to our own bishops in that way, but He will talk to you?"

"It's too much to explain and now's not the right time. With your leg hurting and . . . we're both tired." Marianna looked toward the cabinet in the dining room where the Bible was kept.

She was just making excuses. She'd read a passage just last week about speaking truth in love. But was Aaron ready for it? A stirring inside told her that if she cared for Aaron in the slightest bit, she needed to talk to him.

"Actually"—she placed a hand on his cast—"that is just an excuse. It's something I've been wanting to talk to you about for a while. I've been reading the Bible more, Aaron. The Word of God is so beautiful. There's so much hope and promise inside."

She didn't mention that it was an English Bible she'd been reading. It didn't really matter. Not to her. "The more I've read, the more I've discovered that it's not the outward stuff that God appreciates—our dress, our good deeds, our traditions—it's what's deep in the heart. Jesus wants a relationship with each of us. It's not just about going to church and living as our ancestors taught; it's about trusting Him, turning to Him in prayer every day. It's deciding to live for Jesus because of who He is, and not because of the traditions of my parents."

Was she mistaken, or was Aaron's face softening?

"Are you saying that those things aren't important?" he finally asked. "That you're going to stop being Amish?"

She shook her head. "Of course I'm not saying that. It's not like I'd have to give up one for the other. Instead it's just a way that I look at life. Rules will still be there—there are ways God wants us to live, things He wants us to avoid—it's just where I put my focus that has changed."

Aaron let out a slow breath. "It's hard to be angry at you when you're talking about God like this."

"You're angry?"

Aaron nodded and swallowed hard. "I saw the way you looked at him, Mari. Saw the way he looked at you."

"Aaron, Ben Stone has been a good friend to me, and to my family, since we arrived. Of course I care about him. But you must know I would not break my parents' heart by caring for an Englischman. They've been through enough already with my sisters, with Levi."

"Just telling you what I saw. That's all."

She took in a deep breath. Dat always said her first response and last option should be the truth. "You have to know since the sixth grade, when we spent those days fishing by the pond halfway between my house and yours, I knew you were the one I wanted to marry. And I—" Her words caught in her throat. "Not a day goes by that I don't regret not going to see the cabin, the one you built."

He listened and he waited. She could tell he wanted to hear more. She owed him that. She'd been keeping so much to herself.

"I've enjoyed having you here. I knew you to be kind before, but I've seen the truth of that more than ever. There are many who would have complained, but you've never questioned why this injury had to happen. You've been brave despite the pain, and I've seen even more what a *gut* man you are."

"But that hug . . ."

Marianna lowered her head. "You saw that?"

"Everyone saw it."

Color rushed to Marianna's cheeks. She placed a hand on her face but lifted her head to meet Aaron's eyes.

"Ben was saying good-bye. He's leaving to pursue his music. He said he wasn't sure when he'd return. He wanted me to know that if I left before he got back, that he'd enjoyed meeting me."

Ben had whispered more in her ear. He'd confessed that as much as he'd tried to hold back his feelings he couldn't do it. He'd confessed he cared deeply for her. But she wouldn't tell Aaron that. Couldn't tell him that.

"He's leaving?"

"He is. And as you can see, I'm still here. Does that make you feel better?"

Aaron nodded, but she could tell he didn't believe her completely. Well, at least he'd go to bed tonight knowing she had no intention of marrying Ben. And that was the truth. After seeing the pain Levi's leaving had caused, she had no choice in that.

She felt better too. She'd told Aaron about her deepening relationship with God and he seemed to accept that. Accept her.

Marianna rose, wished Aaron a good night, and then hurried upstairs, joining Ellie in the bed. Unlike Aaron, she had questions. And complaints.

God, why did this have to happen? I know Ben is the one who pointed me to You, but why did my heart have to wander toward him?

"Take away my feelings for him," she whispered into the night. "I want to do what is right, and having such feelings for an Englischman will only lead to pain for Aaron, my family, and . . ." Marianna sighed.

She wanted to believe it would lead to pain for herself, but she just wasn't sure. Pain would come—caring for two men meant she'd have to decide. But she could not yet believe drawing close to Ben would bring as much pain as drawing away from him already caused.

CHAPTER TWENTY-SIX

arianna sat at the dining room table with her grandmother's quilt wrapped around her. She should have been warm. The woodstove was putting out plenty of heat. The quilt was thick and comfortable. She should be happy . . . but she wasn't. She'd prayed last night for God to take away her feelings for Ben, but this morning they were there just as strong.

Ben is leaving. He cares for me, and he's leaving.

Dat sat across the dining room table. Aaron must have gotten up early, dressed, and made his way to the couch, where he'd dozed off once again. The kids were still sleeping.

"Marianna, I want to talk to you." Dat spoke low, she thought so Aaron would not hear if he happened to wake. "There are rumors. People in our community are talking."

"I wondered when that would be the case. I'm sure not many young women have a suitor living under the same roof with her and her family." Marianna's voice was no more than a whisper. "You made it clear Aaron is sleeping in my room, but I'm not in it, didn't you?" She tucked the quilt under her chin and rested her elbows on the table.

"That is not what they're talking about. It seems that there's been talk about you and Ben."

Her heartbeat quickened just hearing his name. "I don't understand."

"People can see things, Mari."

"See what? I've done nothing. I've hardly seen him. We rarely speak."

"Sometimes looks, glances, speak volumes. More than words."

Marianna swallowed hard. Tears filled her eyes. It wasn't fair. She had been trying. She'd attempted to protect her heart.

"People need to keep their thoughts to themselves," she spat. "Do they not have enough to do? Is the frigid weather so mild they need to put their tongues to work?"

Dat glanced out the window, to the snow and the mountains. "You know how it is. We all watch out for each other."

"I know." She folded her arms over her chest. "If you fall short of perfection, you'll be trampled by good intentions or by gossip shared over the grocery store counter or with the movement of a needle in one's hands. And no one seems to understand the pain of their words. The way they knead the heart, pierce it."

As she sat there, she wished she hadn't met Ben. Things would be easier. Then again, she wouldn't have the relationship she had now with God.

Mem entered the kitchen, poured herself a cup of coffee, and joined them.

"Do you wish to end up a *maidel*?" Dat stroked his long beard. He glanced at Mem and then back to Marianna. "If you hold Aaron at arm's length, that might be what happens."

"There are worse things than being unmarried."

"Is that what you think now? Just months ago . . ." Dat licked his lips and looked at Marianna again, then at Mem. Mem nodded. She was minding herself. From her gaze it was clear she wished she could grab Marianna up, take her to the front porch, and shake her out like a rag rug, attempting to shake out her foolish thoughts. Even though Mem stayed silent, her gaze bore deep.

Marianna looked away and focused on her sturdy black shoes sitting on the mat by the front door, realizing for the first time how much she disliked them. The thought surprised her.

Before, her plain clothes had always seemed like a blessing rather than a curse. She hadn't needed to waste time deciding what to wear or worrying what others thought. Today, though, the sameness felt like a trap. Suddenly, her whole life narrowed down to this moment. She could either heed her parents' advice and walk in the familiar path in familiar shoes. Or she could try to get a message to Ben. To tell him not to leave until they had a chance to talk—really talk.

To step out and explore who she could be, and how she could be loved.

Marianna crossed her arms over her chest. The words that threatened to break through surprised even her. "This is still my *rumspringa*. I haven't joined the church. If I choose to dress different . . . or go without my kaap . . . isn't that what this time in my life is for? Maybe walking another way for a time will bring me back stronger. Will help me know."

Dat stood and turned his back on her. "You've seen the pain walking away has caused."

She nodded even though he couldn't see her. She stared at his back. The light blue fabric pulled tight against his broad shoulders. She wished he'd turn back to her, so she could see the expression in his gaze, but she supposed this is how things would be. Not only for this moment, but for life. To walk away from being Amish meant leaving her family. There was no way around that.

She thought about David, Charlie, Josiah, Ellie, Joy. She covered her face with her hands, even now smelling the baby lotion she'd rubbed all over Joy's tummy and legs after her bath last night.

Levi had walked away one night—just packed a small bag, swung it over his shoulder, and walked out on the dark country road. Later she'd heard from Rebecca that friends had been waiting down the road by the stop sign in their car. The guys who'd picked him up were former Amish too. All of those guys had walked away from their lives and their families. Levi had only seen the kids once, and he'd never met Joy.

Did she really want that?

Her stomach tightened, pulling all her emotions into a tight knot. Then, as quickly as they tightened, they loosened again. It became clear what she had to do.

It's not the worse thing to go through life without a husband, she wanted to say, but she didn't.

"Dat, listen." She pressed her feet against the cold wood, curling her toes. "I know you care about me and want what's best. I know the best is not Ben." As hard as it was to say those words, she realized that was the truth.

Dat nodded and then turned back to her. He approached, placing a hand on her shoulder.

She looked to Mem and saw tears in her eyes.

"I couldn't do it," she whispered. "I couldn't walk away from everything."

"Community is like an old coat, Marianna." Dat squeezed her shoulder. "You're not aware of its need until it's taken away."

"I know, Dat. I understand what you're saying. I don't want to leave everything for Be—" She paused, unable to say his name. "I'm committed to serving the people God birthed me into."

"That's a good choice." Dat nodded. "They may not be pretty at times, but like that coat, they are functional, and they'll keep you warm."

Marianna thought about that as she rose and dressed, getting ready for the day. She could choose who to love. She could choose to dwell on the thoughts of what she was missing out on . . . or to love as she should. And would loving Aaron be so hard? She didn't think so. She just had to be willing to surrender to what her heart had been pointing her to since she was a child.

While doing his morning chores Dat answered a phone call from Annie. Jenny had a large electric bill to pay and needed more hours, did Marianna mind not coming into work today?

Marianna would rather have gone to work. She mostly missed the walk there though the snowy, silent world. That was her best time to think, to pray. It was hard to do at home with the younger kids running around—with Aaron's eyes on her. Yet Mem could use the help, so when Mem carried the large basket of washed clothes upstairs, Marianna joined her.

It took just a minute to hang the clotheslines across the room. They worked quickly to get the damp items hung before Joy started to fuss and Ellie got bored of coloring.

As they worked, Marianna's chest still felt heavy. Ben was

leaving. And she'd hurt Aaron. Deciding to love him was the easy part. Realizing she'd been failing in that area was harder. To walk away from one, meant turning to another. How was that possible? She thought about Mem and her confession weeks ago. Marianna bit her lip and turned to her mother.

Should she bring it up?

"Mem, I know we've had a full house, yet, but I've been wanting to ask. You said something a while ago about an Englischman . . ."

Mem's hands paused with a clean diaper halfway to the clothes line. She glanced to Marianna, then pinned the diaper up. "Well, it's nothin' really."

"Mem, I can see from your face that's not the truth."

Her mom took another diaper from the laundry basket, shook it out to straighten it, and then hung it. She did that three more times while Marianna waited. Just when she was sure Mem wasn't going to respond, Mem pushed the basket to the side and sat on the bed, patting the mattress next to her. Marianna hurried over and sat.

"Marianna, I'm gonna tell you something I've never told another living soul." She swallowed hard and looked at the pair of baby socks in her hands. "I was in love once before—or at least that's what I called it. I'm not sure it was love, but the emotions were powerful enough."

Marianna continued to finger a damp dishtowel, pressing it open on her lap and smoothing it. She held her breath, afraid to speak. She didn't want to do anything to keep Mem from telling the story.

"My family, as you know, lives on the edge of the Amish community. Their farm was next—was close by." Mem cleared her throat. "Mark was a good friend. He'd helped out when my dat became ill once. Our Amish neighbors helped too, don't get me wrong. But Mark was there first thing in the morn to lend a hand. Then he slipped out before any of our Amish neighbors arrived. I cared for him, and when he confessed his love . . . well, I had to make a decision."

Marianna had to ask. "But before that. Before you made the decision, did you question joining the church? Did you ever consider leaving, starting a life with him?"

Mem's hand's trembled, and she tossed the socks into the small wicker basket with the rest of the damp laundry. "I'd already joined. I was engaged to your father."

Marianna's body numbed as if her soul were lifting out of it, reaching for Mem, pulling her into an embrace. But her body didn't move. Her arms hung heavy, as if they weighed a thousand pounds each. Her jaw dropped and she told herself that she shouldn't be surprised—everyone faced temptation.

"I did things I shouldn't have. Things I ought to have confessed. But I refused. I was too proud. I didn't want others to know what was in my heart." Mem balled her fists and rested them on her knees. "It would have shamed your father too. He's a good man. Didn't deserve . . ." Tears came then, breaking through quivering lips. "I finally walked away, but it wasn't easy. I didn't realize once I gave away pieces of my heart it was almost impossible to get them back."

"Mem, God will forgive you, if you ask Him." The words came out of Marianna's mouth before she realized. "The Bible says if we confess our sins to God He will forgive them. I do not know where those words are, but I've read them." Yet even as Marianna said the words she felt conflicted inside. Ever since she was a child she knew the right way of confession was to go before the bishop, the church. Was she giving Mem bad advice? Were there other Scriptures the bishops knew that she didn't?

Men placed a hand on top of her kapp, as if trying to keep it in place. Or perhaps trying to keep burning coals from falling on her head.

"It's too late, Mari. That's why He took the girls. I didna confess, and He found His own way to punish me for my sin."

This time Marianna's arms moved, reaching, pulling her mother to her chest. "Mem, no."

Tears came then. Silent tears that wet Marianna's shoulder. She wished Mem would just open up and let everything out. But like the good Amish woman she was, even in her grief she remained reserved.

Marianna cried too, at the pain in her mother's heart. Is that how Mem saw God—as someone who watched and waited for her to fail so He could judge her?

Growing up she heard the whispers among the women, speaking of someone who'd gone astray. "She'd better watch it now" or "They better live right or else." Marianna hadn't really thought too much about those comments. She thought them to be just sayings, but if this was what Mem truly believed . . .

The past opened up as if it were on a scroll, unrolling inside her thoughts. All Marianna had grown up with now made sense. Her mem had been distant from her, not wanting to show favoritism. Dat had explained that on the train. But there was something more Dat hadn't understood. Mem believed her sin had caused her daughters' deaths. A cry forced its way from Marianna's throat and emerged from her lips. "No, Mem. You can't believe that—"

Her mother pushed back, wiped her tears with her fingertips, and then looked into Marianna's face. "I know every sin brings judgment, but I know something else too. Something I wish I'd known sooner." Mem reached up and stroked Marianna's face, making her feel five again.

"What, Mem?"

"I know now that I shouldn't have even let my mind and my heart wander. I should have trusted God more." Mem reached down and took Marianna's hands into her own. "God created each of us. We know that. It's a foundation for our beliefs. And He placed us in a family. He chose my parents to raise me." Mem squeezed. "What I realized, what I finally learned—and the reason I walked away from Mark and walked toward a life with your father—is this truth. If God wanted me to be Englisch, He would have birthed me into another family. He can do anything, Marianna. He can choose whatever family He likes. Staying Amish is trusting God's ways are best. There are things I question about our faith, everyone has those questions. But God has called me here for a purpose. My days have been spent trying to follow Him the best I could."

Marianna studied Mem's face, knowing the words she spoke came from deep in her heart. Marianna couldn't remember another time Mem had been so frank, so real. She also said these things because she feared her daughter would make the same mistake. But was caring for Ben a mistake?

Marianna still wasn't sure. It didn't feel like a mistake, but then again, when could one's feelings be trusted? What she did know was that she had a lot of thinking to do. A lot of praying.

The churning in Marianna's gut also told her she'd been far from fair concerning Aaron. She hadn't given herself time to get to know him—not really. He'd been in her home and she hadn't taken full advantage to really get to know his heart.

Maybe that was the purpose of him being here. Maybe the accident happened so she wouldn't walk away from God's designed plan.

"I'm sorry I blubbered on."

Marianna rose and shook her head. "I'm thankful you've opened up to me. I needed to hear these things. But you have to know that Marilyn and Joanna, their deaths are not your fault. You—"

From the bedroom next door, Joy's cry split the air. Mem rose. She wiped her face again and placed a hand on Marianna's shoulder. "I know."

But as Mem hurried away, Marianna had a feeling she didn't know. Well, maybe she knew it with her head, but not with her heart. Marianna let out a low shuddering breath. Mem carried so much with her still. No wonder she didn't want her daughter to get too close to an Englischman. She knew the cost of such a mistake.

⟨∽⟩

Dear Journal,

I heard a confession today I'm finding hard to believe. I won't mention the person's name because I don't want this journal to be picked up by someone and have her secret there for all to see, but it was something I'd never guessed.

Sometimes it's easy to forget there was a past before we existed. More than most people, we Amish know about our ancestors. We heard the stories of their seeking and their persecution. We understand their desire to follow God and not the ways of the world. Yet sometimes it's those closest to us who we do not understand. We are quick to display our right living on the outside, but hide what's hurting most deep within.

Am I doing the same? I have to ask myself. The answer I'm afraid is yes. If I were to live what my heart tells me, I wouldn't be following the ways of those who've gone before me—not completely any way. I never thought I'd ever face this battle. I had everything planned. Yet the planning means nothing when one's heart feels like it's ripping in two.

CHAPTER TWENTY-SEVEN

*ot long after Dat left for work, Ellie was the first one awake. She wandered downstairs holding notebook paper and crayons. Marianna made her toast, but Ellie wasn't interested. So Marianna sat at the table and watched her little sister draw a picture of a family. Their family, she guessed. She noticed the brown fluffy creature she assumed was Trapper.

"Is that Mem and Dat?" Marianna point to the man with the beard and the woman with the kapp.

Ellie giggled. *"Nein.* Yer silly."

So, not their family. Marianna glanced to the couch where Aaron slept. "Is that Aaron?" Aaron had blond hair not brown, but Ellie was only three.

"Nein. Ben."

"Ben?"

"Ja."

"But Ben doesn't have a beard."

"He will. When you get married."

Marianna looked to Aaron again, just to make sure he slept. Then she leaned closer to Ellie. "But Ellie, I'm not going to marry Ben."

"Ja. Ben lobes you."

"Nein, he doesn't, Ellie. He's just a friend."

"Uncle Ike says he should."

"Uncle Ike said that? Were they talking about this yesterday when they were upstairs with you?"

Ellie nodded. "I say yes!" Ellie put down her crayon and stood on the wooden bench. Marianna laughed and pulled Ellie into her arms. The little girl giggled, but Marianna struggled to understand. What had Uncle Ike been thinking? If anything, he should have discouraged Ben.

She prepared to probe for more details when she heard movement behind her. Aaron sat up, reaching for his crutches. His face wore a scowl. As bad as it sounded, she hoped the scowl was because his leg ached and not because he'd heard their conversation.

He rose and, movements slow, made his way to the small, indoor bathroom. Before he was halfway across the room a new thought hit her. Would Ben become Amish? Was that why Ellie drew him with a beard? Had Ben and Uncle Ike talked about him growing one? Very few Englisch joined their church, but she'd heard it being done.

Did Ben love her enough for that? Would he give up all comforts to win her heart?

No, it was impossible. No matter how Ben tried, he could never be Amish. He'd have to give up his music, and she could never ask that. Besides, a wonderful Amish man loved her. She needed to remember that. God had already given her what she desired.

Still holding Ellie, Marianna watched Aaron cross the room. He was a good man. He would make a wonderful husband. He was what she needed.

Marianna pulled Ellie tighter into her arms, remembering how Ben had held her last night as he'd said good-bye . . .

She pulled her rebellious thoughts back into line. "It's Aaron." Her whispered words were firm. "It's been him all along. And it will always be him."

◦◦◦

Two hours later Marianna's lips curled into the slightest smile as she washed up the breakfast dishes. She was thankful she had a later shift today. It had given her time to spend with the kids before rushing off. It had also given her time to make Aaron a nice breakfast, including a breakfast casserole—and he'd come back for second and third helpings. That was *gut.* Maybe doing that for Aaron helped make up for what happened the other day with Ben. It helped her feel better, anyways.

It was a beautiful walk to work. The sun was bright. Yesterday the snow had been wet and mushy, like half-melted ice cream, but today all those ridges and swirls had frozen solid.

It was only a week before Thanksgiving, so a long winter still stretched ahead. Even so, today's sun was a pleasant break, though it gave no warmth to the air.

She enjoyed the snow, despite the chill. When spring came, she was going to miss this. Either the snow was going to leave, or she was. Maybe both. Walking the snowy road to work had become her time to dwell on what was on her heart and mind. The snow muted the world, in a way, making her thoughts louder. And when she prayed, she dared to make her words to God louder too—her voice lifting through the tree branches splayed over the road.

The wind picked up as she went along, and Marianna walked with brisk steps, her teeth clattering. A cold fog filled the air, as if clouds had left the sky and decided to hang around on the ground for a while. The sunlight she'd so appreciated was first muted, then blocked off.

So much for her nice walk.

A rumble of a truck's engine met her ears even before she could see it. She stepped to the side, partly climbing a hill to get out of the road. But instead of moving past, the truck stopped.

Her heart pounded and she turned—Ben? But no. This was a large, brown truck. Edgar's smiling face peered from over the steering wheel. He motioned for her to get in.

She moved to the door, yanking on it to open it.

"Jump in. I'll give you a ride before you freeze that bonnet to your head."

She didn't have to be asked twice.

"Thank you, Edgar, I appreciate it." After slamming the door shut, she pulled her mittens off her hands and then blew into her hands, warming them.

"At least it's warmer than yesterday, and it was sunny then! Why doesn't the sun bring heat?"

Edgar put the truck into gear. "It does, but what the clouds bring is insulation. Like a blanket in the sky, they keep the heat on the ground." Edgar shook his head. "I hear folks at the store complaining all the time about the clouds, but sometimes they don't realize that's what's helping them."

"We all do that, I think," Marianna said as the truck turned, heading onto the main road to the store. "We complain about what we have, not realizing the alternative could be worse. Far worse."

Like her. She'd been complaining that she cared for two men, and they cared for her. It could be worse. She could have no one to share her love.

But you don't have to worry any longer. Now you have one man to care for. You've made your choice, and it's right.

That was true. And yet . . . she still couldn't make the ache go away. She looked out the window.

Ben was leaving today. The thought pierced her through. Maybe he'd already left. His absence was like the clouds closing in. Yes, in a way he'd made life more difficult for her, as she battled her conflicted feelings. But Ben had brought a warmth to her life and heart. A warmth unlike any she'd ever known. A warmth she couldn't explain.

Like the clouds, he'd been a protecting presence. And she'd miss that, even though the sun continued to shine.

⁓

Ben strode up the stairs, down the hall, and to the media room. He walked in, almost expecting Carrie to be sitting in there. He let out the breath he'd been holding when he saw the room was empty. He wanted to talk to Carrie and make things right, but today was not the day. On the drive down to Kalispell he'd done the hardest thing he'd ever had to do.

He'd faced the fact that things were not going to work out with Marianna. That they never would.

Now, as he moved through the media room, he found the studio door open. Roy sat at the soundboard, fiddling with the controls.

"Got some good news," Roy stated flatly without looking up.

"Oh yeah? What's that?"

"My buddy in Nashville loves your song. He doesn't want to wait for the complete album. He's going to push it out there as a single and get folks interested in you. Should be hitting the air-waves around Christmas. He wants us to keep working on more songs. Maybe even consider a video."

"That's good news." Ben sat in the chair next to Roy. "So why don't you sound too thrilled?"

Roy glanced up and his eyebrows almost met in the middle. "Why don't you guess."

"Carrie told you we had a disagreement." Ben rubbed his brow. "I'm sorry. I didn't mean to hurt her."

"C'mon, Ben." Roy stood, cursing. He turned his back to Ben, his fists balled at his side. "I'm not worried about my princess's broken heart. That's nothing new. She'll mend. But what both-ers me is this woman that you're supposedly in love with . . . is Amish?" Roy turned around, narrowing his gaze. "Tell me Carrie made it up. If not, that's the stupidest thing I ever heard. A chick with a bonnet. Tell me you're not serious. How am I supposed to market that to your audience?"

"Listen." Ben forced his words to remain calm. "I know. You don't have to say it."

"You *know?*" Roy pointed a finger at Ben's chest. "I've already put up with your running away to the woods. Why? Because dur-ing your comeback tour, it'll be a great story to tell. Fans dig that stuff. I've been patient as you've headed back up in those moun-tains to pray. Haven't I been patient?"

Ben nodded. Roy could rant—he'd seen it before—but he wouldn't interrupt. Roy needed to get it off his chest. All of it.

"Seriously, I don't care if you hook up with some Hannah Montana wannabe. Fans will eat that up. They'll want to see what you're doing and who you're with. But some Amish girl? She can't even get her photo taken . . . and those clothes. No makeup?" He shook his head. "Please tell me that you've been considering this. You've changed your mind."

Ben sighed. "Actually, I have."

Roy's arms dropped to his side and his eyes widened. He opened his mouth, then pressed it shut. It was obvious he still had half of his rant ready to go, but with Ben's confession he wasn't going to get the chance.

Ben leaned forward, resting elbows on knees. "You have to understand, I went into the woods for a simpler life. Someone like Mar—um—like this woman fits that perfectly. But I've realized it isn't going to work. Our lives are too different. There is no way it would be possible unless one of us leaves our way of life behind."

"So this chick's out of your life?" Roy plopped back down into his chair.

"I still consider her a friend, but . . ." Ben wiped his hands on his jeans, trying to wipe the sweat off his palms. "I'm pretty sure it's not going anywhere."

"That's the best news I've heard all day." Roy pressed his hands against his face. Then from between his fingers, laughter spilled into the room. "Last night I had a nightmare of girls in bonnets and aprons dancing in your video, but what scared me most was when I woke up and realized Amish can't dance. It's not allowed." His relieved laughter continued, and Ben joined in, not because he thought the situation was funny, but because he told himself to pretend.

Pretend his heart wasn't breaking.

Pretend he really cared about his song.

Pretend this is where he wanted to be. Right here.

Not sitting in the West Kootenai Kraft and Grocery, watching Marianna hum his music unaware.

CHAPTER TWENTY-EIGHT

arianna hurried toward the small, log school-house. A thin trail of smoke wound its way out the silver stovepipe, corkscrewing up into the gray, dreary sky. She opened the door just a crack and slipped inside. The air was warm and moist. The creak of the door opening broke the silence, and a dozen heads turned.

The schoolteacher Miss Emma Litwiller was hunched over, helping a student at his desk. She lifted her head and turned. Her features softened when she noticed Marianna standing there.

Marianna slipped out of her coat. "Got off work early. Jest waiting for my brothers for some company home."

Emma nodded, and Marianna sat down to wait.

She hadn't worked more than five hours. She'd told Annie she wasn't feeling well, which was the truth. The more it settled in her mind that Ben was gone, that they'd never be more than friends, the more her stomach ached.

Annie let her go home early. Yet, she didn't want to walk home alone. To do that would be to let her thoughts carry her away. Besides, she had a good excuse for coming and waiting. It was Charlie's first day back at school after his accident. Seeing that Charlie had his nose in a book—and didn't seem to be having any discomfort—she turned her attention to the room, which was similar to their schoolhouse back in Indiana.

Colorful student artwork covered the walls. Arithmetic problems filled a chalkboard. Fourteen students from first to eighth grade sat in handmade desks. Emma's homemade posters and lessons were also tacked up. Marianna looked at one closest to her.

Bees can sting, oh, this is true,
But bees can make good honey too,
And that's the kind we have for you.

She smiled as she read the rest of the poster that talked about how to "bee" reverent, "bee" generous, "bee" thoughtful. It was just the type of poem she'd hoped to share with her children some day. She looked around. This was just the type of place and education she wanted them to have, which only confirmed she made the right choice.

"Class, please rise and we will conclude by singing *In der stillen Einsamkeitâ*," Emma said.

"*In der stillen Einsamkeitâ*," Marianna repeated in a whisper. Her favorite. As the children stood and sang together, she joined in.

In quiet solitude,
You will find your praise prepared,
Great God hear me,
For my heart seeks You.
You are unchanging,
Never still and yet at rest.
You rule the seasons of the year.
And bring them in at their proper time.

Marianna replayed the last few sentences in her mind as the children finished their song. How many times had she sung that song. Hundreds? Thousands. She'd sung it in school at least a couple times a week as a child, but now . . . how easy to forget those words. Maybe God had led her to the school today for this reason—to remember.

The brush of butterfly wings tickled her heart. Then the feeling grew and turned, churning up emotion that refused to be frozen by the cold outside. *Never still and yet at rest,* the song said.

Are You speaking that to me, Lord? I'm busy with many things—work, my family. But since You told us to love and care for others, that's what I've been doing. But inside . . . is it possible to have rest there?

Marianna thought of Ellie on Dat's lap. Her little sister's favorite way to snuggle was with her cheek pressed against Dat's chest, close to his beating heart. Although Ellie lay awake for at least ten minutes before he took her to bed, her hands hung limp to her side. If her feet moved at all, it was in rhythm of the rocking chair. It didn't matter what storm raged outside the window. The wind could howl. The trees creak and sway, but Ellie was in her father's care.

The children sang the song again. Marianna joined them in singing the last two verses. Hearing her voice, a few of the children turned. They waved and smiled.

"You rule the seasons of the year. And bring them in at the proper time," she sang again in a soft whisper. Like the year had its seasons, her life seemed to go in a similar cycle. Fall hit her hard and winter hadn't come, but spring . . . maybe spring held new hope?

Earlier today she'd been sad to think of the snow melting, but the once-frozen snow would water new life. Her talks with God wouldn't be wasted, even if she was not getting answers. Her prayers were useful, even if they were just being stored up until God was ready to use them to water the changes in her life, at the good and proper time.

She smiled. As much as she enjoyed spending time with her Englisch neighbors, she couldn't forget who God brought her to first—the Amish community that cared for each other so well. That taught their children what was right and good.

She had to be thankful for that.

On the walk home the clouds were spread thin against the canvas of the sky. It was as if an artist had dipped the tip of his paintbrush in white and whooshed a light-handed yet broad sweep across the sky. She glanced to the red-nosed boys walking with her. Did they notice? Of course not. They trailed sticks behind them, drawing lines in the snow and making a competition over who could make the straightest line.

"Do you think anyone will follow our trail?" Josiah's voice raised in pitch. "Maybe if they're lost they can come, and Mem will give them something to eat."

David nodded but didn't comment. Marianna could almost see his response in his gaze. *If someone were lost, would our line make a difference? Especially a line in the middle of the road.*

Marianna smiled, and then her lips fell. If only she had a clear path to follow on her own heart's journey. Even a thin line nearly hidden in white snow would help. Would it lead her to Aaron, as she expected? Of course it would.

She just needed to remind her heart.

Aaron was alone downstairs when they entered the house. Mem was upstairs with the two younger children, and the boys decided to stay outside and work on their snow fort before it got too dark.

Marianna went to sit by Aaron on the couch. "What are you doing?"

"Just writing home. My mem asked what my plans were. I was telling her as soon as my leg is mended, I'll be heading back. Dat's been having an awful hard time keeping everything running without help."

Marianna nodded. "You know, I don't think you should go back by yourself. I mean, even if the cast is off, you're not going to be completely better. I was thinking when you do go back I should go with you. I can stay with Aunt Ida, and I've been wanting to look at that cabin anyways. I think it'll really help with some of the decisions I have to make."

Aaron's eyes grew wide. "Really, Mari?" He took her hands in his and gently kissed the tips of her fingertips. "You've made me so happy."

She smiled and pulled one of her hands from his, stroking his face. "I'm happy too, Aaron." She spoke the words with a smile.

If only she truly felt them.

CHAPTER TWENTY-NINE

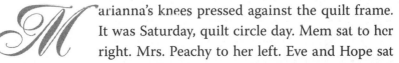

arianna's knees pressed against the quilt frame. It was Saturday, quilt circle day. Mem sat to her right. Mrs. Peachy to her left. Eve and Hope sat farther down, lost in their own conversation. Across from her sat Sarah.

Marianna couldn't count the number of hours she'd spent in quilting circles like this. She'd started when she was ten or so. Through the assistance of the ladies in the circle she learned how to sew, how to set pieces, how to do a running stitch, how to appliqué. She enjoyed the task, it was true, but she enjoyed the conversation even more. Here, she learned how to be an Amish woman. She listened to stories about chores, and family, and baking, and caring for kids. She heard about talk of husbands and tips on cutting expenses.

Quilting day was something she wouldn't miss unless she was ill, and even then some women showed up with a fever. Men weren't allowed. Even if a husband gave his wife a ride, he'd get out of there as fast as he could. The one time her granddaddy had come in—trying to get out of the cold and hoping to be sociable with the women—she'd thought for certain the women would chase him out with a broom. It didn't come to that, but close.

Marianna looked down at the quilt in front of her, moving her needle through the quilt top, batting, and backing.

Mrs. Shelter spoke up first, as usual. Even though she had a soft voice, she got her point across. "I know that many of us have been helping Jenny with childcare. I've seen it's made a difference, haven't you?" Apparently she'd asked the question not expecting an answer, as she continued on. "I took Kenzie home the other day because she'd had an accident and soiled her pants. While I was there, I noticed their cupboards were nearly bare. I thought if we all had a few jars to share . . . Canned goods. Extra flour."

The women murmured their agreement. Not one woman protested, even though Jenny was an Englischer.

"She doesn't cook *gut.*" At Marianna's comment, all eyes turned to her. "Not saying anything against Jenny, she jest never learned. I'm teaching her some at work, but I thought if you could include an easy recipe."

"I hadn't thought of that. Thank you, Marianna." Mrs. Shelter's expression was both appreciative and thoughtful. In the Amish community, a young girl growing up not knowing how to cook was unheard of.

Mrs. Peachy spoke up next, talking about the dinner she was going to prepare for all the bachelors at Thanksgiving. Marianna worked to hide her tight-lipped smile. It seemed the Peachy family was more interested in the single men than vice versa, but she guessed if the family tried hard enough, they'd find beaus for their girls.

Marianna looked down at the quilt she was making. This one was for Annie. It was nearly ready to stick in a frame. After that

. . . should she make the wedding quilt Aaron designed? She teared up at the thought of using their handprints for the border. But even as that idea moved her, she couldn't help but think of the quilt she'd given Ben.

Will he ever be out of my thoughts? Will it always be this hard?

When she'd first started quilting, she'd planned for that original quilt to go into her hope chest and—if everything went as planned—use it on her wedding bed in her first home. She'd always pictured Aaron as her groom. Now . . .

Heat rose up her neck. She'd given her wedding quilt to an Englischman. What had gotten into her? Giving her quilt to Ben was giving him a piece of her heart. Yes, that's what it was. Each passing day that she hadn't heard from him confirmed that fact.

On some days she'd convinced herself that she'd just given him the quilt as a way of saying thank you. He'd helped them in so many ways. He'd also been the one to talk to her about God—to model what a closer relationship with Him looked like.

But on days when she was more truthful with herself, Marianna knew she gave it to him because she wondered what it would be like to cuddle under the quilt with him as her husband. It was a shameful thought and one she'd confess to no one, but that didn't mean she hadn't let her mind wander there once or twice. She just didn't let her mind dwell there when the thoughts did come.

"So, Marianna, how's your young man coming along? I hear he had an awful break."

"Oh, Aaron, yes." Marianna pushed Ben out of her mind. "It was a pretty bad break, but he's getting better. Not in so much pain. He's up and around."

"So are you returning with him to Indiana when he gets better?" Mrs. Peachy's hand moved her needle through the layers of fabric in neat stitches.

Marianna scanned the faces—all leaned forward, awaiting her response, slight smiles on the women's faces.

"I'm still thinking about that. I think it will happen, although there are no exact plans—"

"Is it true he's already built a cabin for you?" Eve Peachy's eyes were dreamy. "And to think he came all this way. I suppose it's nice."

"I haven't seen the cabin, but I'd like to some day." Marianna turned her attention back to her stitching, hoping they'd get the hint. "Aaron is a nice man. I've known him since we were in school."

And that's where her storytelling started. Before she knew it, Marianna had shared about when her and Aaron played Joseph and Mary in the school Christmas pageant. She'd talked about the herd of cattle he was building, the youth sings, and the way they'd watch each other over the fire. She even shared how he'd watched their train leave from the platform as they left Indiana. And with each story she remembered again why she'd cared for him so.

Hours passed, more stories were shared, and when they were finished Marianna joined the ladies around Mrs. Peachy's kitchen table. They'd all decided they'd be working on Marianna's quilt next month, the one she was making for Annie. While the women passed around the plates of cookies, Marianna busied herself by helping Mrs. Peachy with the tea, spooning loose leaves into a strainer and boiling the kettle on the kerosene stove. While Marianna handled the tea, Mrs. Shelter sliced thick pieces of apple bread and apologized for her younger daughters not being there. Both were up the road caring for Hannah Shelter, who'd just had twins. Marianna smiled. What a gift for Sarah's older brother and his wife. She also shook her head. She couldn't imagine caring for two babies at once.

"Mari, we should be leaving." Mem approached, tension clear on her face. "Dat just showed up with the buggy."

"Already, so soon?" Marianna glanced over at the desserts. "But why did he come already? We never leave this early."

Mem leaned close, lowering her voice. "I asked him to. Tomorrow's church at our house."

"Mem, the house is already clean. We've been working on it for days." But from the look in Mem's eye, it was no use to complain. So Marianna rose and said good-bye to the others.

Besides, remembering that tomorrow was church had made her anxious. Not that the house wasn't clean enough—but nervous about what Dat was going to say.

He'd been reading the English Bible, would it be evident in his words?

CHAPTER THIRTY

Their family had hosted church in their home many times over the years, but Marianna hadn't ever been as nervous about it as she was today. The bench wagon arrived last night, and volunteers brought in the benches and set them up. Then today, as morning dawned, their neighbors arrived. The women sat on one side, in the kitchen area, and the men gathered in the living room. The service began with song.

Marianna joined the others in singing the words from the Ausbund, their special hymnal. *"Mer mis-se gla-we an sell was un-ser Harr un Un-ser. Hei-land Je-sus Cri-sti uns g'saagt hot."* And as she sang, the words translated in her mind. "We must believe in that which our Lord and Savior Jesus Christ has told us."

Next came the *'S Lobg'sang,* "The Hymn of Praise."

O Gott Va-ter wir lo-ben dich
Ynd dei - - ne . . .

O, God, Father, we praise Thee,
And extol Thy many blessings;
That Thou hast, O Lord, proved

Thyself again so merciful to us;
And hast brought us together, Lord,
To exhort us though Thy word;
Grant us Thy mercy.

As Marianna sang the words, they resonated in her heart. These hymns were old, written by martyrs who lost their lives in the sixteenth century. They represented deep humiliation and dependence upon God, their deliverer. This was important, but she'd never liked before how the words were sung with great sorrow and loneliness. Now she understood. The message was supposed to be sad. Giving up something you loved was hard.

Yes, she had to give up Ben. But her ancestors gave up their families, their lives, their homes. Should she be consumed by such a small thing as surrendering her love for one man? It was big in her heart, yes, but not so big when she considered she'd still have someone to love and spend her life with, and that they'd live in a community that cared for each member.

One more song was followed by a short sermon by one of their neighbors, and then all knelt for silent prayer. More often than not, Marianna's mind wandered during this prayer time. As a child growing up she'd often count, seeing how high she got before the minister stirred and rose, alerting others to do the same. Later, she often used this time to think about Aaron. She replayed in her mind any looks or glances passed between them. She thought through the week and considered any conversations they'd had. And she imagined all the things she'd say when they were older and could share their feelings unhindered.

But today her heart seemed to crack open within her. Everything she'd been holding inside all week poured out to God in prayer. The thoughts filled her mind, and her lips moved as she pictured Jesus sitting there, listening to every word. Yet it wasn't in her home, next to her that she imagined Him. In her mind's eye she saw Him at the pond behind her home. She imagined it was spring again, and they sat side-by-side on a log. She didn't see His face, now as she could look into Aaron's or Ben's faces, but she felt His smile upon her. He wanted to be there for her. He wanted to listen and, in listening, carry her burdens too.

From somewhere in the room Marianna heard Joy fussing, and children shuffling in their seats. As the prayer time ended, Marianna couldn't hold back a smile. Her soul held a lightness that hadn't been there that morning. She rose, renewed, as if she'd just taken a sip from a cool spring.

They all stood for the reading of a Scripture—the women facing their bench, and the men facing the opposite direction. Uncle Ike was reading today. He opened the German Bible and read the Scriptures in High German—just as had been done from the time of their ancestors. As he read the words, tears filled his eyes and Marianna's heart clenched tight within her.

What caused those tears? Many of the bishops and other ministers back home cried and poured much emotion into their message, but that hadn't been her uncle's way.

His pitch and tone rose, and the emotion in his voice did too. Deep down Marianna had a feeling his tears came from finally understanding what he was reading. It was not just words—just tradition. The words were written for *them*.

Next came the longer sermon. Dat rose to preach. He stood by the front door so he would have a clear view of both groups, and all eyes were turned upon him.

"We will be reading from Acts, chapter 4 today, but first I must tell you I have more questions than answers. I'll be speaking of caring for our neighbor, and too often I've fallen short. I'm unworthy to share a message with you today, but I hope that maybe just a few of my words will be worthy of consideration."

The people around the room nodded, as they did for any bishop or teacher. One would never start a sermon in a prideful way. Instead, ministers let the others know they were flawed humans, with many weaknesses of their own.

Marianna held her breath as Dat reached down to the bench for his Bible. Did he dare bring the English book out? Seeing the German Bible, she released a breath, surprised at the disappointment that struck her. Reading in English would have helped everyone understand so much better.

"The passage I'm reading is from Acts 4:32–33. *'Alle in der Gemeinde waren ein Herz und eine Seele. Niemand betrachtete sein Eigentum als privaten Besitz, sondern alles gehörte ihnen gemeinsam. Mit großer Überzeugungskraft berichteten die Apostel von der Auferstehung Jesu, und alle erlebten Gottes Güte'."* After he finished, he paused, scanning the crowd.

"And for those of you who would appreciate hearing the words in English, I have memorized it for you." He cleared his throat and then continued. "'All the believers were one in heart and mind. No one claimed that any of their possessions was their own, but they shared everything they had. With great power the apostles continued to testify to the resurrection of the Lord Jesus. And God's grace was so powerfully at work in them all.'"

It was not good to be prideful, and yet that's what welled up within her. Dat hadn't brought out the English Bible, yet he'd shared its message. Marianna scanned the crowd, looking for anger on the faces. Amazingly everyone continued to listen as Dat talked about how the Amish community supported each other in numerous ways. Folks in the room seemed to be listening intently.

As her father preached, he presented his message in the singsong manner of the Pennsylvania German dialect.

"*Ya, ich glaab sell isz recht*," Uncle Ike called.

All eyes turned to him. Though he'd only said he thought what Dat was preaching was right, the other men looked displeased. Calling out like this was not their way, yet Marianna wished she was brave enough to do the same.

When it was time for the second, longer sermon, Marianna's full attention was on her father. His face seemed flushed. Had the room gotten too warm for him? Or maybe it was all the eyes upon him.

Dat paused, as though to collect his thoughts. Like every other minister, he spoke without notes. "The Scriptures, we know, speak of judge not that ye be not judged. It is important, and I believe as a community we can be an example to others. I'm not only talking about being an example to other Amish, but to the Englisch. It is not accident that God has brought us here to live among them. Yet are we living the type of lives they could model themselves after? 'Tis a good question to ask, *ja*?"

Marianna looked around the room. As always happened, a few of the older men had dozed off. A few men—Uncle Ike and Sarah's father, Mr. Shelter—nodded. But most of the others seemed distracted. Small children snacked on cereal. One mother opened her handkerchief to show her child a small toy tucked away. The woman gazed at her son as he played, and from the look on her face she didn't even notice Dat was speaking.

"Even though we have chosen to live by the traditions of our ancestors, we must remember our salvation comes through Jesus Christ alone." Dat scanned those listening. "We do not judge each other because that is not our place. But some day Amish and Englisch alike will stand before God in heaven and He'll have one question to ask, 'Did you know My Son?'"

Dat continued for an hour, sharing stories from God's Word about men and women who'd done great things for God. He also shared stories of those who'd failed at having faith in God as they should. After each story, he returned to the point. "They too will be asked the same question. Jest like you and I. Jest like our neighbors down the road. 'Did you know My Son?'"

When he finished, Dat followed tradition and asked for *zeugnis*—for other men to testify that what he'd preached was God's word. Marianna's heartbeat quickened as many men shared their encouragement.

As the service came to a close, announcements were made about the women's Saturday morning gathering at the West Kootenai Kraft and Grocery, and the fact the service in two weeks would be held at the Shelter's home.

The service ended, and everyone rose and spoke among themselves. A few men hurried outside to grab the legs that would convert their benches into tables for lunch.

Marianna moved to the kitchen, opening jars of church spread, which was a combination of peanut butter and marshmallow cream. Other women set out knives, cups, and water. Some sliced thick pieces of bread.

Sarah came to stand next to her and helped open jars of red beets and pickles.

"I liked your dat's sermon very much."

"Thank you. He only desires to serve."

"What he said is true about us loving those in the community. We have much to be thankful for. The way they've helped us. The way they point us to God. I bet your dat would like the prayer meeting too."

Marianna noticed Mrs. Peachy approach and cleared her throat. "So, Sarah, do you work tomorrow?"

"*Ja.*" Sarah followed her lead and changed the subject. "I do work, so I'll see you there . . . and maybe in the evening too."

Marianna knew what she was asking. Sarah wanted her to attend that prayer meeting. Tension built inside Marianna, but she knew the answer she wanted to give. "*Ja.* Maybe you can come stay the night over. We can do some baking."

Sarah nodded. "I'd like that."

Marianna didn't have time to talk to Sarah about the details before her Uncle Ike approached. "Marianna, can I talk to you?"

His brow was furrowed. His eyes flashed deep concern.

"*Ja,* of course." She looked around, but there wasn't anywhere they could go to be alone. Uncle Ike pointed upstairs and she followed him to Ellie's room. A few toddlers played with Ellie's toys in the corner. They'd never understand their Englisch words.

"I hear that you were talking all about Aaron yesterday at the quilt circle. That you're considering returning to Indiana with him."

She cocked her chin. "News travels fast, but yes . . . I suppose that is no surprise."

"What about Ben?" Uncle Ike stroked his beard. "Do you not care for him?"

"Ben? When did you become concerned with Ben? Wasn't it just a few weeks ago that you came by my work and brought me home to visit with Aaron?"

"*Ja, ja* but that was before I understood the depth of Ben's feelings. He's spoken to me about you."

Marianna shook her head. "Uncle, to have a relationship with Ben would be to leave the Amish. You would not wish for that."

She waited for him to agree with her.

Instead, her Uncle Ike glanced out the window. "I know Ben's love for God. He is a good man. He would be a *gut* spiritual leader."

"And Aaron . . . are you saying he wouldn't?"

Uncle Ike sighed. "Aaron is a good *Amish* man. There is a difference."

"Marianna!" Mem's voice called up the stairs. "Are you up there? I need your help. Can you come watch Joy? I need both hands for this food."

She walked to the doorway and called down to Mem. "*Ja*, I'll be right down. Just checking on the toddlers up here."

"*Denke.*"

Marianna turned back to her uncle.

"I know what I want. Who I want. I know the type of life I want to lead. I'm not sure why you doubt that."

Uncle Ike didn't respond, but she could tell from the way he crossed his arms over his chest that he didn't agree.

She hurried downstairs, but thought she heard him saying something after her. She wasn't sure, but she thought his words were, "I will pray for your soul . . ."

CHAPTER THIRTY-ONE

o matter how many times he played, a little buzz of nervous energy echoed in Ben's chest as he approached the mic.

Tonight was no different.

The venue was half coffeehouse, half bookstore. The place was twice as big as the restaurant area of the Kootenai Kraft and Grocery. It didn't seem like it, though, once the people filed in, packing the house. They dressed in designer clothes—men with $5,000 watches and women with rings worth ten times that.

Whitefish, Montana, was only sixty miles from West Kootenai, but it was a world apart.

Most people came to Whitefish to get away, but they didn't do too well at that. They bought second homes with the same luxuries as they'd left in places like L.A., Atlanta, and New York. Roy had mentioned having connections, but Ben hadn't expected anything like this. If someone in this crowd liked Ben and his songs, they could no doubt get on the phone, make a few calls, and he'd be on a jet plane to Nashville or Los Angeles by tomorrow night.

Ben approached the stool and leaned in to the mic. "Thank you so much for being here. Tonight I'm going to share some songs I wrote. I've lived north of here for a couple years now, and I don't know about you, but this place inspires me."

Whispered approval and acknowledgment carried through the crowd.

"The first song"—a quiver in his voice brought him pause—as did memories of his performances in Los Angeles. He'd gotten wrapped up in the fame, and in women. It was hard to believe that had been his life, but he wasn't like that now.

This time it would be different.

"This first song came about after I spent the day chopping wood for a family. I thought about the simple things in life, the things that matter most. About the good ache after a hard day's work. A cup of hot coffee after coming in from the cold. The sight of a loving smile." Marianna's face filled his mind. "And wanting to share my cabin with someone."

Ben started the refrain on his guitar. The voices of the crowd quieted even more and he began.

"Got my cabin deep in the woods
But need somethin' more to call it all good
To fill the aching hole in my life—
Cuz every warm cabin
Needs a good wife . . ."

He finished the song, and for a moment the room was silent. Then applause filled the room. He glanced around and noticed tears in the women's eyes. A few folks had their cell phones out to take photos of him. He noticed some guys approaching Roy in the back. Roy nodded and gave Ben a thumbs-up.

Ben smiled as he settled into his stool even more. He started the next song—one of his old ones that he and Roy had reworked.

The room stilled. He started singing about not realizing he'd seen love until he saw it through the rearview mirror and realizing it was too late. He sang with emotion, passion—and could see how the crowd was awed, moved.

He should have been ecstatic. But . . .

He was doing exactly what the song said. Leaving love.

Just as he was about to start his third song, Ben scanned the crowd and stopped short on the beautiful woman standing near the back. Carrie offered him a slight smile and wave. He could read an apology in her gaze. He guessed she was here because her father had told her about Marianna—and Ben's decision not to pursue her any longer.

The songs flowed from his lips and between each one he talked about going into the woods, talking to God, and discovering life in new ways. Roy was right, the crowd loved it. They all stayed until the last song, then, when he was done, gave him a standing ovation.

Ben smiled and shook hands, and then put his guitar away. He was introduced around—to important people—but in the back of his mind all he could think about was Marianna.

What was she doing? Would she bake cinnamon rolls in the morning? Did she think about their last time together as often as he did? Did she remember the feeling of his arms around her as clear as he remembered her settling into his embrace?

When almost everyone else had cleared out, Carrie wrapped her arms around him. "I'm so proud of you. That was fantastic."

"Yeah, it was a good night." He stepped back from her hug.

"What's wrong?" Carrie's eyes searched his face.

"Just tired I suppose."

"You staying at my dad's tonight?"

Ben nodded, but he took another step back. He didn't want her to get the wrong idea. He wasn't pursuing Mari, but he wasn't pursuing anyone else, either.

"Great." Carrie threaded her arm through Ben's and squeezed. "I've been practicing and I can make some great French toast."

The wheels of the buggy squeaked against the snow. It was the only sound in the night. Marianna held her breath, hoping that the sound of the horse and buggy hadn't woken Dat. She couldn't believe they were doing this—sneaking out to go to a prayer meeting.

When Sarah arrived earlier with her ankle bandaged up from a fall on the ice, taking the buggy to the prayer meeting had been their only choice.

Marianna considered staying home, but something inside told her to go. She needed prayer. She needed the peace of God. She needed the support of others. And so, thirty minutes after everyone had headed for bed, she and Sarah snuck out to the barn, hooked up the buggy, and headed out.

They crested the hill and a ways down the road she saw the Carashes' house. At least a dozen cars and a few buggies were parked outside. When they neared, Mr. Shelter was waiting.

"Hello, Marianna, welcome. Why don't you and Sarah get inside. I'll take care of the buggy for you."

"*Denke*." Marianna handed him the reins. She climbed down and took in a deep breath, holding it as she entered. She'd eyed the vehicles as they approached and hadn't seen Ben's truck, but as she walked though the front door she couldn't help letting her eyes scan the room, just in case.

Ben wasn't there.

Many people greeted her. Most she knew from the store. All of them smiled and told her and Sarah they were glad they were there. They chatted for a while before Mr. Carash asked them to find a seat. Marianna moved to a chair in a far back corner. Sarah joined her.

"Thank you for coming. For those of you who are new here, we don't have a schedule we follow. Every week we just come together and pray. Sometimes we share requests and take turns praying for each other. Tonight—with Thanksgiving so close— I wanted us to pray silently, thanking God for what He's done in our lives. In a little while I'll close us in prayer. At that time if you want to join in and pray a word of Thanksgiving out loud, feel free to do so."

Marianna watched as everyone lowered their heads, and she did the same. So far, this wasn't much different from the Amish silent prayer. As she sat there, she thanked God for her family. For keeping Aaron safe in that accident. For being raised by parents who loved each other and loved their children. For making her able to work and help others. She also thanked God for Ben's purpose in pointing her to God, and she prayed that God would be with Ben wherever he was.

After a while Mr. Carash prayed out loud. "Thank You, Lord, for those in this room. I thank You that we are allowed to meet together in prayer. I thank You that we know of Your ways and Your love and we don't have to try to walk through life without You."

When his words stilled, other voices around the room spoke up.

"Thank You that we live in such a beautiful place."

"Thank You for our need for each other."

"Thank You for Your Word."

"Thank You for warmth on cold days."

Sarah reached over and took Marianna's hand in hers. Marianna nearly jumped, and she realized she'd almost forgotten she was in this room. For a moment it felt as if her heart had been carried close to God in heaven. She didn't know what to think of that, but she knew she'd never felt so close to Him. The more prayers of thanksgiving she heard, the more her heart joyfully agreed.

"Thank You for seeking hearts," Sarah said.

Marianna nodded, and even though she didn't speak it out loud, her heart had a specific prayer too.

Thank You for showing me that when I seek You, I always discover more.

When they'd left her house earlier, Marianna had looked behind to make sure no one woke. Now, as they drove the buggy back, with Silver's coat reflecting in the moonlight, she hoped that still was the case.

Peace filled Marianna's heart. She'd enjoyed gathering with the other believers, getting to know them better, and lifting up their voices together. At first she'd worried that she'd feel uncomfortable or that they'd want her to pray out loud, too. Instead, the more everyone prayed, the more her heart longed to join them. If she kept attending, she might just pray out loud one of these days.

Marianna held her breath as their house came into view, and the quiet earth seemed to be holding its breath too. Above the topless buggy the stars hung like lamps under a dark barn roof. It was beautiful.

Movement caught her attention. A fox darted across the road. Seeing it, Sarah let out a cry, and Marianna noticed Silver's ears perk. Before she knew what to do, the horse reared his head, pulling the reins out of her hands.

"Whoa, whoa, Silver!" It was no use. There was no way to stop the animal.

But instead of running down the road, Silver set his sights on the barn. The only problem was—there was a forest between where they were and where the barn stood.

"Silver, no!"

The horse raced through the trees. Marianna grasped the side of the buggy, holding on for dear life. Sarah's hands tightened around Marianna's arm, another squeal escaping her lips. The buggy rumbled over the forest floor. Silver's hooves trampled brush. The buggy bounced as it bounded over logs and rocks covered in snow.

The world was a blur around her, and then Marianna's eyes widened. Up ahead, behind the house, were two trees. The space between then was wide enough for the horse—but not the buggy.

"Whoa, Silver!"

Her cry went unheeded. Silver raced through the trees and the buggy hit hard. Even though the buggy stopped, the horse's motion pulled the traces tight. A crack sounded and the single tree, where the traces were attached to the buggy, snapped. Marianna's eyes widened as the horse ran out from the shafts. The broken piece of single tree trailed after the horse—and she thought she'd be sick. It was broken.

She broke Dat's buggy.

Even in the dim light she saw something else trailing the horse—the harness. It dangled behind the horse, whipping through the air. The horse raced into the darkness and a new fear gripped her. What if Silver never came back?

How would she explain—sneaking out, losing the horse, breaking the buggy? Tears filled her eyes and the movement of Sarah on the seat beside her reminded her that at least they were safe, uninjured.

She let out a breath. "You okay?"

"*Ja*. You?"

Marianna looked down at her trembling hands. At least she was in one piece. It could have been worse. Would Dat understand?

Marianna looked to the house, expecting lantern light. She thought she saw movement in a downstairs window and leaned forward to get a better view. Before she could grasp a handhold, Marianna tumbled forward, falling into the snow. She gasped for breath as her face hit the snow. Then she heard it. Laughter bubbled from Sarah's lips, filling the air.

Marianna pushed up to her hands and knees. She tried to stand in the soft snow, but one foot sank to her knee, then the other.

They were just behind the house. "Quiet, shh . . ." Marianna hissed.

Hearing that made Sarah laugh harder. She climbed down from the buggy and tried to stand but sank into the snow.

"The horse?" Marianna looked around. She'd heard rumors. Horses were known to run away never to be found. The harsh terrain—and the predators—saw to that. Marianna brushed the snow from her face and bonnet. "Did he run away?" She pictured Dat's anger.

"Look, Silver circled around. He's over by the barn." Sarah panted and pointed. "He wants to be let in." She shook her head and looked at Marianna. "You should see us. We look like elves! We are short, stuck . . ." Her laughter sounded again.

The cold began to seep through Marianna's shoes and stockings, and she didn't think it was funny at all. It was bad enough she'd taken the buggy without permission, but to take it so she could attend an Englisch prayer meeting? Dat may understand, but Mem wouldn't.

Not ever.

"What are we going to do now?" Marianna climbed out of the hole, inching across the snow on her hands and knees.

"Put the horse away and get out of the cold, *ja*?" Sarah crawled behind her.

"And the buggy?"

"It'll be here tomorrow, I can guarantee that. Just make something extra good for breakfast. You'll need to beg for your dat's forgiveness."

CHAPTER THIRTY-TWO

⁓

The first rays of pink dawn stretched over the mountains. Marianna hurried outside, hoping to beat Dat to the barn, to figure out how bad off things were—and how to confess.

She hated to consider what he would say when he knew what she'd done. Not only did she sneak out to an Englisch prayer meeting, but she'd wrecked something that cost a lot. Even worse, she'd put her life and Sarah's in danger. She'd been foolish, but she still didn't regret going.

Even after the accident, the peace from the prayer meeting had remained. It was a miracle.

She hurried into the barn, taking in the scent of leather, hay, and wood. But then her feet stopped short. There, walking into the barn ahead of her, was Aaron.

She stared. "What are you doing?"

He lifted up the broken harness. "Isn't it obvious? Fixing a buggy." He pointed to the broken single tree. "I found some spare parts in the shed. The new single tree is already on the buggy. If you give me a few hours, I can have this harness fixed too." He cocked an eyebrow. "I can fix it, but you'll need the help of your dat and a few other men to get it unstuck."

"You can fix it all?" She still couldn't believe what he was saying—and that he'd be so kind to help her. Still . . . "What are you doing out of the house? How did you even know?"

Aaron brushed his blond bangs back from his face. "I knew because I heard you and your friend—Sarah, is it?—leave last night. I'm not sure what you were up to, but for all the noise you made I'm surprised you didn't wake the whole house."

She neared him. "Did you hear—"

"The commotion? The runaway? The crash in the woods? Yes." He chuckled.

"Really? You were awake?"

"Of course. Had to make sure you'd get home safe." He glanced up at her, humor in his gaze.

"But how did you get out there to fix the buggy? I mean, with your leg." Marianna noticed the bottom of his cast was damp and dirty, and his toes were bright pink from the cold.

Aaron glanced over to Silver. "Wasna too far. And I'm thankful the snow was frozen solid this morning." He winked at her. "Didn't have the same problem you had last night with sinking into it."

"But your leg." Marianna hurried forward.

Aaron rubbed the spot over the cast. "I've been getting mighty good at hopping on one foot. Also a good thing, the woods are filled with lotsa trees to lean on for support."

"Does it hurt?"

"It aches some. I'm not used to being upright this much."

Marianna rushed to him. "Here, let me help." She moved to

his side and wrapped his arm around her shoulders, then guided him forward.

They moved along at a slow pace, Aaron taking small hops. As they neared the front door of the house, Marianna saw Aaron's smile reflected in the window glass.

She paused.

"I saw that smile. You're . . . you're enjoying this."

"Of course I am."

"So you're not in pain."

"Pain?" Aaron tipped his face down closer to her. "I forgot about that." Then he sighed. "If this is what it took to get a hug from you, I shoulda prayed you'd sneak out weeks ago."

"Do you even want to know where I went?"

Aaron's eyes gentled. His gaze moved to her lips. "I suppose not." He cleared his throat. "What matters is you're safe." He leaned down and kissed the end of her nose. "What matters is you know I love you and . . ." His voice fell to no more than a whisper. "That I can see in your eyes you love me too."

Then, as soft as warm air, Aaron's lips touched hers. A rush of emotion, longing, moved through her. This was what she'd been waiting for. He was what she'd been waiting for.

The kiss deepened, and Marianna wrapped her arms around Aaron's shoulders.

This was the man she was going to marry. Everything within her told her it was so.

⁂

Abe Sommer had helped get the buggy unstuck but had yet to talk to Marianna about it. She'd headed off for work early and before she was due home, he and Ruth and the children had walked down to Carashes' for dinner.

Devon Carash passed Ruth a dish. "Has Abe talked to you about our Monday night prayer meetings? We'd love to have you come some time. I know that some of our beliefs are different—but we love and serve the same God."

"Prayer meeting? No, he did not mention it." Abe could see Ruth biting her tongue. He'd mentioned it to her and she'd refused, but from her sweet smile it was clear she didn't want their neighbors to know she was against the idea.

Susan Carash joined in. "I'm sure things have been busy for Abe—with the work, children, helping to care for that young man staying with you. Your brother-in-law Ike has been coming for months, and it was wonderful seeing Marianna last night."

"Marianna?" Ruth looked to Abe, and he felt himself sinking in the chair. He'd heard their daughter leave last night and guessed where she was going. He'd just been trying to figure out how to spill it to Ruth. He supposed he didn't have to worry about that now.

Susan placed a hand over her mouth. "Did you not know?"

"Oh, yes, of course. I just forgot. She's quite independent now with work and friends."

She sounded calm enough, but Abe could tell from the glint in his wife's eyes that this subject was far from closed.

⊂✄⊃

Dat, Mem, and the kids had been invited down to the Carashes' for Thanksgiving dinner, joining the family for a second time that week. At first they'd refused to go, saying they didn't want to leave Marianna behind. But when Marianna insisted, Mem looked deep into her eyes and a knowing crossed between them. Marianna needed time with Aaron. They'd been together a lot, but always surrounded with family. They needed time to talk. To plan.

With a smile on her face, Mem had packed up the children, the food, and they were off.

Marianna had a surprise too.

"Now that I know you can get around, I have an adventure for us." She brought Aaron his coat.

He cocked his head and tried to scowl, but it was impossible to hide his grin.

Dat had hooked up Silver to the buggy—recently fixed—for her and it waited by the front door. Marianna had already piled warm blankets on the front seat and packed a thermos of hot cider. It took some maneuvering to get Aaron inside, but they finally did and they set off.

Aaron closed his eyes and breathed in fresh air. "Where are we going?"

"The question is where are we *not* going. This place is so wonderful, and so far all you've seen has been the inside of our house. There's so much to show you."

She took him in the direction of the West Kootenai store, and on the way they passed the one-room schoolhouse. "It's cozy and warm inside and the teacher seemed real nice." She glanced over at him and tried to imagine Aaron being a father. He would make a good one some day.

She pointed to the store ahead. "It doesn't look like much, but it's the gathering spot for everyone in the community. After you get your cast off, I'll show you around inside. There's a small store and a craft room and a restaurant. They make delicious food if I say so myself." She chuckled.

Aaron seemed to be enjoying every minute of it. He leaned back against the seat and wrapped his arm around her shoulders.

"Where are we going next?" He scooted closer to her.

"You'll see." She turned the buggy around.

They drove toward Lake Koocanusa. It was a few minutes' drive, and she took the time to point out the trees, the trails, and the rivers she'd learned about. She also told Aaron about the town that used to be in the valley—the one covered over by water when they put in the dam. Finally, she held her breath as they crested the hill. When they reached the top, the road continued on, traveling down to the lake, but Marianna parked the buggy there. "Well, what do you think?"

Aaron's eyes widened, and he scanned the area. The mountain ranges in the distance, covered in snow. The forests of pines that met the edge of the lake. The crystal blue water.

"It looks like something from a dream. I've never seen anything like it. I saw the lake when your dat drove me home from the hospital, but I was in too much pain to appreciate it. Now I can't believe I'm actually here with you. No wonder you love this place, Marianna."

She blew out a breath and smiled. "It's something, isn't it."

"Yes, I'd say so." There was a tenderness in Aaron's voice, and when she turned she noticed he was no longer looking at the lake, but at her. He leaned forward and kissed her cheek, and she smiled at his closeness, his warm breath upon her.

"There's another place I'd like to show you someday. It's a special place I like to go and pray."

"I'd like that, Mari." His voice was almost a purr. "Sounds nice."

Yet even though he said the words, it was clear from the look in his eyes that he was more interested in kissing than praying.

"Thank you for doing this, Marianna." His tone grew husky. "I appreciate you showing me what you've come to love about Montana . . . and when we get back to your house, I have something to share with you too."

Marianna had cooked a simple meal for the two of them. She hadn't wanted to spend very much time in the kitchen—especially when Aaron said he had a surprise for her after dinner.

Then, when they settled down before the woodstove, he asked her to go to his room and retrieve the small box.

Marianna's fingers trembled as she carried it to him. Aaron's eyes glowed as he took it into his hands.

"When you left Indiana, I didn't know what to do. I cared for you, Marianna. I wanted to let you know, so I started writing letters."

"Letters?" She sat down beside him. "But I don't understand. Why didn't you mail them?"

Aaron lowered his gaze. "I wanted to know for sure how you felt. I didn't want to get my heart broken. I was sure you were going to come here and find someone else."

"And now?" She studied his face, his smile.

"Now . . . well, I have a feeling I've won your heart."

Marianna nodded. In the back of her mind she thought of her journal, all the questions and concerns she'd written within those pages, but she didn't want to think of that now. All she wanted to think about was Aaron. Being with him.

She stretched out her hand. "Can I read them?"

"We'll start with two."

"Two?" Marianna pouted. Then she leaned forward, resting against him, tipping her chin on his shoulder. "But why only two?"

Aaron chuckled. "Because I want more of this. I don't want our romance to end, Mari. I want each day to be beautiful, filled with something special."

Marianna straightened and reached out her hand again. "Okay, I'll take two."

With a smile, Aaron pulled out the first two letters, handing them over.

Marianna leaned her back against the sofa. She opened the first letter.

As she read about Aaron's struggle to accept her absence, and about her brother crying the day they all left, Marianna's heart broke and tears filled her eyes. When she read Aaron's words of love for her, her heart warmed. What would have happened if he'd mailed this note months ago? Would her heart have been open to it?

"Thank you, Aaron, for letting me know about Levi. I miss him. It makes me want to go back." Then, with a soft hand she stroked his cheek. "I love you too."

"There's one more. This one's better."

Marianna nodded and opened it.

❧

Dear Marianna,

To say that life here in Indiana is empty without you is only the beginning. Everything seems empty, the house, my day.

I went to town yesterday for more materials for the house and I found myself wandering over to the train station, just to check the price of tickets. If I knew you'd be happy to see me I'd be there in a minute.

I've been working on the house and each little thing I consider how you'd like the best. Would Marianna like a tall window? Would she like a deep sink or a bigger porch?

I also look to the view of the meadows, the trees, and the sky. I have the perfect place for a swing and I bought the materials, too, to make one. I'll start that project tomorrow. Keeping my hands busy helps my heart. And I can't wait to think of us swinging there together. Not just next year, but for the rest of our life.

Love,
Aaron

Marianna turned to him. "Did you build the swing?"

He eyed her. "Don't you want to wait and find out in the rest of the letters?"

She folded the letter and put it back in the envelope. "I don't want to wait."

"Yes, Marianna, the swing is sitting near the trees next to our—"

He paused, but she knew what he was going to say.

"Our home."

She scooted closer, knowing what she wanted more than anything. *"Ich will hem geh."*

"You want to go home? Do you mean . . . ?"

Marianna nodded. "To Indiana. I'm ready to go back now."

"Because of Levi? Do you miss your brother?"

She shrugged. "That, too. But . . . well, I just have a feeling I need to be there. I feel that this community has given me so much—a new faith. It's something I want to share."

"I have seen a difference in you." Aaron stroked her cheek. "I like it, *ja*."

"Looking back, I see that there are no accidents. I was fighting for my own way"—she thought of Ben but pushed him out of her mind—"but now I'm ready for God's plan."

What was God's plan? Marianna didn't know exactly, but she had an idea. Maybe God brought her to Montana to test and see if she'd be faithful wherever He wanted her. Without doubt she'd come here to deepen her relationship with Jesus, but maybe that wasn't just for her. What if the reason for her deepened faith was to return to her family, her friends, her community and share the good news with them? They didn't listen to outsiders. They'd never listen if someone like Ben were to come and share his hope and passion for God. But they just might listen to her . . .

"You're returning with me, Mari?" Joy rang in his words, filled his face.

"Yes, Aaron, as soon as you're ready."

"Does that mean you . . . you'll come see the cabin. You'd consider being my wife?"

She nodded and lowered her gaze, heat rising to her cheeks. "*Ja.*"

"*Ja*, you'll consider it, or . . ."

"*Ja*, Aaron. If you're asking I'm saying yes. I'll be your wife."

Marianna had nearly talked Aaron into letting her read one more letter when she heard her family returning. She glanced at the windup clock on the mantel. "I know they've been gone almost all day, but I wish we had longer."

Her dat entered first, followed by Mem. David was next, carrying a whole pie, excitement shining on his face.

"Mari, we got a letter from Levi!" Charlie hurried in. "The Carashes got it in their mail a few days ago and they gave it to us tonight."

They all entered and closed the door behind them, taking off their coats as if eager to share the news. Marianna rose. There was only one thing that would make her family so happy.

She hurried to Dat. "Is he—"

Dat nodded and laughter poured out. "He's returning, *ja*. Levi is returning to the Amish."

It was everything she'd hoped for, but something tempered her father's words.

Marianna looked from her father to her mother, seeing more in their faces than they wanted to share. There was joy there, but something else too.

"Is . . . is everything okay?"

Dat pulled the letter from his pocket and then handed it to her. "Yes, Mari. Or at least, it will be. Sometimes pain and wrong decisions are what bring us to God. You better read this, and then you'll understand."

Marianna went to sit on the couch beside Aaron. She'd been so excited about Levi's letter she hadn't thought to tell her parents about her and Aaron's decision to marry. Not that she'd tell them tonight anyway. Amish couples didn't tell their family and guests until a few weeks before the ceremony, and they still had time for that yet. Plenty of time.

Aaron leaned close as she opened the letter and began to read.

Dear Dat, Mem, and Marianna,

I'm writing this letter with news you will be excited to hear. There is other news I know will surprise you. First of all, I've spoken to the bishop. I've confessed my wandering, and I've asked to be baptized into the church.

Second, Naomi and I will be getting married soon, we are doing so because she is expecting a child. It is not what we'd planned, but we know every child is a gift. When I considered raising this child I knew I had to do it the only way I knew—in our community—as Amish.

Naomi hasn't been feeling well, and I'm also writing to ask Marianna to come and to help care for her during the rest of the pregnancy. Naomi is staying in the Dawdi Haus, and I will not join her until we are married. I do not wish for her to stay alone. So Mari, would you come?

That is all my news for now. I'll write more later. I know you will find this news a surprise, but I bet you'll be happy all the same. It's what you wanted. Maybe, now, the whole family can return.

Love,
Levi

Marianna folded the letter, unsure what to think. "A baby." She turned to Aaron, noticing his wide eyes.

"Some news, isn't it?"

Aaron swallowed hard and then nodded.

She took his hand. "Looks like we'll be returning home sooner than expected. Think you can travel?"

Aaron looked at her, his brow furrowed. He didn't answer.

"Well, unless you don't think . . ."

"Yes. I'm sorry." He leaned over and pulled her head against his chest. "I can't wait, Marianna. It'll be good to go back. It'll be good to show you our home."

"Our home," she whispered. "I love the sound of that. Our home."

June-Sevenies,

>*I know this letter may come as a surprise to you, but I'm returning. I'll be back in Indiana before you know it. Aaron went to the doctor and the doctor was pleased by his progress. He put Aaron in a walking cast so he can get around much better. It should make the trip easier for us both!*

>*There is other news I have to share, but I'll do so when the time is right. I just want you to know that even though there have been many challenges over the last few months God has shown me more of Himself. He's also shown me the man I'm destined to be with is the one I've loved for as long as I can remember.*

*Sorry this note is so short. I need to run to catch the
mail. I've enclosed Aunt Ida's address. You can reach me
there in a few days—imagine that, a few days!*

Love,
Marianna

Abe turned and wrapped his arm around his wife. It had been
a Thanksgiving unlike any other, but he was proud of her. He
snuggled closer and kissed her shoulder. Her nightdress smelled of
soap and of smoke from the woodstove. Although Abe didn't mind
the scent, he was eager for the scent of spring. Spring held so much
promise—a representation of the new life growing inside the earth.

He smiled at his wife. "I enjoyed tonight. It was good to share
a meal, to see the kids having fun."

"Did you know Marianna went to a prayer meeting?" Ruth's
voice was tense.

"I overheard. And that explains what Aaron was up to, fixing the
buggy. Explains why it got stuck. It looks like she had a bumpy ride
through the woods. Silver must have gotten spooked." He smiled.

"This is no laughing matter. First, she's meeting with the
Englisch, praying words *out loud*. And what next?" Even though
Ruth asked a question she didn't wait to answer. "Our daughter
will go the way of the world, that's what will happen. And then—"

"What, Ruth?"

"Two children lost. Levi left for a time. Marianna next."
They'll say we did this to our children—that we had no right having them."

"You're letting your thoughts run away like a scared horse.

Marianna's going nowhere. She's curious. You have to admit we were too at that age."

Her back stiffened, but instead of releasing her, he clung to her. "Besides, you saw her and Aaron tonight, didn't you? If anything she's drawing closer to him—and to her own baptism."

"We need to be setting an example of what is and isn't Amish. It's too easy for things to get confused in this place." She pulled away, scooted closer to the edge of their bed. "The children need to know . . ."

Abe clenched the quilt in his fists. They'd shared much under this quilt. Years ago they'd shared dreams. They'd fought some, but not often. Mostly about small things—things not worth the air to speak them. But now . . .

This was different. What he had to say mattered.

Abe leaned up on one elbow and gazed at his wife's brown hair in the moonlight. "That is why we're here, Ruth. So our children *will* know. Being in Indiana made it too hard to show them what was important. Everyone watched their neighbor without looking at the concerns of one's own heart."

Ruth shifted but didn't speak.

"Our children are learning what's important. Didn't Jesus Himself say to love thy neighbor? I'm not sure He just meant those similar to oneself."

"It's not right, that's all I'm saying."

Abe lowered back down and rested his head on his pillow. "If it's not one thing, it's another."

"What's that supposed to mean, Abe Sommer?"

"It means that if things aren't exactly your way, they're not good enough, godly enough. I imagine God doesn't know how to run the world on His own." He sighed and lowered his voice. "Good thing there's always an Amish woman or two around to help Him out."

CHAPTER THIRTY-THREE

*E*dgar hobbled into the restaurant kitchen and pulled two cookies from the cooling rack. He headed back to his place at the cash register. He didn't seem to notice the women circled in the kitchen, sitting in chairs. A few people shopped, picking up items from the store shelves, but the women in the kitchen paid them no mind. Sarah, Jenny, Annie . . . their eyes were fixed on Marianna.

She bit her lip as she glanced at them and swallowed hard, noticing tears in Jenny's eyes.

Annie eyed Marianna. "Are you sure this time?" She smoothed her apron.

"*Ja*, Aaron and I are set to leave in a few days' time."

"I'm sure your parents are pleased Levi will be joining the church." Sarah leaned forward, her eyes fixed on Mari's. Both knew her words were an understatement.

Jenny crossed her arms over her chest. "I don't understand. Your parents are happy that your brother got his girlfriend pregnant?" A low, harsh chuckle burst from her lips. "Wish they could have talked to my parents. As soon as they found out I was pregnant, wham! They gave me the boot. I was on my own. They even changed the lock on the door. If it wasn't—" Words caught in her throat. "The love I've been shown in this community has made me trust in love again." She reached forward and took Marianna's hand, squeezing it hard. "I'm going to miss you."

Marianna nodded. "*Ja.*" She wanted to tell Jenny that she'd miss all of them too, but heat rose up her neck at the thought of sharing her feelings like that. She decided to change the subject and talk about Levi and Naomi. She could do that without tears.

"Jenny, please don't misunderstand. Pregnancy outside of marriage is not encouraged, but people know it happens. Usually the couple marries in a simple ceremony. No one speaks of it, but they have only a lunch without the wedding dinner. Only later, when the baby comes too soon, do others realize what happened. But bed courtship, well, it's an old tradition that sometimes leads to other things . . ."

Jenny cocked an eyebrow. "Bed courtship?"

"It's how an Amish boy and girl date. He picks her up at her house and takes her home or to a friend's house. They spend the night together, you know, to get to know each other better. With everyone working so hard during the week on their farms and jobs, weekends are the only time for young couples to get together. They want to spend as much time together as possible."

"I bet they do." Jenny smirked. "And I thought . . ." She shook her head. "Well, I thought different of your people."

Annie joined the conversation. "Traditions are traditions, and sin is enticing to everyone—no matter how you were raised. Sexual impurity is wrong, but each of us must make the decision to stay strong. I'm just thankful Levi's making a good choice and that he'll be there for his child."

"Did the letter say when the baby's due?" Sarah asked.

"In a matter of months."

"Really? That soon?" Sarah's eyes widened. "I thought they weren't together." Her eyes bored into Marianna, and she could read the question in her friend's eyes. It was the same question that met Marianna on the walk to the store this morning. Last night she'd been so excited about Levi's return. Her heart had been so light with the idea of becoming a bride that she hadn't taken the time to think about Naomi's pregnancy. The slow walk in the chilly air had awakened those thoughts.

"I'm not going to get into their business. I just wanted you to know that my brother and my friend—they need me. And . . . while I'm there I'll be planning my own wedding."

A gasp escaped Jenny's lips. "To Aaron?"

"Yes, of course. Who else would it be?" Marianna laughed but the look on Jenny's face made the answer clear.

It was a look of relief that Marianna was not marrying Ben.

A pang struck Marianna's heart. She started. Was she . . . jealous? No, of course not. What did it matter if Jenny ended up with Ben? In fact, it would be a good thing for them both. They each deserved someone good.

Marianna forced a smile, then turned back to the pie crust she'd been rolling out. She had a beautiful future to look forward to . . . she needed to be thankful. She needed to see this time in Montana as the way God helped her finally understand where she belonged.

⚬⚭⚬

Marianna waited until everyone else was in bed to ask Aaron the question that had pounded in her head all day. She sat in the rocking chair by the fire, close enough to see his face but far

TRICIA GOYER

enough to buffet the pain if she didn't receive the answer she was hoping for.

"Aaron, there's something I need to ask you. About Naomi."

The color drained from his face.

"Were you wondering when I'd ask?" She leaned forward, resting her elbows on her knees.

"Not really. I didn't think—"

"That I'd hear?"

His cheeks reddened. "No. Not really."

"You should know better, Aaron. I mean, you heard about me—about what people were saying about . . . well, you know, Ben." She had a hard time saying his name and ignored the deep stirring inside.

"But that's different. Every time I was with Naomi, we were alone."

Somehow that wasn't comforting. "Girls talk, Aaron."

"It was nothing. We were just keeping each other company. My heart ached so with you gone."

She wanted to tell Aaron she understood and, in a way, she did. That's why she'd been so drawn to Ben. She was sure of it now. She'd been lonely. She was looking for someone to fill the hole that being without Aaron had caused. She didn't blame Aaron. He needed to be admired and appreciated—even though it was clearly a sin for a young Amish woman to desire such things.

As for Naomi, with Levi breaking up with her, it was only natural she had turned to Aaron. Even so . . .

"Did you kiss her when you were together? I have to know."

Aaron lowered his head. He didn't speak, but he didn't need to.

"Did you do more? Did you treat her in a way a husband treats a wife?"

"No." The word shot from Aaron's lips. "It—it wasn't like that."

Marianna studied his face, trying to decide if she believed him. She had no choice but to try. She'd made mistakes too. "So, where do we go from here?"

"If you want to talk to Naomi, you can. Just so you know I'm telling the truth."

"I wasna thinking about that. I mean, now that we know we are both human and that we are prone to mistakes. I suppose we should expect shortcomings. I have no doubt we'll continue to fail each other. We're not perfect."

"You're not mad?"

"I have to admit my heart is a little crushed, but I understand. I left you, Aaron." She looked into his face. "And an empty heart is always looking for things to fill it."

Aaron stepped forward and placed both hands on her shoulders. Then he pulled her toward him. Though his touch was gentle, his urgency as he drew her into an embrace was not. "Do you promise you'll never be apart from me again?"

She leaned her cheek again his chest, amazed to hear the beating of his heart through the rough cotton of his shirt. "I cannot promise that."

"Yes, I know. But least you're returning with me, right? And you'll come see the cabin." He stroked her neck under her kapp. "And then will you let me court you proper-like?"

"You mean sketching me before the fire and allowing me to wash your hair isn't a proper courtship?" She chuckled, trying to ignore the pain she felt. Trying not to think that Aaron may have held Naomi like this.

"No. I wanna do it like I've been planning for two years."

She pulled back from him and looked into his face. "Really? How is that?"

"I can't tell you. It'll ruin the surprise."

"Well, if you don't tell me, I will not let you have a piece of apple pie." She hurried to the kitchen, where the pie cooled on a wire rack.

"You wouldn't . . ."

"I would."

"Okay, but let's sit by the fire."

Marianna took his hand and followed him in to the living room, facing him on the sofa.

He smiled. "Well, there was going to be the typical rides down the country roads. Sitting side by side at youth sings. I might have come a time or two and woke you up to go visit with friends. Then, when I was sure that you were dreaming of a wedding as much as I was, I was going to take you to my house—our house. I was going to show you the barn first and my herd that was growing. Then, as sunset neared, we'd walk though the trees to the house itself."

Marianna smiled and closed her eyes, picturing it all as he talked.

"I'd show you the front porch, then I'd take you inside to the kitchen and living area. I'd show you the indoor bathroom and the small side room for our first child. Then I was planning on taking you to the bedroom—our future bedroom—and give you your first kiss."

Marianna swallowed, her gaze on Aaron's lips. His hand reached up and cupped her cheek, then slowly—so slowly she thought she'd pass out waiting for him—he leaned forward. Her eyes fluttered closed and she lifted her chin. As his lips touched hers, a bolt of lightning shot through her, down her body, zapping her heart.

He pulled back, but she refused to open her eyes. She focused on the warmth of his breath. His touch. "I love you, Aaron. I've waited for these kisses from you. I'd always planned for them to be like this . . ."

Then, unbidden, another face filled her mind.

Naomi's.

Stop it. It wasn't anything. He said so.

The fact that Aaron and Naomi kissed wasn't what bothered her, not really. Marianna was no fool. She knew few young men kept themselves pure through *rumspringa*. But the idea that Naomi had unwrapped the gift that Aaron had been saving for her . . .

Naomi saw the cabin. She'd seen the sunset through the trees. She'd enjoyed Aaron's embrace. All before Marianna had. Her wave of happiness was replaced by a nauseous feeling in the pit of her *gut*. She pushed away from Aaron and rose.

"What's wrong?" He stood, favoring his good leg.

"I'm tired, that's all. It's been a hard day."

"You're lying, Marianna. I can tell. You've never been a good liar."

"I just wonder why I had to come here at all. I should have stayed. Things would have worked out. You wouldn't have kissed Naomi in our place—the cabin—where you should have been kissing me. And . . ."

Marianna stopped there. She didn't want to continue. She didn't want to talk about how her heart was wrapped up, or who it was wrapped up with. She didn't want to picture Ben's face or long for his smile. She didn't want to admit that even as Aaron's lips were on hers she'd wondered what it would be like to kiss Ben. She blew out a soft breath realizing that she regretted not trying at least once. She hadn't been baptized to the church yet after all.

She sat on the couch, snuggling into the corner. "I feel sick."

"I'm sorry, Mari. Sorry I failed you, but I have to admit I don't understand. Weren't you the one who just said it was good to know neither of us is perfect?"

"I know." She wrapped her arms around herself. "I just . . . need some time, Aaron."

He nodded, and left the room.

CHAPTER THIRTY-FOUR

*A*aron sat in the corner booth feeling as out of place as if he were walking on the moon. The Englisch and Amish sat together in the booths, talking with each other about things like the weather and how the hunting season was going. It was Marianna's last day of work, and everyone gathered to wish her good-bye. She moved around the room, taking time to talk to each person.

Aaron picked up his knife and brushed butter over the thick slices of bread. He'd have her all to himself soon.

Ben blew warm air into his hands as he stood on the porch of the store and watched a buggy approach, not wanting to go inside. How long had he been standing there? Fifteen minutes? Twenty? He wasn't sure.

The horse's hooves crunched the frozen snow and the buggy rolled under the street light. Ben sucked in a breath—the icy air feeling like razor blades in his lungs. That's when he saw Mr. Sommer in the buggy. Abe waved a mittened hand, and Ben waved back, forcing a smile to his face. He hurried up to help with the horse. He'd have to go in now. No more hiding in the darkness.

"What are you doing out in the cold, Ben? Aren't you going to come in?"

Ben took the horse's reins and patted the animal's side. "Oh, I saw you coming and just thought I'd see if you needed any help." It was a lie, but he didn't think Abe would care for the truth.

"Not really. I'm not staying long. Just picking up Aaron and Marianna and getting them home. They have an early train tomorrow." Mr. Sommer tied Silver to the hitching post and then waved Ben to follow him in.

Ben's eyes scanned the restaurant, and his eyes fell on the one he was looking for. She stood there, with her simple blue dress, her apron dingy from a day working in the kitchen, her woolen stockings. Her clothes were pinned. Her face held not a hint of makeup, but she was beautiful in a way none of his old friends from Southern California would ever understand.

She hugged a few people, then moved to the table where Jenny and Kenzie sat, taking time to give them both a long hug. Ben watched as she slipped an envelope from her pocket and pressed it into Jenny's hand. He was pretty sure inside the envelope was the money she'd received for the quilt she'd made for Annie. It was only a guess, but it was something Marianna would do.

Voices, loud laughter, and the sound of the radio filled the room. Annie didn't have the radio on often, but no one wanted to miss news of the upcoming storm. And then Ben heard it, his voice, his song. On the radio.

The pounding of his heart increased and he looked to Marianna. She paused, lifting her head as if recognizing something familiar.

She looked up at the ceiling, as if trying to concentrate, and just then someone approached. The tall man walked with hardly a limp. He placed one hand on her arm, in the other he held his brimmed hat. She turned and a smile filled her face. He pointed to the back door, and that's when Ben saw them. Two brand new suitcases, most likely for their trip.

Marianna wrapped her arms around Aaron, clearly excited, and placed a kiss on his cheek.

Tears filled Ben's eyes and the blue dress blurred before him.

"Every warm cabin needs a good wife," his voice on the radio sang. Hot emotion tightened Ben's throat. A tear slid from the outward corner of his eye, and he wiped it away. He'd been gone too long. He'd missed too much.

Lord, is this how it's supposed to be? If so, why does my heart hurt so much?

Ben watched as Marianna hurried to Annie, offering a warm hug. Then others—Jenny, Edgar, Mrs. Peachy—rushed forward, each waiting their turn.

"Good-bye," Marianna said to everyone. Aaron stood to the side, waiting. A soft smile filled his face and his love for her was clear.

Why did I have to fall in love with her, Lord? Why did it have to come to this?

He'd done everything God had asked. He'd walked away from fame. He'd been content to serve others. He'd loved God, shared his faith. So why had God brought Marianna here? To hurt him? To test him?

God, do You want to know if I love You most?

His mind told him he did love God more. But his heart?

Ben watched as Aaron returned his hat to his head and placed his hand on the small of Marianna's back. She paused, looking back over her shoulder, scanning the room one last time as if she were looking for something—someone. Ben stepped into the kitchen before her gaze reached him. He couldn't let her see him like this. He'd always told her he believed God had a perfect will. He couldn't let her see the anger, the pain in his gaze.

Why, God?

Morning light shone through the windows. Marianna hadn't looked at the photo of her and Ben for weeks. Knowing it was tucked away in her journal—protected by her wonderings, questions, and prayers—helped. Like armed sentries, her words would not accuse because the photo was there. A few times she thought about digging that journal out from beneath her other things. Once she reached down and touched the leather of the book but then pulled her hand away.

She had to stay strong.

Seeing her joy in the photo, and Ben's gaze upon her, would do her no good. It would puncture her heart again and replay accusations of her mind. *I should have known better.* Becoming too friendly with the Englischer had been the cause of most of her pain.

She knew that now. The boundaries her community placed on outside things—outside people—were for her own good.

So why had she kept the photo? Would Mem have kept a photograph of the Englischman she once loved? After all, photos were slices of reality, unlike the dangerous nature of one's fanciful thoughts.

She looked down at Aaron's letter in her hands.

She'd almost missed it. She'd almost walked away from a love that was true, one she was created for. In a few day's time she'd be back. In Indiana.

She placed a hand over her heart. In a few days she'd see Levi. And then . . . she imagined walking through the home designed for her.

Marianna rose and dressed, then tied up her snow boots, slid on her coat, and headed out into the chilly morning air. The light filtering over the mountains seemed to sharpen the white around her, causing it to glow. She walked behind the house, and even though she could no longer see the trail to the pond, she knew the way. Trapper trotted by her side, stopping every now and then to sniff a thicket. Even though the world was quiet, life was buried deep under branches or in the ground. That's what things seemed like lately—that true life was hidden under the surface.

She made her way to the pond and noticed it was frozen over, still. The beaver dam was there, and she smiled thinking of the creatures safe and warm inside. For so long her mind seemed frozen with questions. But today things were different. Today life had thawed and hope had sharpened everything, just like the sunlight through the trees. She would return home. She'd help Levi, she'd spend time with Aaron and get to know the man she was loving more each day.

But there was more than that. Truth had come to her in the night as she'd prayed. She was going back different. Not only did she have new friends and a different outlook on life. God had changed her inside, and that was something she wanted to share.

Marianna reached down and plucked a small pinecone off

a broken branch, tucking it in her pocket. Just as one pinecone could scatter many seeds and grow a forest, maybe the truth she wanted to share would plant new hope in the Amish community she'd grown up in.

She started back to the cabin, her steps quickening. Suddenly she couldn't wait to go back with Aaron. She hoped to have another day making pies with Rebecca. She wanted to sew baby clothes with Naomi and work on mending by the fire with Aunt Ida, and as she spent time with them, she wanted to share about what she'd learned here. Not the fact that Amish and Englisch were more alike than she thought or that some snow was so wispy and light that it couldn't be formed into a snowball—although those things might come into the conversation.

Instead, she wanted to talk to them about God, His word and His goodness. Faith wasn't about their dress and their ways. It wasn't about doing things like their ancestors. It was about learning that the One who created and brought order to the world was the One who loved in deeper ways than she could imagine.

Excitement filled her. It would be impossible to sleep. Was Aaron awake? They could talk about their trip, and maybe he could tell her more about the cabin.

Her heart ached. How she must have hurt him by not going to see it. He'd worked so hard on it.

Warm heat hit her cheeks as she entered her parents' cabin. As she hoped, Aaron was awake. He sat on the couch as if waiting for her. When he glanced up at her, she noticed his smile. She took off her mittens, coat, and boots, and joined him.

She smiled back, a cold blustering filled her stomach as if a winter storm stirred inside. Amazingly, it was a welcoming feeling. It showed her she was on the right track.

Aaron extended his hand to her and she reached for it, taking slow steps forward. She looked around at the simple house and imagined the place Aaron had built for her—the type of place she'd always pictured growing up.

When did I forget those dreams?

This is where I belong. With Aaron.

She let out a slow breath . . . if only she'd realized it sooner. If only all her feelings for Ben would vanish with the morning dawn.

"Ready to go?"

She met Aaron's gaze. "Yes, I believe I am." She put her hand in his and followed him out the door. To the train.

To her future.

Epilogue

arianna scanned the crowd—and then she saw him. Levi, the man—no longer the boy—strode to her. Tenderness for her brother, still with close-cropped hair and Englisch clothes, tugged at her heart. But as Marianna approached, she saw something. A shadow of stubble on Levi's face. The beginnings of a beard.

Her heart leapt.

Marianna held back the questions on the tip of her tongue. She wanted to know about his plans, about the wedding, yet she waited. Other Amish milled around. Such things as she wanted to know were shared in private, around family. Only after the engagement was published a few weeks before the wedding would they be able to talk about it in public.

Even though it wasn't ladylike, Marianna lifted her skirt and ran to him.

Levi opened his arms to her, and she stepped into them. His T-shirt was soft on her cheek.

"Thank you for coming, Mari. I can't tell you how much it means."

She swallowed hard and nodded. Her lips parted to answer, but the quiver of her chin stopped her words. She looked back and noticed Aaron gathering their suitcases. He looked at her, waiting, giving them time before he approached.

"Are you crying?" Levi's hands touched her shoulders and he pushed her back to see her face. "You don't have to cry. I'm all right and Naomi will be too. We're figuring things out." He wiped away a stray tear from her cheek with his thumb. Levi's touch was gentle. "Don't cry, Marianna."

"They're happy tears. Levi, you have to know that. The days to come . . . I can't even imagine, how full of happiness they'll be."

"Yes, Marianna." Levi hugged her again. "I suppose it's what we've always wanted. We just didn't know."

"We do now, Levi." Laughter replaced her tears. "We do now."

Hamburger Potato Dish

2 pounds hamburger
1 medium onion, diced
1 can cream of mushroom soup
1 can water
6 medium potatoes, peeled and cubed
salt and pepper to taste

Brown hamburger and onion. Add soup, water, potatoes, and seasoning. Bake in casserole or cook in a skillet, stirring occasionally. Meal is done when potatoes are tender.

Corn Bread Meat Pie

1 pound ground beef
1 large onion, chopped
1 can (8 oz.) tomato sauce
1 teaspoon salt
1 tablespoon chili powder
1/2 cup chopped green pepper
1 3/4 cup water
1/2 teaspoon black pepper
1 can (12 oz.) whole kernel corn
Corn bread mix (prepare as on package but do not bake)

Brown ground beef and onion in skillet. Drain. Mix in the other ingredients and let simmer for 15 minutes. Pour into a greased casserole dish. Top with corn bread mix. Bake at 350 degrees for 20 minutes.

Amish Peanut Butter Pie

———————— ⬡ ————————

3/4 cup powdered sugar
1/2 cup creamy peanut butter
1 cup sugar, divided
3 cups low-fat milk, divided
3 large eggs, separated
6 tablespoons cornstarch, divided
3 tablespoons flour
1/4 teaspoon salt
2 tablespoons butter
2 teaspoons vanilla, divided
1 pie shell, baked
1/4 teaspoon cream of tartar

Beat together the powdered sugar and peanut butter till the mix is crumbly; set side.

In a large, heavy saucepan, combine 2/3 cups sugar and 2 cups low-fat milk; heat to scalding or possibly till bubbles start to form on the bottom. Don't let it boil.

Meanwhile, in a medium bowl, beat the egg yolks to mix; blend in 3 tablespoons cornstarch, flour, and salt. Stir to make a paste.

Whisk in the remaining cup of cool low-fat milk, whisking till the mix is smooth.

Pour in some of the warm low-fat milk mix, stirring to combine.

Add in mix in bowl to the low-fat milk in the saucepan. Cook over medium-low heat, stirring constantly, till the mix bubbles up in the center.

Add in the butter and 1 teaspoon vanilla. Remove from heat and let the custard cool.

Preheat oven to 350 degrees.

Sprinkle 2/3 of the crumbly peanut butter mix in the bottom of the baked (and cooled) pastry shell. Pour the cooled custard mix over the top.

In a large mixer bowl, place the egg whites, cream of tartar, and remaining 1 teaspoon vanilla. Beat till stiff peaks form.

Gradually, while beating, add in the 4 tablespoons remaining sugar and 3 tablespoons remaining cornstarch. Continue beating until the eggs whites are very thick and glossy.

Spread meringue on top of pie; sprinkle the remaining peanut butter mix on top.

Bake for 10 to 15 minutes; watching carefully, or possibly till the meringue is golden. Chill and serve.

Amish Caramel Pie

3 cups brown sugar
3 cups water
2 tablespoons butter
1 cup all-purpose flour
3 cups milk
6 egg yolks
2 pie shells, baked

Mix together flour, milk, and egg yokes. Set to the side. Boil brown sugar, water, and butter together for 2 or 3 minutes for a good strong caramel flavor. Slowly stir flour mixture into boiling syrup, stirring constantly until it comes to a boil. Remove from heat; cool 5 minutes and stir once. Pour into 2 baked pie shells. Top with either a meringue from the egg whites or allow pie to cool and top with whipped cream.

Amish Breakfast Casserole

1 pound sliced bacon, diced
1 medium sweet onion, chopped
6 eggs, lightly beaten
4 cups frozen shredded hash brown potatoes, thawed
2 cups shredded cheddar cheese
1 1/2 cups small curd cottage cheese
1 1/4 cups shredded Swiss cheese

In a large skillet, cook bacon and onion until bacon is crisp; drain. In a bowl combine the remaining ingredients; stir in bacon mixture. Transfer to a greased 13 x 9 x 2 baking dish. Bake, uncovered, at 350 degrees for 35–40 minutes or until set and bubbly. Let stand for 10 minutes before cutting.

AUTHOR'S NOTE

Dear Reader,

During the writing of *Along Wooded Paths*, as Marianna was adjusting to life in West Kootenai, Montana, I was doing some adjusting of my own. I'd just moved from Kalispell, Montana, to Little Rock, Arkansas. Like Marianna, I started making friends with people very different from me. While I missed my old friends back home, my heart had plenty of room for new relationships, too. Moving away, I wasn't giving anything up . . . instead I grew in my knowledge of a new place. I also found my place within a new community.

When I started working with single moms in inner city Little Rock, I thought I had something to offer them. What I didn't realize was how much those relationships would change me. Just like Marianna found with Jenny, it was a special give and take. The laughter and hugs of those young moms is something I'll always cherish.

Sometimes in life we have an idea of what God's plan is. And other times His greatest plan is simply for us to love the people He's put in our paths.

Who has God put in your path? It may be someone who's facing a challenging time, like Aaron. It maybe be someone who just needs a little help, like Jenny. Next time someone enters your life, consider how your love and support can make a difference. The truth is, sometimes you'll be the one who is impacted most of all . . . just like Marianna. Just like me.

With care,
Tricia Goyer

TEASER CHAPTER FOR BOOK 3,
BEYOND HOPES VALLEY

aomi's parents' big, white clapboard house was newer than other houses in the community. Marianna remembered when the new house went up. The Dawdi Haus—the smaller, older farmhouse where Naomi's grandparents once lived—was in back.

From the porch of the Dawdi Haus, Marianna could see the trees her parents planted after her sisters' deaths. And beyond that she could see her parents' property and house. It didn't feel like home any more.

To her, *home* was where her parents were, where her siblings were. And Montana was very far away.

She'd get over to the old place soon enough. She still had a hope chest filled with her things upstairs in her room. She thought again about the many journals she'd written. It would be interesting now to go back and see what she'd written. Did her words come across as sad as she'd always felt? Would she read the weight of trying to live her life to make up for two sisters lost? It would be interesting to find out.

Naomi paused next to a trunk on the porch of the Dawdi Haus. "I'll be setting everything up for after the wedding, of course."

Marianna looked from Levi to Naomi. "So you'll be living here? Near your parents' place? I hadn't thought to ask."

"*Ja*, it's a *gut* home. It's been empty in the year since my grandfather passed. Levi got a job on the Stoll farm. Aaron gave a recommendation."

Marianna nodded. "Did he now? That sounds like Aaron."

"With the house and the income, s'pose we'll have enough to make it. And after the wedding, as we go around visiting, we should get enough for me to keep a home." Naomi rubbed her round belly. She talked like things were happening no different than with every other Amish young couple. The truth was, it wasn't uncommon for Amish girls to get pregnant before they married. What was uncommon was for their boyfriends to come back from the world.

Naomi sniffed the air and rose. "I think my pie's done. I'll be back in a minute."

She smiled at Marianna and Mari smiled back, but as soon as Naomi was out of earshot she turned to her brother.

"Are you certain, Levi?"

"Certain?"

"With this decision."

Levi looked deep into Marianna's eyes. She could see he knew what he ought to say, ought to do, but that didn't mean it would be easy. Gazing into Levi's eyes was like looking into her own soul.

Levi sighed. "Love is a choice, not a feeling, Mari. Didn't you write that in one of your letters to me?"

"Yes, it is a choice, and you're not making an easy one." Marianna forced herself to ask the question she'd been wanting to ask. "It isn't your baby, is it?"

Levi sat up straighter in his seat. "Why would you say that?"

"There is something different about you two. Distance. She . . . it's as if she's worried you're going to walk out at any moment. And you—you have the same look in your eyes as when you were ten and Dat gave up on that newborn calf. You stayed with the calf day and night for a week, feeding it at all hours until it was strong enough to nurse. You were proud. You were weary too, but that didn't compare. It was as if the sacrifice was worth it. It's as if this marriage to Naomi is out of duty, not love."

"You're seeing things where they ought not be."

"Am I? It's me you're talking to, Levi. I've come all this way to help. Shouldn't I know the truth?"

He studied her. "And you'll not speak it to anyone."

"Of course not. You know me better."

"I have not slept with her, Mari. I may not have followed the Amish ways, but I believed Dat when he told me that union ought to be saved for marriage."

Marianna's trembling fingers touched her lips.

"Whose? Whose baby is it, then?"

Levi shrugged and lowered his head. "Would you believe me when I tell you I won't ask? I don't want to know?"

"But why? How could you not want to know?" Marianna felt a sickness coming over her stomach.

"I want to love this child like my own, to think of it as mine. As far as everyone else is concerned, it is." He covered his mouth with his hand and then wiped it, as if wiping poison off his lips. "I don't want to think of her with another man. Don't want to think what I'd say to a man who would do such a thing. Who would do that, Mari? Who would leave a young woman pregnant and alone?"

Marianne had no answer. Not one that she would speak aloud. But she feared she knew.

And it was tearing her apart.